THE RAINBOW CHASE

Kris Karron

Plantation, Florida

EXCLUSIVE DISTRIBUTION BY
PARADISE PRESS, INC.

ISBN #1-57657-236-6

Printed in the U.S.A.

May she be granted beauty and yet not
   Beauty to make a stranger's eye distraught,
   Or hers before a looking-glass. . . .

   —W. B. Yeats

Against the beautiful and the clever and the
   successful, one can wage a pitiless war, but not
   against the unattractive.

   —Graham Greene

THE
RAINBOW
CHASE

Chapter One

JEANNE LATHROP LOOKED down and watched her brand new red Nike trainers make tracks on the trail in Washington's Rock Creek Park. Overhead a cloudless blue sky let the October sun smile down on her. She was out for a five-mile run and she felt great.

The Nike trainers weren't the only new things about Jeanne. She had a new body, a new face and a new spirit. Only a year ago she had weighed eighty pounds more than she did today. It was hard not to shout out to every runner, bike rider and pedestrian she passed: Hey, look at me! Look at the new Jeanne Lathrop! Everyone would know soon enough, though, when the *Playgirl* article came out.

Next July *Playgirl* would run the article Jeanne had written on how running had transformed her life. You've got to sign that article with a pseudonym, whispered her old self. No way, countered the new Jeanne. Every once in a while that old self spoke up. But Jeanne could handle her. Handle her calmly. Okay, she'd been fat. She had hidden not only her fears but her abilities behind that fat. Now she was thin and running strong toward a new life. She got an awful lot of good thinking done as her legs covered mile after mile.

Jeanne took out the handkerchief she carried in the pocket of her red nylon running shorts and wiped her forehead. It certainly was warmer here than it had been last week in Elmton, South Dakota, when she had jogged the roads where she'd once ridden her bike to school.

A week ago she'd stood at high noon on her parents' doorstep in Elmton and asked sweetly, "Does Jeanne Lathrop still live here?" The wide front porch shaded her, and the old screen door through which Mom peered filtered the view. Looking blank, there stood little Mom in a blue-flowered dress, pleasingly plump at sixty-one. Dad had approached the door, his silhouette floating through the fragrance of roasting beef. He, too, stared at the stranger on the porch. The Lathrop nose gave his face a wonderful strength. It had ruined Jeanne's smaller countenance.

Until she got rid of it.

She'd dressed very carefully in the motel that morning, after throwing up her breakfast pancakes in a sudden fit of nerves. A designer shirtdress of nubby brown wool. Wide gold earrings below the short hairdo named after Dorothy Hamill. Most of her silky, straw-streaked brown hair was feathered forward toward the bangs. She'd applied dark brown eye shadow and a soft blusher, and lip gloss to match her rose nail polish. Perfume, too—Halston. She'd surveyed the transformation. Sandals with medium-high heels. A dangly bracelet. No more braces on her teeth. She'd worn braces all the way through college on the advice of Aunt Lily, her mentor and the source of funds for the new clothes and the new blue Porsche that had made this eventful trip home. Eyeglasses were abandoned in favor of a contact lens in each hazel eye. Her waist was cinched to twenty-three inches.

Jeanne told herself that to stand at one's own door after two years' absence and not be recognized by one's own parents was an experience granted to few.

"Jeanne?" said Mom, who always rhymed the name with *teeny*, the basis of many cruel highschool jokes. "She's back East being a magazine reporter. She works for a running magazine. About lady runners." The discontinuity of her speech showed she was catching on but didn't know yet.

Jeanne relished the experience of anonymity for a moment more. A linguist at George Washington University had taught her to suppress her Midwestern twang so thoroughly they hadn't even known her voice.

Then resolution gave way to the surge of love within her, and Jeanne cried out, "It's *me*, Mom, Dad! I'm home! It's Jeanne!"

Four hands struggled with the latch while Jeanne stood grinning like an idiot. No more pardon-me-for-ruining-the-view Jeanne. Wow!

Her very own parents hadn't known her!

She replayed that delicious moment again and again in the busy theater of her mind. They hadn't been told that on July 6 Dr. Andre Lewissohn had broken her Lathrop nose and removed half its bones through her nostrils. He'd also freed the short upper lip that had given her the look of a bird. Now she had a small childlike nose—said one acquaintance, "like a piece of candy."

"Don't try for beautiful," she'd told the plastic surgeon. "I can't hack that. Try for cute. I'm only five-four, and I've got my youth to enjoy. I want to look about twenty, because if you succeed, Doctor, I want time to do everything my mad Aunt Lily did and more, and she was going strong at fifty-nine.''

Not just living at fifty-nine. Loving, too.

Inside the house Mom had wept, and Dad had kept holding her at arm's length and then fiercely hugging her.

"We are so *glad!* So glad for you," they said in unison. How many times she had heard, "You'll be a handsome woman in your middle years." "Look how many friends you have because of your wonderful personality, your wit and charm."

What had personality gotten her but loving pity, all those devoted girlfriends, and jobs like being decoration chairperson for the sophomore ball—which she attended without a date, busying herself at the punch bowl, hoping against hope for just one boy to ask her to dance before the evening was over—but no one did.

Her grades and her personality had landed her a spot in the freshman class at George Washington University, where she'd taken up photography as a hobby. What better place to spend dateless Saturday nights than in a darkroom?

After college she found a job in one of Washington's many government offices but spent most of her time hiding behind the filing cabinets. At lunchtime she brought her substantial brown bag lunch to the Mall, where she began to notice her fellow bureaucrats jogging up and down the paths that connected the Capitol Building with the Washington Monument. She marveled at their svelte forms, their rosy cheeks and the enjoyment they seemed to be taking from their exercise. Freedom, she had thought. That's what it must be like to be free.

With more determination than she had ever felt in her entire life, Jeanne began jogging. She borrowed her friend Amy's circular driveway, which was shielded from the street by a tall, concealing hedge. Round and round for months, jog, walk, jog, walk. Then jog, jog. Then jog, run, jog, run. She started losing weight, and her fatal addiction to chocolate donuts loosened. It was a marvelous shrinking year for the incredible shrinking woman.

Men began to look at her approvingly. Then Aunt Lily's bequest bought her both a shrink and a nose job. So far, though, she hadn't had her first real date, her first real kiss or anything else in the way of romance. But she was ready. Fairly bursting, to tell the truth.

Jeanne remembered shocking her folks by jogging clad in only a T-shirt and blue nylon shorts. After all, she couldn't break her streak.

"You *streak*, too?" her incredulous parents asked in unison.

She burst out laughing. "No, my streak of running every other day without a break. It's lasted quite a while now."

"And you've even given up smoking?" asked Dad.

"Yep. It's not too late for my lungs or my legs."

That was when Mom pulled the bedroom door shut behind them and gazed intently at her half-naked daughter. "Now, Jeanne, you know we love you as much as we did before. But I'm worried that you'll let these good looks of yours make you forget the training your father and I gave you. I hope all this running business won't make you start running after men. I know you spent a lot of time with your Aunt Lily and that you loved her. Now Lily was my sister and I loved her too, but that doesn't mean I approved of her ideas and the things she did. You're a good girl, Jeanne, and I want you to stay that way."

"Don't worry, Mom. I know you and Dad love me, and I won't do anything to make you unhappy." It was the best she could do to assuage her mother's fears.

She kissed her mother's cheek and watched her head toward the kitchen where a freshly baked chocolate fudge cake was cooling. It was Jeanne's twenty-fourth birthday, and later that night she had licked every candle clean, not wanting to waste a drop of the luscious chocolate butter-cream icing. And she had eaten two large slices of the cake. Oh, well, one didn't turn twenty-four every day, she'd rationalized, pledging an extra three miles to burn up those calories. Chocolate was her nemesis. But those days were over. An occasional indulgence, sure, but no more pigging out, no more seeking comfort in chewy chocolate chip cookies or spongy fresh donuts covered with chocolate icing.

Jeanne's mind returned from Elmton to Washington, eagerly anticipating tomorrow when she was to interview a gorgeous Finnish doctor for *Fancy Free*, the new woman's running magazine where she was editor, reporter and jill-of-all-trades. She'd met Ron Liu, *Fancy Free's* editor-in-chief, through her running club and had shown him her new-life-through-running story—the one that had subsequently been accepted by *Playgirl*.

Ron, quick, sharp and Chinese, called Jeanne "a new convert" and "a true believer," which described her quite precisely. She couldn't dispute it. Running had changed her life. When the *Playgirl* piece was published, everyone would understand her the way Ron did. Not only would they understand, they would see. The piece was to run with color photos of Jeanne before and after. Jeanne's enthusiasm for running and her *Playgirl* piece were enough for Ron to offer her a job at the magazine, even though she had no experience beyond her work on the Elmton High School literary magazine.

When she started work the magazine didn't even have a name. How they had argued over it! The phrase "footloose and fancy free" had come up time and time again. Finally the owner, Ron and the three staffers had settled on *Fancy Free*.

Because the magazine was new the pay was low, but Ron allowed Jeanne and the other staffers to arrange their time so that they could supplement their incomes with other freelance assignments. *Fancy Free* was more a family than a business, and everyone shared. There was a profit-sharing arrangement to make up for the low salaries, which also made everyone work extra hard to make *Fancy Free* a success. There was always something to do: write, edit, proof, take pictures, develop them, lay out copy and ads, draft letters to advertisers, answer letters to the editor. You name it. Jeanne's knowledge of photography and darkroom procedures made her doubly valuable to the magazine, as they saved the cost of hiring a staff photographer and sending film to a commercial darkroom.

Ron was their "beneficent" dictator, as he inaccurately called himself. He set the standards and he set them high.

"Women don't want to flip past stories about men's track teams and male sprinters and how to protect the scrotum on below-zero runs," he said. "They have different interests entirely."

When first hired, Jeanne bought copies of all the major women's magazines and busily studied their contents. She learned quickly. During her fat years, her reading had run to *Time*, *Newsweek* and the *Geo-*

graphic. She'd never been very interested in cosmetics and the cutaway bras, feminine sprays and baby oil. But now . . . babies? Aha! How about an article on the minimum age at which children could begin jogging?

Her mind never stopped churning out ideas for articles. Recipes? A before and after jogging menu. Hair care? Fight hair loss and dullness through increased scalp circulation. (Her first side effect from jogging had been a tingling scalp, back when her buttocks were turning from jelly into muscle, and her hair from strings to shiny waves.) More ideas. Why sauna? Why meditate? Why practice yoga? Why break legs skiing, break necks riding horses? Why spend a lot of money? Running is practically free, once you've bought a pair of sponge-soled trainers, limousines for the feet. Some of these articles she could write herself, others would go to Kerry and Nancy, her fellow staffers. Ron might farm out one or two of the more technical stories to freelancers.

The story on the Finnish doctor was up in the air. Dr. Erkki Haukkamaa was doing research for the National Medical Institute on ultramarathoning. Ron might use it if she stretched the woman's angle, or she might try to sell it somewhere else. It never hurt the magazine to have her cited in the credits for her freelance assignments as an editor and reporter for *Fancy Free,* the nation's newest running magazine.

Jeanne's already accelerated heartbeat gained a notch or two as she thought about Dr. Haukkamaa. He had spoken on ultramarathoning at one of her running club's seminars. Haukkamaa was a medical doctor doing physiological research on the effects of running ultradistances: 31, 50, 62 and 100 miles. As he stood before the group, clipboard in hand, Jeanne had been mesmerized. His heavily accented English had a choppy rhythm, and it took a lot of concentration to understand what he was saying. She could picture his incredibly pale blond hair and eerie gray eyes. He didn't look so much a Scandinavian as he did a tall, slim, handsome Japanese with strange light coloring. It was the combination of his arresting appearance and startling voice that had made the Finnish doctor the object of many of Jeanne's fantasies in the past weeks.

After the lecture, Jeanne had taken a couple of deep breaths and approached him, introducing herself as a reporter for *Fancy Free* and asking if she could interview him for an article on the study he was conducting at the National Medical Institute. He had been polite, telling her to telephone his office for an appointment.

Jeanne was no stranger to fantasies. She had lived vicariously through her elaborate fantasy life for years and years. The imagined phone call to Dr. Haukkamaa became grander and grander each time she played it through.

The phone would ring in his chrome and glass office at the Institute.

"Dr. Haukkamaa."

"Good morning. This is Jeanne Lathrop. We met at the Georgetown Road Runners Club seminar."

"Of course, the beautiful young writer for *Free and Fancy*."

"That's *Fancy Free*, Dr. Haukkamaa."

A small laugh. "I am confusing my English, Miss Lathrop. Now I believe you wanted to make an interview with me for your magazine. I am most anxious to show you my laboratory. How is tomorrow at four o'clock of the afternoon? When

we are finished, it will be the end of the day and
we can perhaps dine together, yes? I have more
of interest to show you than my laboratory."

"Four o'clock would be fine. And dinner would
be fine, too."

And after dinner . . . her first Finnish sauna? What
a way to go.

But that wasn't the way it had gone at all. She had
called the Institute several times, left messages which
were not returned. When she finally reached Dr. Haukkamaa, he had no recollection of her whatsoever. She
was crushed. And explaining who she was and what
she wanted was excruciating. But an interview had
been set up for tomorrow, and she would do her best
to make an impression on him then.

Aunt Lily's clothes would help. Jeanne called them
that because they had been purchased with a bequest
from Aunt Lily's will. Twenty-five thousand dollars
for her "to spend foolishly within the next six months.
Otherwise, the bequest will benefit the political party
that our family has never voted for." No one was sure
which party that would be, but Lily's intent was clear.
Spend it or lose it foolishly.

It was because of Lily that Jeanne had come as far
as she had. And it wasn't just the money that had
bought the Porsche, the psychotherapist, the new
nose, the clothes, the hairdo and makeup. Aunt Lily
had been her friend. Jeanne had never met her before
she arrived at George Washington University. Knowing her mother's disapproval of her flamboyant younger
sister, Jeanne was reluctant to call Lily. But when Lily
phoned, inviting her to dinner at her home near Washington, Jeanne accepted more out of curiosity than
anything else.

It was the first of many evenings she was to spend sitting up late with Aunt Lily, smoking the fragrant Turkish cigarettes Lily was so fond of, and discussing men. Lily said love was beautiful, wonderful, sublime, the best thing in life. She had buried two husbands, divorced a third and, at fifty-nine, was never without male companionship. She practiced what she preached. She was gay and careless and had died suddenly in a car crash because she hadn't fastened her seat belt. At least there had been no lingering illness, no prolonged suffering. Jeanne missed Lily terribly.

When the swelling in her face had finally gone down after her rhinoplasty, Jeanne did the most foolish thing she could think of. She booked a room at the Hotel Pierre in New York and spent three days doing the New York beauty scene. A haircut and manicure at Kenneth's; a body massage, facial and makeup consultation at Adrian Arpel. Long days in the designer collections at Bloomingdale's buying dresses, sportswear, exotic lingerie. She topped off each day by running through the Pierre lobby in shorts and Nikes, across Fifth Avenue to Central Park for a long slow run. Once around the hilly park was six miles. The blue line marking the last couple of miles of the New York City Marathon remained on the asphalt surface year round. Maybe next fall she'd return to Central Park to cover the twenty-six point two mile course through the five boroughs of New York City. It would mean qualifying in another marathon first, but she could do it. She knew she could. If she could train with Dr. Haukkamaa, she was positive she could run a marathon.

After a long training run they could shower together, soaping each other, kissing as the water ran down over their faces. Warm and relaxed, he would carry her into the bedroom, lay her face down on the bed and massage her tired calves and thighs, his strong thin fingers expertly kneading her squeaky-clean flesh. Then he would gently roll her over, kiss her from her toes to her face, caressing every inch of her.

Jeanne was jolted back to reality as she nearly tripped over a rock. How much longer would she retreat into such daydreams, block out the world as if she'd walked into a pitch-black theater, sat down and turned on the projector? When she was jogging or driving, it was dangerous. The habit had caused bike accidents when she was riding to and from school in order to avoid taking the school bus. Though she could never avoid the bus entirely. Pedaling along, munching a candy bar, braced for the passage of the yellow bus with a screaming head at every window, she'd hear "Fatty!" "Lookie, it's the Blob!" "The Incredible Hulk!" Then the bus would pass, and she wouldn't see the boys any longer—or the girls who, out of pity, tried to shush them. She'd busy herself imagining Jeanne as a slip of a girl—Mom's phrase—blond, bosomy, beautiful. No, absolutely gorgeous. Lithesome, mindless, irresistible to men. All men. All handsome men, that is.

Her fantasies had been grandiose, but they had helped her survive a very unpleasant reality. It was not at all nutty to live on fantasies as an alternative to neurosis. Dr. Tinsley didn't have to tell her that; popular books said so. Dr. Tinsley helped her analyze her daydreams. He handled her symbolic creations delicately and didn't always delve into the past to help her understand her current pangs and problems. Her looks had done a lot to damage her, but she had also had decent parents—strict but loving—and a stable community to grow up in. If only she had been an attractive girl. A plain one, even. Her sudden change to being pretty made her unsteady sometimes, distrustful, worried that her new world would disappear—and guilty.

She and Dr. Tinsley had examined this guilty feeling. She had abandoned the old Jeanne, left her back there among the chocolate donuts in South Dakota, weeping in her blubber and drying her oversized nose. Jeanne felt this pain most often when she caught herself judging a stranger by his or her appearance. Vastly preferring beauty to its opposite was normal, not a betrayal, Dr. Tinsley said. Under his calm and gentle questioning, she could put the old Jeanne to rest. The new Jeanne had so much to live for, so much to do. Here and now.

Jeanne slowed her pace on the autumn carpet of yellow leaves. Breathing heavily and feeling flushed and glowing, inside and out, she walked back to her car and drove back to her apartment overlooking the Potomac River. She still hadn't solved the problem of what to wear tomorrow to meet the fascinating Finn. He was not handsome in the American sense, but oddlooking, with that pale hair and oriental features. There was something almost cold about him, impenetrable, with his runner's body, hard and long. She shivered. Warm, she thought. I'll wear something bright and warm.

Chapter Two

NO FLANNEL SWEATS and track shoes for her interview today! Jeanne wore a cashmere dress of dark rose, fine gold chains tangling inside the open collar and gold hoop earrings. She knew what he'd think of the graceful high heels as she clippety-clipped up the steps. She entered the marble hall of the building that soared within sight of the Mormon temple off the Capital Beltway. It was surrounded by evergreens and green lawns on this crisp October day. She ran her eyes down the directory.

Haukkamaa there, 604.

No need in the elevator to touch her hair or glance in a mirror. Her hair was cut so well that it fell perfectly into place with only a quick blow-dry. And stayed that way. Though painstaking at first, she now applied her makeup with a deft hand and needed only to reapply lipstick as the day wore on.

Jeanne entered Suite 604. As she sat in the carpeted anteroom, she hoped that Dr. Haukkamaa would not sit for the inteview in a wrinkled lab coat, needing a shave. He did not disappoint her. After ten minutes' wait, she was directed down a white corridor to his office. Surprised not to find an antiseptic lab, she surveyed the dim, deeply carpeted room, lit by two cubical frosted lamps on low tables. It was walled on three sides with bookcases. He sat behind a large desk, looking at her as if he hadn't expected her to look the way she did.

Dr. Haukkamaa rose as she entered, his lean face under the pale hair hinting at several conflicting emotions. He slowly took off thick-rimmed reading glasses and laid them on an open book among stacks of letters and notes.

"Dr. Haukkamaa," she said in her best clipped accent, wishing he were not quite so tall, so imposing, so slow to respond or to do more than study her and her outstretched right hand. She pulled her hand back. Perhaps Finns did not shake hands with strange women. He dipped his head to indicate the nearer of two leather chairs by his desk.

She sat down, clipboard in hand, studying that unsmiling alien face.

He has to register each January at the post office. He's an alien, like Mr. Spock, she giggled to herself.

The man bore a vague resemblance to that personage, despite being so blond. Strong jaw. Sealed lips. Skin smooth as honey. He wore expensive gray trousers, sharply creased, and a closely fitting gray vest. The blue shirt beneath it seemed new, its sleeves crisp and full, fastened at the wrists with agate cuff links.

"You come from that magazine, I presume?" He rolled his r's like a Scot.

"Yes."

"May I ask your own name?" he said, eyes narrowing, arms now folded across his wide chest.

"Oh, excuse me," she said, angry at herself for the oversight. "I am Jeanne Lathrop."

Hearing his accent again startled her. The Finnish accent was not at all Scandinavian but seemed more akin to Chinese or Japanese. The voice itself was a deep and pleasant one, like none she'd ever heard.

"I learned just this Monday of your desire to take an interview," he said to her as coolly as if he considered his English perfect. "I am little prepared to tell an organized description of our work here. I will need more time to manage that. What I can tell today is only an oversee . . . overview."

Then he stared at her, the narrowed gray eyes wider, unblinking. It was a fixed and riveting gaze that left Jeanne breathless. Did he always unnerve strangers this way? She murmured "May I begin with some questions that I've prepared?"

He dipped his golden head again, magisterially.

He was seated now, leaning back in his desk chair, feigning patience.

"I would like to begin by asking about you yourself, Dr. Haukkamaa, since you have so recently come to our country, and since you are also a marathoner like the people you study."

"Your first line will say, 'From the land of Paavo Nurmi and Lasse Viren, comes here a student of the medical effects of long distance running.' "

"That is not what I had in mind," she said, miffed. But she noted the true Finnish pronunciation of both names she'd long been mispronouncing.

"To start off," she said, "How does one pronounce *your* name, Doctor?"

"You say it almost correct. 'HOW-key-mah,' not 'hake.' "

"And your first name?"

"I am tired of hearing 'Eric.' It is 'AIR-key,' such as you feel the air blow, and you put the key into the lock."

"I see," she said, writing down "air-key."

"Now I hope you have a more interesting question," he said.

"May I ask your age?"

"And yours?"

"Mine is not at all relevant, Dr. Haukkamaa. Yours is. Americans expect to see an age listed in an article extolling your own distance-running abilities. You are not yet in the Master's category, I assume?"

"In a half dozen years."

She hid a smile and wrote down "34." He looked older.

"*Miss* Lathrop, I presume," he said, eyeing her ringless left hand.

"Are *you* married, Dr. Haukkamaa? Is your family here with you in Washington?"

"That is another fact not relevant to the laboratory."

"But it is interesting to the readership."

"Which is the magazine you interview from? Again?"

She told him in accents as clipped as his that *Fancy Free* was her own magazine, but the *Journal* had expressed an interest in his laboratory on the basis of her inquiry letter. God, was he a sharp-toothed shark in that blue and gray, with square white teeth! Cold as the ocean depths. This was not going to be easy.

She sighed, and the gold chains over her breasts jingled faintly. She noted his glance at the open neckline of her dress, and then he scowled down at her stiletto heels.

Jeanne opened her mouth to defend her shoes, then decided not to speak up. "A runner too," she said instead, "and your work with ultramarathoners interests me a great deal. It seems that everyone is curious. Incredulity over marathon runners is fading, and interest increases in the ultradistances, particularly in women who can achieve such distances and who may eventually better the men's record."

"Not likely," he said. "The female body owns a far lower percentage of muscle than the man's."

"And a higher percentage of stored fat to burn over fifty or a hundred miles of running. Women might become competitive at those distances if they put in the same hours of training as men do."

He didn't move an eyelash, but the set expression reminded her of their relative ages and educations. He was the physiologist, not she. And the marathoner too.

"To return to the preliminaries, Dr. Haukkamaa, I would appreciate it if you could supply some personal information. Such as how many children have you? Surely that—"

"The work here is the only thing I wish to discuss," he said firmly, gesturing for emphasis toward the corridor. Scowling again at her.

"Then tell me about the work here. Maybe later you will feel more relaxed in my company."

"After a drink?" he said, brows going up and down quickly. It was only eleven in the morning.

Jeanne wished she'd done some research on Finns. All she could remember were the stereotypes. They are silent, take saunas and are great drinkers.

"Are you prepared to understand the vocabulary?"

he asked. "Such terminology as endorphins, triglycerides and HDL?"

"Yes," she said. "High density lipoprotein was the last acronym. It is a type of fatty substance that tends to be elevated in runners and indicates low danger of arteriosclerosis to come. Triglycerides give the opposite picture when found in high quantities in the blood. Endorphins are produced in the brain by stress and shock, and apparently by runs beyond forty to sixty minutes in length; they resemble morphine, giving a sense of elation and well-being."

His brows went up. "The end of the examination," he said.

"I wouldn't be here if I were a perfect ass."

The words just popped out, but they did bring a faint smile to the chiseled lips. He dipped his head, for an instant closing his gray eyes. Then he laced his fingers together behind his neck and amazed her by propping his heels on the desk.

"All right," he said softly. "Let us begin. I hope you write the shorthand."

"I use a tape recorder, Dr. Haukkama."

"I see."

What she felt like asking just then was, "Speak a little Finnish for me." But she didn't dare.

When her machinery was in order, he frowned at the bookcases opposite and began a highly technical overview of the Institute's findings in regard to ultra-distance runners, which she captured by thumbing a button. The facts that struck her as especially intriguing she jotted down. Otherwise she never took her eyes from his profile, sharp and golden against a backdrop of thousands of weighty tomes shelved from ceiling to floor.

The goal of his own research—"personally," he said

with emphasis—was to gather data that indicated man's and woman's requirement for regular strenuous exercise, especially in modern cultures tending to overweight and stress. If doctors realized the value of sustained exercise, they would not be so hesitant to prescribe it. And to prescribe fewer medications. "My days as a clinician are gone," he said oddly and paused for several beats of her heart. "Finished. I wish to work with healthy bodies now, not with doomed and dying ones." Then she saw him shake his head as if to clear it of a bad dream. "If we have family histories and blood chemistries upon many runners for many decades, we will be able to compare with the average American. And Finn."

Ultramarathoners, he explained, interested him because "any healthy body can run twenty miles, and with a cheerful crowd, twenty-six-point-two. The runner has complete recovery in a day or two. But at fifty kilometers, one hundred K—kilometers—we expect to see some long-term physiological effects."

Speaking of his work and hopes, he became almost animated; the cold mask disappeared. Then he said abruptly, "It is time for lunch," and swung his feet down from the desk. "There is not time now for you to see the facilities."

So she was dismissed? Just like that?

"I go only down to the Institute diningroom. Will you accompany me?"

He rose, reached into a closet for his suit coat, and put it on.

Of course she would. Jeanne sprang up and slid her reporting tools into her leather bag. He stared at her feet.

"You shall bring ruin to your feet in that way," he said. "Your shoes are abdominal . . . abominable."

"I know it. I prefer running flats, but for business, well—" She sneaked a glance up at him. "One wears skis to ski, and snowshoes to—"

"But you came to talk of running," he said very logically as he steered her out the door.

The sudden light touch of his hand on the middle of her back felt like an electric charge. Her cheeks burned, and she feared that the way he watched her, tilting his head to see her face, he had noticed it.

He didn't speak again until they were seated in the glass and marble diningroom among white columns, well away from other diners. They unfolded crisp red linen napkins.

"You seem very young for what you do, Miss Lathrop," he said, placing his on his lap. "In what suburb of Washington is your residence?"

"I live in the city," said Jeanne. "In Georgetown."

"I am in Bethesda. You can write that, but give no address. I wish privacy. I have a house lent to me. I built there this summer a sauna."

"Oh," she exclaimed. "How very Finnish of you!"

"There is a great deal more to Finland than saunas and Nurmi," he said, his eyes cold again.

He ordered a crab sandwich and a glass of New York sauterne. She opted for shrimp and avocado salad and the same wine.

Try again, Jeanne.

"That is why I wanted some human interest for this story, Dr. Haukkamaa; we know so little about Finland. It's a shame. Just a line or two on differences you perceive between Finland and America—"

"This is not America; there are two continents called Americas. This is the United States."

"I stand corrected," she said tartly, and then sighed. It wasn't getting any easier.

"In July," she said brightly, "you travel to Helsinki where the international hundred-mile race will be held?"

"In June," he corrected her, his head bowed in assent. "We have on file now many Finnish and United States runners who will have tests before, during and long after the race. They will permit rest stops with blood sampling and metered intake and output."

"I suppose there *is* a great deal of walking during a race of a hundred miles. Bill Rodgers stops to drink and to tie his shoe laces in the midst of marathons run in two-ten."

He seemed to feed everything she said into his mental computer, as if she were his patient, having her output calibrated. His stare was disarming, and Jeanne wished he wouldn't look at her with such open desire.

She now recognized it as desire and she felt queasy, picking at her food with difficulty. It was still a novelty for her to see that emotion in a man's face, and he very obviously didn't want to give himself away. She was scared and excited at the same time.

"It is too bad," she said, not glancing up at him, "that the race cannot be run in the States, so I could follow up on this story."

"Go to Helsinki, then," he said as if it lay right around the corner, gesturing with a large but lean right hand. "Summer is tourists' season, and warm. There is no darkness."

"Midnight sun, uh? If I could manage fifty miles, I might try to *run it*," she joked, watching his face.

"So you do run distances?"

"A half marathon is my best so far," she responded. "I've been running for only twenty months, and I'm up to at least eighty-five miles a month. Is that acceptable?"

He considered her, stroking his temples with his fingertips, but didn't answer.

"May I ask if you are married?"

"I am not married and have never been."

That sounded like an uncompleted sentence, and she hid a wince. His face remained stolid.

"One cannot judge anymore, from a woman's name or her rings. Liberation."

"We will be liberated when the Olympic Committee permits women to run races longer than a mere 1500 meters."

"Ah, that issue rises up again."

"I should think your research would put you on our side," she said hotly. "Open all Olympic races to women, especially the marathon. We've cut our marathon record time by an hour since 1964, while the men's record has hung up at 2:08:34 since 1969."

"I held that same opinion," he said curtly, "when you were not yet out of school." He gave her a long, hard, interrogator's look.

"I'm not that much younger than you," Jeanne countered. "You needn't bite my head off."

"I am old enough to remember the hard times in Finland when my country was to struggle to repay its war debt. To save the province of Karelia, the province of my family, Finland took the side of Germany. Germany was defeated, and much money was to be paid by my small country to Russia. It was very difficult. I have seen much hard work and suffering in my life, and you worry only if women will run an Olympic marathon."

Jeanne withered under his sudden attack.

He stopped speaking and bowed his head. "I am

ashamed, Miss Lathrop. My words run away with my feelings. Please forgive me." He reached across the table and took her hand. A moment's pressure from his long slim fingers was all she could stand before she jerked her hand away and dropped it, burning, into her lap.

They finished the meal in strained silence, then ascended to the lab, where she knew she'd find stress testers, chromatography and spectrophotometry equipment, dials and electrodes. He touched her back again briefly and held her arm. Jeanne closed her eyes for an instant, walking beside him, and hid a not unpleasant shudder.

Why the strong attraction? She knew practically nothing about him. Every time she asked a personal question he changed the subject. What was he hiding about his life? Was he married? She didn't want to start her new life fooling around with any married man. Or did he have a different woman every night at his house with its sauna?

The laboratory hummed. Elderly men ran on two treadmills while wires radiated from their chests. Young women in white lab coats among sterilized glassware jotted notes, and gave Dr. Haukkamaa the eye. Some of them, she noted, wore running shoes. He pointed out charts and graphs and talked of cholesterol and testosterone, of cardiac output and vegetarianism, emphasizing facts of interest to women readers.

Then he took her back to his snug office and again mentioned the sauna.

"The Finnish sauna," he said, as she was about to gather up her notes and depart, "is not what Yankees think. It is not a spiritual retreat. Not religious. It is not for sexual orgies. It is merely for taking a bath."

"And what is that supposed to mean?" Jeanne retorted, standing as tall as she could, but even in heels half a head shorter than he.

"Put that as 'personal' in your article. A footnote, at the bottom. State that in sauna, Finns bathe. That is all."

He was having fun with her.

"I shall come over and see for myself someday," she said, hardly believing those words came from her own mouth. "When I need a good bath."

"You are certainly welcome to visit, Miss Lathrop."

"Perhaps I would if I knew where you lived."

"You I will tell. Or shall we go out to dinner Saturday night, and talk more, and then the sauna. Is that agreeable?"

"You move fast," she noted, brow raised, hiding her violently accelerating pulse.

"We are alike," he observed, leaning against the doorjamb, hands in pockets, eyes narrowed. "You impress me. We may discover we like each other."

Feeling as if she were a foot off the ground, but with her brow furrowed, Jeanne left the building. *Wow. Wow and wow again!* The interview hadn't started out very well, what with her shoes and her defensive arrogance, but he had been attracted to her all along! He had to be or he would not have delivered that blockbuster of a proposition.

So why aren't I jumping for joy?

Because he seemed too much to handle. He was older, a foreigner, experienced, a puzzle. So they'd have dinner out Saturday night and then a sauna. On the first date? Was it proper to take a sauna with a man on the first date? This was a time she could really have used a talk with Lily. But she was on her own.

A run was in order before returning to the office. She had a lot of things to think about before Saturday night.

Chapter Three

JEANNE WAS TRANSCRIBING her tapes of the Finn's maddeningly attractive voice. She thought of him as Air-key as she typed frantically, switching off the recorder on the floor with one bare toe. Then, catching up, she turned it on again to hear more. Taping beat shorthand, and she had his voice forever in her possession.

Too fidgety to face the *Fancy Free* office, with its crisis-a-minute atmosphere, she'd phoned Ron and told him she was working at home on the Haukkamaa interview. She had some ideas for the piece and wanted some quiet time to think them through. Okay, Jeanne, Ron had said, we'll muddle through without you.

She paced her way through Thursday and Friday. She could only sit at the typewriter listening to his voice for a few minutes at a time. Once around the apartment and back to the desk. She jotted down ideas for follow-up research, for angles for the article.

Mostly, though, she worried. It was very possible that she would lose her virginity on Saturday night.

The thought of Erkki's touch as he guided her down the halls of the Institute made her covet more of him, his tall, golden, runner's body. She didn't want to seem a ninny, though, a silly virgin at twenty-four. He might laugh, be amused. He was no boy of sixteen, proud to take a girl's virginity. He might be scornful of her. She was a career woman. She'd shown him she knew her terminology cold. She'd done her homework, but not in bed. She could always treat Saturday night like a pop quiz and do the best she could with the limited knowledge she had.

On Friday night she had a sudden mad impulse to go out to a singles bar, pick someone up and sleep with him, just to get that first time out of the way, let it not interfere with whatever else was happening between herself and Erkki. Instead she curled up on the sofa on Friday night and watched *Casablanca* for at least the twentieth time. "You must remember this, a kiss is just a kiss . . ." Maybe she was making entirely too much out of this. She should relax, let nature take its course. Easier said than done.

On Saturday she cleaned her apartment within an inch of its life. She scrubbed kitchen and bath, polished furniture, vacuumed rugs and furniture, even washed the windows. And all the time she thought of Erkki Haukkamaa and his double-whammy stare. Here was an absolutely dazzling man to excite and enjoy her new body. She wanted everything to be perfect. She yearned for perfection beyond anything she had experienced in her fantasies. She wanted a real man, real caresses. But could she respond in kind? She just didn't know.

Jeanne watered the plants on the sills of her tall

windows and looked down at the slow, mighty Potomac. No matter what happened tonight, the river would be there tomorrow. Life would go on. She turned the plants to give their leaves a chance to reach for the sun in another direction.

For lunch she managed to get down a banana and a cup of herb tea. No need for caffeine today. She was jittery enough as it was. Erkki would arrive at seven. She imagined him walking into the apartment, his piercing blue eyes taking in the room, stabbing at her. She could see his immaculately shaven face and precise jaw over a fresh blue collar. He would be dressed to the nines, sheathing that fine, lean body in an expensive wool-blend suit, tailored exactly to his form.

And what should she wear tonight? The snug black velvet pants with her full-sleeved Chinese silk blouse of emerald green? She tried them on in front of a full-length mirror, added delicate black sandals, and knew at once that she looked good. Very good! It would be cool this evening and Jeanne chose an antique black silk shawl Aunt Lily had given her. It was delicately patterned, edged in long fringe, but genuinely warm as well.

She took a long relaxing bubble bath and scrubbed every inch of herself with her loofa sponge until her skin was pink and tingling. Her skin drank in the scented body lotion she applied after her bath.

Painstakingly she applied a special makeup for evening wear. A pearly foundation, cheekbones accented with dusty rose blusher. Soft gray shading over her eyes, a hint of black mascara. A final touch of almost colorless glossy lipstick would make her shimmer in the dimly lit restaurant where they would dine. Her only jewelry was a pair of Chinese cloisonné earrings that complemented the green of her blouse. She brushed her freshly washed hair until it shone burnished chestnut.

On the very stroke of seven Haukkamaa arrived as expected. He looked around the apartment with that frowning stare, while she admired his surprisingly casual tweed jacket and beige turtleneck sweater. So there was a less formal side to the doctor.

She wondered what he thought of her cozy apartment. She had furnished it with handicrafts from all over the world. A beige Haitian cotton sofa dominated the room. In front of the working fireplace a braided rug, a gift from her mother, brought warmth and color into the room. Her end tables were carved Indian rosewood, and over the sofa hung a handwoven Peruvian rug. None of her furnishings were expensive, having been purchased at the local import stores favored by students and struggling singles.

Erkki gave no clue to his thoughts. He was silent, intense in his focus on her living quarters, and suddenly just as intent on leaving. His hands were quick to touch her shoulder, her elbow, to guide her down the dimly lit stairs of the Georgetown townhouse that contained her third-floor apartment. His car was a sleek, black Ferrari. She slid unsteadily into the bucket seat.

Erkki drove quickly and skillfully, without speaking, to a chic restaurant called The Broker. The Ferrari glided into a parking slot, its engine ebbing. With one deft motion, Erkki brought the car to a stop and turned to face Jeanne. Her breasts swelled a little in their baskets of lace, and the throb of her heart was echoed by a throb lower down. She could not hide the tiny smile at the corners of her mouth, and knew that he noticed it.

"You are happy. You look extremely well this evening," Dr. Haukkamaa said, assisting her out of the Ferrari.

"And so do you," she quipped, because she did feel happy.

He walked her down the sidewalk with his arm across her back and his hand gripping her arm, pressing her against his side. "You have lost some height," he said.

"Stern advice from some big-shot doctor last week," she retorted.

"You have humor," he said. "A sense of humor. You are a very interesting woman."

She couldn't flip back that compliment like a tennis volley. "I've heard of The Broker," she commented. "A very old building; wasn't it renovated—?"

"A recovery, yes," he said, bending down to speak softly to her, his breath ruffling her bangs. Her vision blurred, darkened.

Inside, among the old brick arches like catacombs and the light, naturalwood fittings, she recovered her composure. Without carpeting or insulation, the place was noisy, but marvelous to study. The clientele raised their voices over drinks, so she concentrated on the vichyssoise, the poached sole with prawns, the truffles. She declined the escargots, saying she'd never eaten snails.

He smiled. "So something is new to you, Miss Lathrop? I had thought of you as a lady so perfect, so . . . so very well experienced."

"Not at all," she said, meaning it.

She had a sherry before dinner, white wine with the meal and benedictine afterward. By the time he suggested dancing at the Shoreham, she was feeling warm and pleasant.

"I do not like the Disco. I am old-fashioned," he said.

The old hotel was elegant, set among tall trees. It furnished a dark dance-floor and music slow enough to waltz or foxtrot. Whatever steps he danced, Erkki held her close, her head turned so her cheek pressed against his shoulder. This is what couples did in movies, in books, in fantasies. Cinderella Lathrop at the royal ball had trouble with her breathing.

Now, waiting for midnight to strike and her svelte form to turn into cottage cheese by the bushel and her costume into fabric by the bolt, she put away memories. Only on tiptoe could she see over his shoulder. But who wanted to? He had a strong lead, which was not surprising. His hand slid slowly down her back, moving to caress the silk blouse, the electric flesh underneath. Skillful fingers slid below her waist and drew designs above her hips. She anticipated her first desired kiss. She wanted to nibble, relish, assimilate before devouring. She was thirteen at the beginning of this date; she had reached sweet sixteen within three hours. When the night was over, she might be twenty-one.

He danced well, with economical, rhythmic steps, one long leg pressing strongly between hers. Now he lifted her right hand onto his shoulder and linked his hands behind her waist, half lifting her off the floor against him.

Dancing with Erkki was much different from dancing with a girlfriend in a furnished rec room. Jeanne smiled to herself as she thought of those sessions. But at least she had learned to dance, and she loved dancing with Erkki. Her mind flew to other excitements impending. She nodded against his body, dazed.

In the car they talked as little as before. He drove steely-eyed, focusing on the road. Through Rock

Creek Park he sped, that forest in the middle of the nation's capital, with its bridges and dark tunnels and trees. Her weekend jogging route crossed and recrossed the park.

There were all sorts of things she wanted to know about this man. All she didn't understand rose in her mind, through the silence. Finns might be laconic and drunken, but this one held his liquor well. In fact, he'd fed her more drinks than he'd consumed, and he'd had coffee before the drive home. Sensible. Doctors are all too familiar with the tragic aftermath of auto collision: try a stint in any hospital emergency room. Like the crash that killed Lily—Lily, who seemed to be perched behind Jeanne in the Ferrari now, elbowing aside the hunk of fat Jeanne and urging the new slim Jeanne to march forward with courage into the very jaws of . . . of experience.

He must be married. No man this enthralling could be a bachelor. Divorced? What was the Finnish divorce rate? A lot lower than ours, even with deep snows and dark winters, isolation and depression. She'd looked at a map. Hudson Bay was further south than Finland. She shivered. And they kept warm in saunas. He'd built a sauna, and they'd soon . . .

No man had seen her in less than shorts and a T-shirt.

He turned off the route, fidgeted at stop lights, then entered a winding road, climbed a rise, and whipped the Ferrari into a driveway and under a carport beside a two-story house in Bethesda. It wasn't the ranch style or the Georgian brick she was expecting.

The house was old, constructed of stucco and half timbering, and stood in an evergreen grove. When she called it a troll's castle, he laughed abruptly.

He led her through the carport, ducking under

leafless vine curtains, and pointed out a wooden building against a tall fence that surrounded the sloping back lawn. In the moonlight near the sauna she spied the border of an oval swimming pool. When he switched on the underwater light from the back entry, it glowed like a deep, giant sapphire.

"I have laid the fire in the stove," he said. "You undress while I ignite it."

He directed her toward the sauna, a squat building walled with stacked four-by-fours stained dark. The windows were narrow and high and closed. He emerged almost immediately.

"You go in there," he said. "I shall fetch *vasta*."

"What's that?" She was thinking of wine or towels.

"Birch branches frozen since summer."

She was reminded of *McGuffy's Readers* that spoke of the dreaded birchings for bad children, and he didn't enlighten her. Wow! The girl from *Fancy Free* meets the birch-bough troll?

In a small well-lit room she stood admiring newly built benches that smelled of sawdust and forest and held fresh white towels. Wooden buckets of water stood on the floor. She pushed over the heavy plank door that opened onto a stoveroom—the sauna—and sniffed for humidity. There was none, just a charcoal-hickory smell. She did not enter, nor did she leap out of her clothes.

He returned promptly, carrying boughs crimped with ice and tied in a bundle. He shoved them into the sauna, then stood in the anteroom staring down at her.

"Do you sauna before running?" she asked nervously, picking at the buttons on her blouse without undoing them.

"Not hardly. Relaxed muscles will not run. No, sauna is for after running, to bring blood to the skin from the legs. The sweating sends waste nitrogen through the skin and out of the body to cleanse the blood. Kidney patients are helped the same. You understand?"

"Perfectly," she said.

"You will not endure so hot as I, so sauna is soon hot enough for you. You know saunas?"

"Not very well," she said, which was an understatement.

"Probably electric saunas," he snorted. "That is for city flats. This is a country sauna, with burning wood in a stove and stones on top to be wet for steam."

He began to undress slowly, his back politely turned to her. He eased off jacket and sweater, hanging them on wooden hangers. A glance behind her as she shed her sandals showed her a wonderful bronzed back, slender enough to display a ribcage criss-crossed with muscles that moved with his flexing. His arms were well muscled, unlike most runners' arms.

Most runners, she mused, all leg and narrow-shouldered, resembled kangaroos. Not Dr. Haukkamaa. But he'd told her that his marathon PR—personal record-time—was, so far, 2:46:03. Not exceptional, since he was nearly the optimal age for a marathoner. His time would be close to the best for men near sixty years old. It didn't compare with the women's world record of 2:27:33.

Why was she standing there recalling racing times, as if she were researching an article? To distract herself, of course. Coward. What would Lily think of you? But at least she stayed. She didn't run shrieking from the sauna into the night.

"I shall go in first. You are too slow," he said from behind her as she labored over her buttons. When she didn't turn around, he stepped past her, wearing a small towel wound around his waist. The sauna door opened and closed, blasting her with hot air.

Jeanne Lathrop, late of South Dakota, hung her garments on hooks, wrapped herself in a skimpy towel and pulled the sauna door open, squinting into the dark.

Good girl, Jeanne. Smart Jeanne. Go to it, Jeanne, her mind urged her. She was in. She looked. He was sitting on the highest of three wooden tiers, no longer wearing his towel. That much she could see. She sat down on the hot wood of the bottom bench, her face already sore from the consuming heat and her eyes stinging. He tossed her a birch branch.

"To loosen the dirt," he observed. "And to smell good. Good treatment for the sinuses, also."

"Yes, Doctor," she gasped.

She covered her stinging face with both hands, causing the tucked-in towel to slip loose and slide slowly down her sides to the bench. But she didn't move. He was swishing and rubbing his body with the branches, sitting above her where the heat must be infernal. In any burning house, hug the floor; put a wet cloth over your face. Jeanne gritted her teeth.

"What is the temperature?" she whispered, two minutes later.

"No more than hundred degrees," he said.

"That's ridiculous! Washington is over a hundred in the summer!"

"Centigrade," he chuckled. "That is two hundred and twelve degrees, to you."

Ohmigod! She pressed fragrant, fresh-thawed birch leaves against her cheek and passed them over her breasts and stomach, enjoying the pungent summer scent. Well, maybe this wasn't so bad.

"This is *hikoilu*," he said. "In Finland the dry heat

time may be Fahrenheit 260°. It is for being quiet, traditionally.''

"I'm sorry. I'm not a Finn."

"I like when you talk, Jeanne," he said, choosing this time to use her first name. "Now we sweat much, and I show you *vihtominen löylyssä*, with water for steam."

The low round stove was covered with smooth rocks. Erkki picked up a wooden bucket of water from the bench beside him and tossed the bucketful of water over the stones. Suddenly their dark scorching den hissed and breathed smothering clouds.

Jeanne gasped for breath. She bent over, her hair growing heavy with mist. But pride made her try to sit up. Everyone adored saunas. Joined health clubs to use them; built them in converted closets at home. And here she was in the dark with a beautiful, scary, naked man, anticipating—

"Come up here," he commanded.

She decided to obey, easing herself up onto the middle bench. When she started to descend again, afraid her eyeballs would harden like boiled eggs and her flesh melt off her bones, he reached down and seized her under the arms. He lifted her up beside him, gazing at her so that for a moment she forgot the discomfort.

"Lovely woman," he said, and touched her shiny throat, passing a fingertip down between her glistening breasts, white in the moonlight through the small window.

"I can't . . . bear . . . this heat," she gasped.

He surrounded her with hot, slippery arms and kissed her, but the heat alone was making her faint. He smelled good, like a birch tree.

Not until his big hands had flowed all over her, familiarizing themselves with every curve and fullness and straining muscle of her body, did she escape back down to the more bearable level of the sauna.

"In sauna," he said calmly from his perch, "babies were born in the old days. It was the warm, clean place of the house. Our President, Urho Kekkonen, was born in sauna. Now he invites many world leaders to sauna at his home. Men do not make war talk when they sit, all alike, naked in sauna."

No, thought Jeanne, they only want cool air, and will agree to anything to get it.

Did he bring recalcitrant maidens here and refuse to open the door or dampen down the fire until they acquiesced to his desires?

"Now the pool: *vilvoittelu*. The cold," he said abruptly, springing from his bench down to hers. She was so wet that his hands slipped all over her, gaining no grip. He put his arm around her to keep her with him. They went out of the sauna onto the cold, dewy grass.

The pool of sapphire was close by, and he hesitated only a moment at the edge. Afraid he'd pitch her in before he dived, Jeanne closed her eyes and dove into the deep end. For the first time in her life, she actually enjoyed entering cold water. Their hot bodies must have acted like heating coils, raising the water temperature by ten degrees.

She swam hard to keep the illusion of perfect temperature, but her breath soon caught at the bone-numbing cold. Grinning, Haukkamaa vaulted out of the pool, reached down, and pulled her up and out.

"Once more, the hot," he said.

"Oh, must I?" she responded, hanging back, but the night air was chilling. In the bluish glow reflected from the dancing water, they were Grecian statues, perfectly muscled male and female bodies. He did not pause, however, to admire her, but whisked her across the grass to the now welcome heat of the sauna. This time he was merciful and let the door stand open after only five minutes of suffering.

The hot and cold and hot stunned all modesty out of her. It made a Finn of her, for an hour. As she warmed herself, relishing the smell of crushed birch leaves and hot stones and new wood, he explained that now they bathe.

"It is *peseytyminen*. I fetch soap and water."

With a bucket of cold water, scented soap and a brush, they scrubbed themselves right where they sat. Then to rinse, they had another quick swim. In the anteroom again, he drew water from the sink and gave her a glassful, "to replace electrolytes. You will dehydrate, lose minerals."

In the now cooler sauna, he compromised and sat on the middle tier, putting her next to him. His hand on her back moved up and down, up and down. She smiled at him.

"Perhaps I could grow to like this. The sauna. It's all so new to me."

She meant more than the sauna, but she didn't want him to know any more of her history than he'd soon find out.

"Now is the time for after-sauna *karpalolikööri* and *kaaretorttu*," he said, and explained, "cranberry liqueur and a little cake rolled with berries. But I have only the cranberry Fennica liqueur. No woman I know cooks *kaaretorttu*."

"Some men are actually able to cook, too, I've heard," she retorted.

"Take care," he said. "I cook well. And Finnish women voted in 1908, before any women in Europe or the Americas," he added with pride.

She stared at him. Without further talk, in the cooling

dark sauna, he put his arm around her waist and tipped her face up to his. The contact made her mold her body to his, wanting no more stove for heat.

"You wish to make in my new sauna the Yankee orgy?" he asked softly. He didn't give her a chance to draw away. He kissed her suddenly and then deeply, caressing her with lingering fingers. She could not sit still, so he stood her between his thighs, facing him, with her arms looped down around his neck. He reached up to fondle her high, bobbing breasts, looking at her, his hair drying to gold bullion in the faint light.

"You are very beautiful, but of course you know that," he said. "I believe you are truly a runner. Such a firm body . . ."

His hands explored the firm body where the wide corners of the hips had been and were no more, and the buried places of the fat pads before they, too, became muscle.

"Glorious," he whispered.

Even if he said such things to all women, she chose to believe him, and she loved it. Loved his touch and his words. She swayed a little, so he had to close his legs on hers to hold her upright. After such caresses, her knees were buckling. Slowly he moved her from between his knees, but he didn't stand up. He gripped her legs, spread them wide, and shoved his legs under them, so that she sat on his thighs with her legs over the bench and around him. That brought his hard core to meet her most sensitive point.

Jeanne now learned about kissing. His active tongue pursued hers into the deepness of her mouth, and her pelvic muscles tightened until he felt it and muttered something in Finnish down in his throat. He kissed her ears and eyes and then the line of her jaw when her head fell back.

"You are the most sensuous . . . sensual—" he said, his caresses becoming fiercer. Suddenly he pivoted on the narrow bench and straddled it like a horse. Gripping her small waist between his hands, he began slowly lowering her, arching her backward, so her hands were pulled away from his warm neck and her head tilted back. Still he kept her thighs up on his own legs, and she grasped his forearms, her legs around him. Her shoulders and only her shoulders touched the warm wet wood.

Jeanne groaned and let her head drop back in a nest of hair, her hands dropping limply from his arms. He stroked her with that smooth, warm, seeking—

She exploded. Violently her body rippled with unbearable sensation. The instant the cataclysm struck her, he tensed, watching motionlessly. When she shuddered down into quiet, he pulled her up again to sit facing him.

"What a woman!" he exclaimed, shaking his head in bewilderment. "Never have I seen a woman so . . . loving!"

She had nothing to say. She wanted it all, to be filled and finished, to become a woman in every sense. Her desire communicated itself without words through tender kisses. She wanted him to be as happy as she was. Her legs wound around his waist. She felt herself again being lowered, dizzyingly, and her head lay once more on the warm sauna bench, as warm as a horse's lowered neck. Wide-shouldered, Erkki loomed over her, gripped her hips, lifted them. Slowly, slowly, without violence, almost tenderly, he began to open her.

Jeanne groaned at the unbearable inevitability of it.

"You wait for me this time" he murmured as if smiling. Her eyes were tightly closed. She could not imagine it would feel so impossible. Rings of tension ascended her body again.

Then he stopped.

"*Perkele!*" he cried out. "You are a virgin!"

"Please go on," she whispered, up at him.

"How can this thing be?" he asked dumbfounded. "So sensual, so knowing, and yet—" He didn't move. She felt like screaming in anticipation. Would he laugh at her?

"This be for house, and bed," he said, and swept her upright and into his arms, standing. She lolled, limp as a doll.

The night was still black as he carried her across the lawn from the lighted entry of the sauna up to the house. She covered her eyes. Through room after room, he never paused, his bare feet slapping across the hollow floors. Finally she was laid upon a bed in a softly lit room. He opened the covers from the opposite side and expertly rolled her body over onto the cool, smooth sheet.

When he came back he carried a dark towel in his hand, which he spread beneath her body. Settling himself beside her, lying full-length, he gently opened her eyelids with his two thumbs. "Look at me," he whispered.

She found nothing to say. She touched his arms, tracing the muscles twisting around from the backs of them. The insides of his elbows were soft as satin and warm.

"Have you been a nun? A sister in some order?" he asked.

She was too startled to reply.

"Enclosed in a convent? Is that why?"

"Not exactly," she hedged, willing to say most anything to keep him from guessing her history.

"The convent, then, it is true?"

"It might as well be," she said. She closed her eyes and sighed deeply.

"You should have told me, first. I never saw any woman so . . . so happy in her body, and so ready. The first you entered my office, your eyes said 'make love.' I said to myself, 'that young woman feels quite much passion.' Now I shall teach you what I thought you knew." A pause. "Are you safe against—?"

"Yes. The Pill," she said.

"Ah."

The he ceased to interrogate her. He acted instead, and she lay smiling, feeling him cherish her body. The doctor become a tender teacher. No, a surgeon now, prepping her for an exquisite surgery with a long probe warmed for the purpose.

He lay beside her and stroked her quickly rising ribs and belly with the backs of his fingers, barely touching her, so she shivered all over. He reached beneath her and squeezed her roundnesses, and then spread her legs as he rose and knelt between them.

"It is so long since last I—" he whispered. "This way, for now, and later the more interesting—" His rapid breathing interfered with his speech.

Then he moved over her, blotting out the dim light, and made contact with her ready flesh and parted her. Slowly, slowly, he penetrated.

Jeanne lifted her arms gracefully, and put them around his neck. He lay lightly on her and rocked his body, back and forth, so she began to moan with pleasure. Her toes splayed apart with the sensation and the expectancy.

"Yes," she murmured. "Yes, yes. Please!"

His hands ran under her back and rose to grip her shoulders. He increased the pressure, and she gasped.

"Look at me," he commanded, and she did so. Wide-eyed. He smiled.

It hurt now. It hurt a lot, and she bit her lip, but she wanted the hurt. She didn't want to slide from maidenhood to womanhood like a mother knocked out cold for the birth of her child.

"Move," he whispered. "Move against me to make it easier."

She obeyed. He lessened the pressure and raised his weight, so she could undulate her hips, dance under him. Then, grimacing, he thrust, and she felt the barrier broken. He bowed his back for another thrust, and her nails cut into his fine velvety skin. He still stared down, fascinated, into her face.

"Oh, Erkki!" she cried, almost rolling her "r" as he did.

In, in, in. So much of him! She'd never guessed how deeply a man penetrates a woman, or how awful and wonderful it could be.

Then he pulled entirely free of her body, so she felt collapsed and empty. "Oh, no!" she gasped. "Come, come to me."

Smiling, he came into her again, more easily this time. Now he worked himself round and round, grasping her bosom and then reaching under her and lifting her, so he came further into her body.

"Beautiful woman," he said. *"Kaunis, kaunis!"*

The sound of the strange Finnish tongue did it. She began to squirm with the rising waves of excitement, and he lost control; teeth clenched, he convulsed. She went with him, gripping him to her and crying out her own crisis of joy.

When Jeanne awoke, it was daylight Sunday and she ached from sleeping locked against his side. Before he woke, she lay thinking about what to say. No journalist's questions now, and none about running either. Was it too soon to ask about them—him and her?

Before he could say 'Good morning,' she began.

"Do men like to . . . to have virgins?" she asked, like a very young girl.

"Yes," he admitted. "We do," he said, tracing her features with a wonderful finger. "Do you know how a girl's face looks as she experiences that?" Erkki shook his head unbelievingly. "Or a woman's face, like yours, after waiting for so long? I think you are not twenty. Not more than twenty-five—"

"Twenty-four," she admitted.

"It is wonderful to see," he concluded, sighing.

"Men get all the pleasure," she commented wryly.

"A boy's first time must look wonderful, too."

"Ah, yes." She'd think about that. She wanted no man but him, but yet . . . but yet . . . Twenty-four, and this was her first time, first man, first real kiss.

"I am glad you waited for me," he said.

"So am I."

Jeanne, pressed down into the love-wrinkled sheets, took her second lesson on how to move with him, and how to use her tongue to twist around his. Before noon, she'd learned all she had fantasized, and things she hadn't known were possible.

They showered together. When they went to the kitchen, they found they weren't hungry for food and returned to the kingsize bed.

Jeanne learned to watch his face and marvel at what she could do to it. The cold, stolid, narrow-eyed Finn so entirely in control in his office was a different man today. He lay on his back, sighing and gazing up at her kneeling form, raising those strong arms to grasp the

brass bars at the head of the bed. Jeanne straddled him
and began to revolve in a belly dance worthy of Salome
herself, brushing him lightly. She undulated, her high
breasts rising and falling, her arms rising until her elbows pointed to the ceiling, and her hands lifted her
locks of hair.

"Beautiful angel," he murmured, arching his back
so she was lifted off her knees. "Devil! You learn so
fast, you will become a devil with men. You will leave
me. What did I make of you?"

"A vessel of pleasure," she said a trifle smugly.
What really shocked her, though, was her power over
him. At this moment, she mastered him.

Something of this must have been communicated
through her musing expression, for he gasped that he
could bear no more, jerked her down, rolled over with
her and took aim. She heard herself begging him no,
no, but he did not listen.

"Too much of teasing," he said, "you will learn is
not wise!"

She fought him, but not in earnest. She was as heated
as he, and his spirited entry, with her legs kicking
widly, her hands pinned down beside her head, gave
her a tremendous climax. She began to weep.

"You see," he said, lying atop her and not asking
why she wept, because he already knew. "We are
alike. We cannot get too much of this, and we know
what each shall want."

Silently, Jeanne wished she knew what she really
wanted, and prayed she would learn what Erkki
wanted, too.

Chapter Four

"REMEMBER ROSIE AND the Boston Marathon?" Ron asked Jeanne one day.

Boston 1980. Jeanne hadn't yet begun working at *Fancy Free* in 1980, but she had been running by then. Anyone who ran and read would remember Rosie. Any TV watcher would, for that matter. She nodded. "Of course I do."

"What a way to make women's marathoning famous!"

"I know. I'd give anything to know why she did whatever she really did," Jeanne mused, "and if she herself knew what really happened."

"Be nice to get an interview with someone who'd done a thing like that," said Ron, pushing his jet black hair from his forehead. Even though he was the male editor of a magazine for women runners, he easily commanded the respect of his female staff. He was a wonderful boss.

"Psychology of it intrigues me," he continued.

"First we're trying to get women jogging. For weight loss, for self-confidence and assertiveness, for prenatal benefits, for premenstrual tension, for menopause, for every good reason. So they jog. Then they run. Then they run marathons. Then they pretend to *win* marathons. Where is it going to end?"

"Same place men's running does. Longer races, better times, worse injuries. And the Los Angeles Olympic Marathon of 1984."

"Don't make book on that," Ron said sarcastically. "You know they won't admit that a woman can run twenty-six miles. The Olympic Committee is willfully blind. In 1970, true, three thousand men and no known women ran in a total of seventy marathons. But last year, in some three-hundred and sixty marathons, there were seventy-five thousand men and eight thousand women. Did you know that? Eight thousand women. And the Committee chooses to ignore it."

"You sound like an article," she said, grinning. "Write that as an editorial for the next issue."

"*You* write it, you'll be the one discriminated against."

"I'm more interested in the cheating. Why would anyone do it, when running's such a personal thing? Except for the trophy in each age class, what's there to gain?

"A T-shirt to wear among your sedentary friends," he said.

"Yeah, but some race directors are handing out the shirts with the numbers, *before* the marathon. T-shirts have lost their value."

"It was done before Rosie, you know," and Ron pulled from his encyclopedic backlog of information the example of the Chicago marathon where the first *two* women to cross the finish line were disqualified.

Also a case in Baltimore, one in San Diego, one in San Francisco.

"Enough!" she said. "This cheating stuff really burns me up. I could skin anyone alive who would bring shame to running. It would be so great if everyone could be on the honor system, but with cheaters around security procedures will have to be tightened. Videotapes, checkpoints, bike patrols on the courses . . ."

"Go get 'em, Jeanne," Ron interrupted. "Hey, I have to get back to work. You reporters have all the fun. We editor types have to negotiate with advertisers and coddle the U.S. Post Office."

"You love every minute of it and you know it."

Ron walked away, making his way through the rabbit warren of tiny cubicles crammed into the three-hundred square feet of floor space allotted to *Fancy Free*. She leaned back in her chair for a few seconds and then bolted upright. There was work to be done. First she needed to finish off an article on running during pregnancy that she'd begun the week before—before putting it aside to interview Erkki. When she first came to *Fancy Free*, it had taken her ages to do each paragraph. But now she sat at her typewriter and fairly flew through her work. Practice sure helped.

She and Ron still hadn't made a decision about running the Haukkamaa piece in *Fancy Free*, so she had queried an editor she knew at the *Journal*. "The research sounds good," she'd said to Jeanne. "And this Finn doctor sounds terrific. Do you think he's photogenic? We could run some pictures with the copy."

Ah, yes. Very photogenic. And eugenic, every other kind of -genic. For Jeanne. Wonderful. Therapeutic. She loved him. Already? Stop it, or you'll never get anything done today.

Ron had asked her to cover one of the new marathons for the magazine. They seemed to be popping up all over the place. The big races like Boston and New York got lots of coverage. Her angle for the piece would be the differences between running one of the prestige races and running a race with fewer entrants, less hype, less competition.

November was a good month for marathoning. It was cool enough and usually without snow. When so much blood must go to your legs, there is not enough left to circulate and cool your body. So hot weather races show poorer times for any but the heat-adapted superjocks. And twenty-six point two miles at eighty-five degrees hurts, as Ron would say, "like Hades."

Jeanne looked over the long list of November marathons. North Carolina. Pennsylvania. Georgia. Tennessee. Hawaii. Hmm. She giggled as she thought about asking Ron to pay her expenses to cover a Hawaiian marathon. He would roll his big black eyes and shake his head. "Be serious, Jeanne, for once, will you?"

But seriously, most of the new marathons were far enough afield that she would have to leave Washington—and Erkki—for a weekend.

On impulse, she picked up the phone and called him. When he answered and said "Haukkamaa here" she forgot what she was going to say. There was a long silence.

"This is Haukkamaa. Is anyone there?"

"It's me, Jeanne," she babbled. "I have to cover a marathon and I can't decide which one to pick. The only one I've ruled out is Hawaii because Ron wouldn't pay the expenses." She explained her assignment and the fact that she would have to be away for a few days, probably over a weekend.

"Just do not be apart for long time," he said, and she breathed a little more quickly. "I wish to see you. Right now. After five. Can you be free?"

"I can," she said, before she looked at her pocket calendar.

She could.

"Not to only talk," he warned, and she pressed her legs together in her slacks, smiling in total happiness.

That was not the sort of conversation to make working all afternoon any easier, but she edited Kerry's third draft of a piece on the danger of crash diets and looked through the life story of Babe Didrikson Zaharias for Nancy, continuing to wonder where to go, considering the cost of gas. Anyplace she picked was a shot in the dark. If she picked Delaware, something exciting could happen in Kentucky. Maybe she should decide on the basis of scenery, a new place to run.

Jeanne had been seeing a lot of downtown Washington since she'd begun running to and from work at *Fancy Free*. This increased her weekly distances without eating up too much of her time. She could bring in her changes of clothes on Mondays then run the other four days and shower at the office, courtesy of Ron, who had made such facilities available. The office might be small, but Ron had insisted that a shower be installed in the rest-room. He had also printed up T-shirts with the magazine's crazy name emblazoned in brilliant orange on front and back. The staff was asked to run to and from work in these shirts. Good for PR. And Jeanne did. The words inspired lots of comments. The next shirts, she suggested, should clarify that it was the magazine that was fancy and free. Not the runner.

Pill down, libido up. She thought of Erkki. Erkki ran at noon some days, but most of the time he ran at six in the morning, before work, in his lovely treelined neighborhood full of old houses, rolling lawns and barking dogs. On weekends he did fifteens or twenties, and had already invited her to come along.

To come along to the June ultramarathon in Helsinki, too. Now that was an invitation! Maybe it even implied a future. . . .

No, just enjoy Erkki now, she told herself firmly. And maybe that was part of the thrill. That he'd be going away. His visa was already stretched past the breaking point, he told her. She might think she loved him, but it was too early for decisions. Still, couldn't love occur at first sight and last forever? Didn't it? Mom said it did, but Mom found Dad, and Lily had only Albert, Rutherford and Gary. Etcetera. "Etcetera, etcetera, etcetera," as the King of Siam would say. None of them, Jeanne figured, measured up to her father, strong Sam Lathrop.

But then, Mom and Lily were totally different women, sisters only in name. Which was her best role model?

Jeanne switched off that disturbing meditation and thought instead of running and Rosie.

With Rosie, as someone had said, running had lost its innocence.

Chapter Five

ERKKI HAUKKAMAA HUNG up his lab coat, glared at himself in the glass of the door through which he exited and arrived at his car before his American watch said five twenty. He headed down the Beltway toward Bethesda in the worst of the rush hour traffic. Wise of Jeanne to live close so she could run to and from work.

He closed his eyes for a moment, thinking of her. Jeanne. How could she have come to him at twenty-four in the wonderful condition he found her? Surely she had not been free to know men for long, or another would have initiated her. When she'd walked into his office that day he would have wagered a year's salary that she was experienced—more experienced than he. The first sight of her had rocked him, she in that clinging rose dress and the impractical shoes that made her ankles only two inches across; she with her sparkling, eager eyes. She looked at him as if she knew him already, indeed had already been intimate with him and returned for more. He had wanted her so fiercely that he had used the sauna as a lure, and now that she had accepted his invitation—cockily daring him to follow through—he found the days of waiting terrible.

What if he'd been too hasty, frightened her, mistaken as he had been about her? How did she reach that state of being—what do Americans call it? A foxy lady.

Had she really been a nun? She had not answered his question directly. What did he know of Catholics, of nuns?

He was suddenly back in Helsinki, a Lutheran boy from the countryside, son of refugees, survivors among the dead. How many thousands were killed by the invading Russians, when the Finns stood fast for a hundred days, outnumbered ten to one? He'd been a stranger to churches. But once he had ventured up the long, steep steps—not of the cathedral of his own faith that loomed over the harbor, pale-domed, and as white and immaculate inside as a hospital or mausoleum— but up the steps of the neighboring Uspenski Katedraali, the Eastern Orthodox cathedral built of diagonally-laid red bricks under thirteen onion-shaped golden domes, the flames at Pentecost. It had no pews. The black-clad worshippers stood in the circular sanctuary among baroque icons of filigreed silver and gold, frightening to a boy; paintings and statues in shiny, dazzling colors, so different from the cold white Lutheran marble that it took his breath away. Jewels glistened and winked everywhere, and soulful Byzantine eyes gazed down at him.

Throughout the endless hour and a half celebration, invisible voices sang beautiful monotony in another tongue behind the altar screen, and bearded priests in black did inexplicable things. Could Jeanne's background be the even darker, medieval Roman Church? The boy, Erkki, had not knelt, but pressed himself against the wall, his soul shivering within him at the mysteries of the jeweled icons and the replicas of bloody torture.

So he had become a physician, dedicated to the alleviation of suffering.

Some he had not been able to alleviate, and that pushed him into this research upon healthy, no, superhealthy bodies, to discover why they prospered. No more disease and distraught kin, ooze and stink and deathbeds. He'd thought he could bear it, but he couldn't. The memory of horrors in Helsinki, the guilt, the helpless rage dogged him even here in America.

You are a doctor? You call yourself a physician? His wife's parents had hurled stinging, relentless diatribes at him, all the more insulting for their Swedish idiom. The Swedes had run at will across his land for centuries, suppressing the native peoples, forbidding them a written language, lording it over the Finns, then losing Finland to the power in the East, the Russians, who had killed both his grandfathers and all his uncles.

He rubbed the back of his knuckles over his forehead, swerved fractionally and corrected his steering. Jeanne. Jeanne was a better antidote than the extended visa, letting him escape all that. Not to return to his native land was difficult. Yet all he wanted was to bury himself in Jeanne, *Giinni,* burrow into her gripping, welcoming body, into the dark of her, to make her weep with joy of him. Instead of being cursed to hell for his sins. And they were many. Jeanne didn't know how many, though she had asked. It was fortunate she didn't work at the Institute, didn't know his colleagues there, had no access to the rumors about his past. Her questions he had deflected perhaps too angrily—would this cause suspicion?—but he wanted this one person, this lovely, love-hungry female to be his sanctuary. And she was a runner, too.

What might he blurt out in bed with Jeanne? When they were both in a frenzy, bodies conquering minds? Or suppose that Jeanne became intent upon marriage? What could he say? Already the questions, "Where are your wife, your children?" "Have you wife or children?" had struck him like exploding bombs, and he had been rude, but not so rude as he had wished to be.

Oh, Jeanne, so long pent up. How did they stand it, nuns and priests and neglected women? He could not imagine such prolonged celibacy. When he first came to the Institute he had dated two of the assistants from his group, the pretty ones, one after the other, half for revenge, half to drown his sense of loss and self-condemnation. He hardly remembered them; one hated him now, while the other made cow eyes at him and silently asked for more.

More loveless thrusting. Rock stars had their groupies. He had his. Cecily would roll blue eyes up at him while pipetting reagents from bottle to bottle, and then withdraw the glass tube from her lips and run her pink tongue around the mouthpiece. He'd flee to his office and punch the buttons to bring Sibelius flooding into his ears. Relief, sitting with his head in his hands, letting the music cleanse his soul. Lust had done him in once before. Not again. Not with Jeanne Lathrop, he prayed.

"Do you imagine you can get away with all this?" screamed the voice through the telephone receiver. They used English because they spoke no Finnish, and his own Swedish was poor. By choice. He was proud of his native tongue, albeit a language used by only five million people. And virtually unlearnable by any but an infant who hears it spoken from birth; a language Swedes banned in schools and for polite usage a hundred years ago. When he first came here, the Americans had laughed at his struggles with the odd concept of gender. He had used "she" and "her" in reference to men. That President Kekkonen did it also was small comfort. Now he had mastered the pronouns and improved his pronunciation, but he knew he did not speak English like other educated Europeans. Americans might think him stupid. Illiterate. A peasant. Karelian peasant.

Could the son of Karelian peasants be husband to an American woman? Could he be husband to anyone again? Could he forget the past and make a new future with Jeanne? Precious Jeanne. He would be with her very soon.

Chapter Six

ERKKI WAS COMING! This afternoon! She must run home, carrying manuscripts rolled in her butt pack, a zippered nylon tube strapped around her waist, that bounced upon her rear as she ran. Then she must shower and dress . . . in what? A pegnoir from the Twenties? Jeans and a skimpy top?

She ran on the sidewalk alongside bumper-to-bumper traffic, breathing exhaust. But at least she was running, and that allowed her to eat desserts now and then. Two miles to work and two miles back, except when she was forced to take her briefcase, full of more papers and books than her butt pack would hold.

She raced up the steps two at a time and unlocked the door, shedding her *Fancy Free* T-shirt before she reached the bathroom, stepping out of her shorts while one hand tested the shower temperature. Then she kicked off shoes and undies and plunged in. *Tepid water, yuk!*

Jeanne remembered the sauna, soon to be reencountered, but not tonight.

Splashing herself with lotion, she put on fresh bikini underwear and shrugged into a pale blue silk blouse. It was a wisp without buttons that tied in a soft knot under the bosom. She pulled on slinky black silk jersey pants, reveling in the soft feel of them next to her skin.

Her hair required no more than a quick brushing after she shook drops of water from it. She slipped jade droplet earrings on, made up her eyes, barely tinted her lips.

He rang at six-thirty, and she pressed the button to activate the buzzer that unlocked the main door downstairs. She ran back to her own door, unlocking it, her hand on the knob ready to fling it open the moment she heard him at the top of the stairs.

The second she looked at him she saw his eyes were shadowed with weariness or sorrow. She stretched out her arms and drew him to her.

"Erkki, oh, what *is* it?"

"I have been thinking of you."

"I thought there was something wrong," she sighed with relief. "I've been thinking of you, too. I missed you."

It had only been three days. She stepped back and held him at arm's length. It was so very good to see him again. He wore an elegant shirt with pale blue and beige stripes, sleeves rolled European-style above his elbows. Nice elbows, narrowing in from sinewy golden forearms lightly downed with pale hair over smooth skin.

"That is a nice costume," he said wearily in his foreign voice that continued to thrill her. His face was more gaunt today. His hand, gnarled with tendons, closed around the glass of sheery she poured for him.

"Very sweet," he said, wincing. "Sugar exists in all American food and drinks."

"You don't like it. I have drier wines—"

"Stay. It is fine. I need energy. I shall have use for much energy, I think."

She remained quiet, but felt her nostrils and eyes flare open like a mare's. The livingroom was not as neat as she would have liked, considering how neat his home and office were. But haste, the need to be pretty and sweet-smelling and seductive, had ruled her. The scattered sections of the *Washington Post* and *The Washingtonians* did not seem to distress him.

"Now," he said, setting down his glass before she had drained hers, "Do we talk of dinner, or do we—"

"The latter," she said, and took his hand.

She would have led him boldly to the bedroom, but he pulled her to a halt.

"Jeanne, I cannot delay to ask you. How did you become as you are? How did your history fail to empty passion from you?"

Jeanne prayed that he never read *Playgirl*.

"I fantasized," she said simply. After all, it was true.

"Ah. Good. That is helpful, even to happy wives."

"I know. I felt very wicked, but it saved my sanity. Now everyone talks openly about fantasies. Luckily I had a dear aunt who was quite avant-garde, even bohemian. She advised me—" Jeanne decided to leave it at that.

"Tell me," Erkki said suddenly, sitting down and pulling her onto his lap. "I would like to know what you liked to dream. Did you dream of heroes coming to you on bended knee and pleading their love? Like in courtly days with knights and queens?"

"Sometimes I did. And sometimes I made up stories

in which I was carried off by a strong, older, experienced man. I was raised strictly and it helped me, uh–"

"It helped take off your guilt."

"It's good to know you understand. Before seeing Dr. Tinsley, I was too ashamed to reveal any of my fantasies to anyone. Can I tell you a secret?"

He nodded and brushed his lips lightly against hers.

Jeanne grinned sheepishly. "I even made up an alter ego named Amelia. Amelia was constantly being swept away by Arabian sheiks on gorgeous stallions, or by Indian braves on the warpath. She hasn't been around for a while. And since I've met you, I don't think I'll need her again. Oh, Erkki, I am so happy I met you."

He kissed her deeply and ran his golden hands up and down the length of her body. "So you like the man who will not be denied, but who will make you like it very much. I did not have to try very hard, as you remember. You liked very much the little that I did—"

"Hush," she said, embarrassed to remember the rapid effect his hands had had on her. "That was the sauna, and such a new environment—"

"Let us not talk," he said.

By now he had her soft slacks down over her hips. He flipped them onto the nearest empty chair. He stood up and held her tightly against him. Suddenly he released her and moved aside.

For a long time he didn't touch her. The tension doubled her desire. With an effort, she did not move, just stared up into his face, seeing out of the corner of her eye his brown hand approaching very slowly, rising, and closing around the knot of her shirt-tails. His hard knuckles brushed the underside of her breasts.

"Come to me," he said, and then drew her to him,

slowly pulling her up and in, across the soft rug, her hands hanging at her sides. He held her motionless, close to him. Now his free hand began to explore her back, and touched the twin dimples above her buttocks. He held her on tiptoe, her body stretched from toes to diaphragm, so he supported half her weight with his fist gripping that knot. She went dizzy with anticipation.

He kissed her casually, savoring lips that reached up toward his. When she could stand it no longer she flung both arms around his neck and he dipped and swept her up off the floor, hand under her knees.

He didn't have to be told where the bed was. He found it and stood her in the middle, her head close under the suspended canopy. He pulled the blouse from her shoulders and let it billow down on to the bed. He tossed it aside. Standing with one arm locked about her waist, he kissed her while he unfastened his shirt. Catching a glimpse of them in the bureau mirror, Jeanne was jolted by the impact. Half-clad girl and fully-clad man. Suddenly—with a few swift motions, an unclad girl and a half-clad man, he laying her on the bed, lying over her with a breast in each hand, murmuring words in Finnish that she didn't understand, and didn't need to.

Jeanne's head fell back, her spine arched, and her bones melted with desire. Half blind, she reached for him. Naked, he lay on her, and teased, teased, kissing her all over.

"Oh, end it!" she begged until he turned her over, pulled her up on her knees, and came to her that way, making her breasts swing forward with each push.

"Oh, Erkki! Oh, Erkki!"

He turned her face toward the mirror, and the disparity between their sizes and the whiteness of her skin against his golden color, the ropelike muscles down his side and loins, bulging and tensing with the strain, filled her with delight.

He lifted her off her knees with his effort, and then he fell on his side with her, crooning, "Sweet, sweet little Jeanne, so warm, so needing. Needed."

They lay cuddled together, Jeanne fighting the inevitable joyous, unbelieving tears. "Just think. Lots of women never once experience this," she told him.

"It is sad. So unnecessary."

"To have it once or twice and then never again would be worse. Like seeing and then going blind."

"Do not think doctors are ignorant. We see the women with the back pains and the headaches and the allergies, and we suspect they do not tell us everything. You might give lessons, Jeanne."

It was her turn to laugh. "Really? *Me?*"

They did not go to dinner until nine. Erkki had to hold her upright all the way down the stairs, so limp was she with love.

"I shall never want to lose this," he said.

"Must you lose it?" she asked, face against the side of his warm neck.

"Of course I must," gruffly. And then more softly, "I should not have it even now."

Chapter Seven

I AM IN love, Jeanne said to herself in surprise. I thought people exaggerated how it felt.

She found herself saying, "Erkki, Erkki, Erkki," over and over, and writing his name in margins again and again. She pictured him piecemeal: his eyes, narrow, pale-lashed and piercing, the square teeth so straight and white. The hands, long-fingered and square-palmed, that knew exactly what to do and where and for how long. She had never seen any man naked, and there he was, long and lithe, with those stunning runner's legs. The tendons behind his knees were iron cables, but the skin between them as soft as a baby's. This intrigued her, the contrasts—the aloof, commanding, foreign strength coupled with the boyish hair and the excitement at discovering her.

Do women in love cease to eat? Running decreased appetite by relaxing away the compulsion to eat, but love cut her desire for food by keeping her queasy with fear. Suppose she lost his affection? Suppose she was just one of a string of women that so skilled a man might obtain? Was he hiding something? Why would he not answer questions about his past? And what had she to offer him above others?

Plenty, Dr. Tinsley would have said. Her treatment had been terminated by mutual consent only recently. She could see him occasionally, when needed, but she trusted herself now to stay off the guilt trips and the Valium she had once needed.

Ron interrupted her thoughts by dangling her car keys in front of her nose. "So what marathon are you going to cover?" he asked.

"Knoxville looks pretty good," she ventured. "I've got a map of the course, and the way it winds through the countryside, crosses rivers, it should be a beautiful run. Perfect weather there right now, too. Below sixty. I could use some new vistas, and I've never been to the hills of Tennessee. First time for the race, too. It's being co-sponsored by the local road runners club and the Knoxville Chamber of Commerce. That's an interesting combination right there."

"Then go for it, kid. Lookin' good." Ron knew how much she loved to hear that phrase. Race spectators lining the last yards of a course shouted it as encouragement to runners nearing the finish line. Often, it was just the lift you needed to pour on that final kick.

The Knoxville marathon was scheduled for the Sunday after next. It would be a long trip, an all-day drive from Washington, but it would be beautiful. She had returned from Elmton via the Pennsylvania Turnpike, with its narrow lanes carrying too many cars through uninspiring scenery. To get to Knoxville, though, she could follow the Interstate through Virginia mountains afire with fall foliage.

Erkki would be attending a conference in Boston

this weekend, so she wouldn't see him. She found a ten K—six point two miles—race in Potomac Park. When she started racing, Jeanne had concentrated on the short Fun Runs which were proliferating madly. But with a 4:30 marathon goal sometime in the next year, she needed to race longer distances. Ten-milers would have to be habitual training runs by winter, moving into some fifteens and twenties in summer.

Saturday Jeanne drove her Porsche to the park and joined the mob for a towpath race up to up to Glen Echo and back. No T-shirts, just ribbons at the finish line and your name in the sponsoring club's monthly newsletter. Gratifying just the same.

At the starting line runners lined up according to their minutes-per-mile time. Feeling feisty, Jeanne found a spot in the eight-minute pack. Her PR for ten K was 54:23, slightly under a nine-minute pace. Her goal today was fifty minutes, a hair over an eight-minute mile. When the starting gun sounded, the runners clapped and cheered as they took off. It took a few strides to hit the open road with so many racers, but as soon as the pack thinned out Jeanne knew it was going to be a good race. Sometimes the first mile was murder, but today her running was almost effortless. Legs, arms, heart, lungs and head worked together.

The carpet of fallen leaves on the path was wonderfully soft after the cement sidewalks she pounded to and from work. Good shoes were indispensable, but they could do only so much. Her orange juice sloshed around in her stomach, and she concentrated on her breathing, creating a four-stride rhythm. In-in, out-out.

At the halfway mark an official was calling the splits; 25:15 he called as Jeanne passed him. Her fifty-minute goal was very much in sight. She lifted her elbows a trifle, pushed off more forcefully with her toes and leaned into it. With a push she might break an eight-minute pace. A mile in eight minutes! When giant Jeanne began jogging, a twelve-minute pace was impossible for even a quarter mile. A quarter mile at a time, in secrecy, around the secluded driveway, so the jiggling jelly-jogger would not be seen by laughing passersby.

What a distance she had come!

At the beginning of the last mile of the six, she decided to try her kick. Fisting her hands, Jeanne poured it on, wondering what her pace was. Surely below eight. Fifty yards before the finish line the nausea she expected to feel began choking her. It was going to last just a moment after she finished, so she endured it, grimacing, plunging over the line as her time was shouted out. 49:56. She had done it! Made her goal with four precious seconds to spare. She was hot today! Nothing better than cheering spectators for the last stretch to put wings on one's heels.

At beer-and-pop time around the keg and coolers, restoring fluids and minerals they'd all sweated away, she asked who might be running the Knoxville marathon a week from tomorrow.

"I am," grinned a compact man with a droopy brown moustache. His smile gave him long dimples, and laugh wrinkles fringed his eyes. He was around thirty, Jeanne calculated. He'd shed his T-shirt to wring it out, showing a narrow, brown, furry chest. "I saw you cross the finish line today. You looked real good. What do you think you'll do in Knoxville? 3:30?"

"Oh, I'm not running," Jeanne laughed. "I'm covering the race for *Fancy Free*. I have to drive down anyway and thought I'd be patriotic and save gas and get some company for the long drive." It was an impulsive thing to do, but she tended to do impulsive

things after a run, things she would once never have
dreamed of doing. She always saved her difficult assignments—awkward phone calls and confrontations
with the landlord or the dentist—for after running. And
this happy runner looked like a whole lot more fun
than the dentist.

"I'm as patriotic as the next fellow. I'm also Dick
Kilmer," he said, extending his hand.

"Jeanne Lathrop. Glad to meet you." His hand-
shake was friendly and warm.

As they walked to her car, they exchanged phone
numbers and made plans for the drive next week.
Jeanne drove off, waving to Dick as she headed out
of the park.

She hadn't gotten very far when she realized what
she had done. She was going off next weekend with
an almost total stranger. Well, not really. She'd learned
a few things about him. He was not married. He'd
made that very clear. He worked for the Bureau of
Land Management. He was a runner. Anyone who was
a runner had to be a good person. Jeanne's loyalty to
the sport was that strong.

And what about her loyalty to Erkki? He was her
first lover, but beyond that what was he? The heady
medicine of Dick's appraising glance, the possibilities
it contained, excited her. There was something warm
and appealing about Dick. He was *not* handsome, not
even oddly handsome like Erkki. Cute, though. About
five-nine, runner's build, blunt nose. The laughing eyes
and tumbled curls made him charming, and his body
was what Lily used to call "poetry in motion." You
can't find fault with that.

Erkki was wonderful. She felt things with him she
never imagined she could feel. But he was so mysterious, an enigma. Dick was just the opposite. He'd

hardly stopped talking, offering information about himself, asking her about herself. Lily had warned her about falling for the first man she met. Didn't she owe it to herself to sample life's pleasures, to make up for what she'd missed? She had promised herself to experiment, to try new things. Tonight she had a ticket to see a troupe of Thai dancers at the Kennedy Center. And she was going alone, not with a girlfriend, not with a date. Her insatiable appetite for food had been replaced by a need to experience the world, to take what was offered her. And Dick was offering, wasn't he?

That night at the Kennedy Center she was astounded by the Thai dancers in their sparkling baubles and rainbow costumes. Barefoot, they gesticulated in impossible positions, squatting, springing, tumbling, and by the end she ached not only from the race but also from sympathy for their adductor muscles and hamstrings.

Tonight, Jeanne imagined, the audience in this immense, palatial edifice must include celebrities and public figures: senators, diplomats, artists. Nervous, she forced herself to move easily among the bejeweled and befurred in her soft purple velvet dress. Men looked, women looked, and the men looked again. She lifted her chin, set what she hoped was a secretive smile on her lips and decided this was nice. To be mysteriously alone, nameless, but worth gazing at. What did people think her? A visiting Frenchwoman? A dancer? She surely moved with a grace she'd never before possessed or ever dreamed of possessing.

How she'd envied the stars on TV, back in Dakota. The ageless figures of Astaire and Channing and Ann Miller, who kicked and tapped and twirled, leaped and glided, and might be fifty, sixty or even seventy years old, while Jeanne at fifteen sat weeping in her useless body. How fantastic to stroll through the lobby of Kennedy Center in a body of springs and levers, oiled and capable of a marathon race—someday. She hugged her elbows against her sides and grinned.

Life. Life as a new Jeanne. Pretty and popular and in tip-top shape, with exciting challenges to meet. Next weekend in Knoxville, covering the marathon, interviewing runners, shooting pictures, sniffing out human interest stories, getting to know Dick. And then back to Washington, *Fancy Free* and Erkki Haukkamaa. She could have it all.

She went home singing, the whirligigs of color and ripples of Asian music still in her head, and threw herself into bed for a dreamless night.

Chapter Eight

ON WEDNESDAY JEANNE went to the Institute where Erkki showed her more of his work, including the battery of tests he was running that day on older male runners; electrocardiograms for heart size, oxygen consumption, cardiac output; chemical analyses for cholesterol lipoprotein, lactic acid and hormones. He did not seem happy to see her, which made her ill at ease and interfered with her reporting. She busily took photographs and left the building without saying adieu to her preoccupied lover.

By the time she got home, the phone was ringing. It was Erkki. "I just got in from work. Yes, I'd like to see you. Of course, come over."

He came over. She was frantic to ask him to explain his coldness at the lab. He'd been colder, if possible, today than on the first day she'd tackled him. But she didn't ask. Why did he run hot and cold this way?

When Erkki arrived, she poured him a glass of the

driest white wine she'd been able to buy—wine the color of his hair—and sat watching him drink it.

"I was surprised when you called. You hardly said a word to me today at the Institute, other than business. I didn't know what was going on."

"There is nothing 'going on,' as you say. At the laboratory I work. That is all. And now the laboratory is behind me." He drew her close and pressed his lips to hers. They tasted of wine, cool and dry. She drank deeply of him and lay back against the sofa cushions, groggy and content, her arm about his neck and his face between her breasts as if he'd smother there and die happy.

Later, much later, they lay beneath the canopy sky of Jeanne's bed.

"I have missed you while I was in Boston. And this weekend we will be apart once more. Have you decided which marathon you will attend?"

She told him she would be going to Knoxville.

"It is a long drive, is it not? You will be all right on your own?"

For a moment, Jeanne didn't know what to say. Should she tell him about Dick or not? Did she want to tell him to hurt him a little, the way his coldness had hurt her today at the Institute? Better to be honest, lay your cards on the table.

"How much do you know this person?" he responded gruffly after absorbing her statements.

"I told you. I met him at the race on Sunday. You don't want me to drive all that way by myself, do you?"

"I have difficulty understanding you, Jeanne. You have no men until you meet me, and now you spend the weekend with a stranger. I do not like it. Not one bit do I like it."

"You don't own me, you know." Jeanne turned away from him. What right did he have to act like this? A few hours ago he wasn't even civil to her, and now he wanted to tell her whom she could and could not spend her time with.

He rose from the bed and began to dress. "It is time for me to return home, I think."

Jeanne watched him, biting her lip until she tasted a drop of blood. "Erkki. I care about you, but this is all so new to me. I need time—and space."

He stared at her, through her with his disarming eyes. His face was set, as if carved in granite. "Enjoy your weekend."

With that he was gone. The silence in her room was deafening. The smell of their lovemaking was pungent in her nostrils, the bed still warm from his body. Jeanne punched her pillow and pulled the covers up over her head. Damn, she thought. Damn.

Dick arrived in his closed brown van with a western sunset painted on each side and in back, oblong tinted windows you could not see into. They had decided to take his van instead of her Porsche, because it would be more comfortable for the long drive to Knoxville and back. As Dick pulled up, though, Jeanne had second thoughts.

"What's the matter, Jeanne?"

"Nothing. I just think my Porsche would get better mileage than you will. We should have taken my car."

"But your Porsche means a nice fat hotel bill. We can sleep in this."

He was already moving down Wisconsin Avenue, so she bit her tongue and only raised an eyebrow in reply.

"You can go into a motel, if you want, but not me.

I've got heavy alimony and child support to pay, and every penny counts.''

"Oh," she said, pitying him. Did Erkki send funds back to Finland for such a purpose? Something was wrong about Erkki. His silences were forbidding. She didn't want to find out, though. It could not be good news.

"Speaking of pennies," Dick said pleasantly, his arm muscles rippling as he turned the nearly horizontal steering wheel, "a penny for your thoughts."

"I was wondering about you, but I didn't want to pry. You're divorced and have a child or two?"

"Right. We got hitched at twenty, and it didn't work out. Same old story. My son's six, and I see him on alternate weekends or when I can get up to Wilmington."

"I'm sorry," she said. She could tell from his tone that he missed his little boy a great deal.

Dick was consistent in his thrift. He didn't suggest eating breakfast or lunch in cafes along their route, but pulled out sandwiches and fruit. She asked him to stop at a supermarket so she could contribute Gatorade and carbohs to stock him up on glucose for tomorrow. He was carbohydrate loading, but hadn't starved himself on a purely protein diet beforehand. Wise man.

He turned on the radio and they both sang along to songs they knew. He glanced over at her with lowered brows, finally muttering, "Who've you got, Jeanne? You live with anyone? No, you wouldn't, not going to Knoxville with me."

"No, I live alone. At present."

They'd taken 211 Southwest through Warrenton to pick up 81 at New Market, near Luray in the Shenandoah Valley. It was familiar country to Dick, and she asked if he knew "Oh, Shenandoah," one of her favorite folksongs. He did, and he sang it in a fine bass-baritone that raised gooseflesh on Jeanne's arms.

"I'd damned well better break three hours tomorrow," he said next. "I've been hammering against that ceiling for years. It's like the four-minute mile for me."

"Which didn't fall until 1954, as I recall."

"You sure know your facts, don't you?" Dick glanced at her with his winning smile.

"When I started to work for *Fancy Free*, I read everything there was to read about running."

He listened with interest to her description of her job, and then gradually told her about his own background and interests. Her picture of him filled in, color by color, like a paint-by-number picture. He made her laugh at tales from the New Hampshire winters of his boyhood, and from his stint in a Texas bootcamp. He had been drafted back in the early seventies. "Try jogging in a heavy pack and boots, carrying a rifle," he snorted.

Unlike Erkki, Dick was jocular, and it took her hours to realize how much of his own unhappiness he was whistling away by his jokes and songs and his eager questions about her own life. The longer she knew him, the more appealing he was, both in actions and looks. In Levis, yellow polo shirt and the most beat-up running shoes she'd ever seen, Dick endeared himself to her without half trying.

This morning the sun silvered the trees and grass, dew hung like tinsel from the branches. On the wide, uncrowded, velvety asphalt highway, the efficient van sang along hill after rolling hill, humming like a busy sewing-machine. They passed Washington and Lee University and rolled into Roanoke in good time. Rest stop. She studied the clean, red brick buildings and homes, the white trim and antebellum pillars and cupolas. The Municipal Building of 1915 dated from the thirty-first year of the City of Roanoke. After Washington's bustle, Saturday's bustle here was noticeably slower.

Out of town, past brown fields, green-black forests, white silos under a pale blue cloudless sky, they drove over rivers on high bridges and followed valleys headed West.

Dick let her take her turn at the wheel and flung himself down on the inflated bed in the van to do stretches. His voice continued from behind her, asking if she, too, ran track in school, if she had sisters and brothers like his six. She found herself telling him everything—about her aunt, her fat, her nose job. She left out only Erkki Haukkamaa. Glancing back, she saw him sitting with one leg extended forward and both hands clamped around the arch of that foot. She hoped he broke his three hours tomorrow. And she wanted to do everything she could to help him get his wish.

The autumn colors of the mountain hardwoods gave way to ridge upon ridge of dark spruces and firs paralleling the parkway. The sun moved ahead of them as they approached Bristol, Tennessee, and as the hills grew longer and flatter, he told her bits of Civil War history that had intrigued him. All the dead and the dying on the plains from Antietam to Lookout Mountain.

His system of snacking on the road rather than stopping enabled them to make good time. He peeled bananas for her, after she tried feeding him orange sections, one by one as he drove. She didn't want him to get a cramped right foot from pressing the accelerator for hundreds of miles, so she drove.

"Watch what I'll do tomorrow," he teased. "Happens every time. Get my only blister on the heel of my accelerator foot. You'll have to drive all the way home."

"I won't mind. I love to drive," she said.

If one got tired, there was always the bed, complete with fresh linens, two fat pillows and a comforter. And the van had a tank for drinking water and a tiny chemical toilet.

"You could live in this van," she said.

"I have. Joey and I do that when I visit him; it cuts down on the time I have to spend with Sylvia. Just toss the kid in back and off we go."

"You want custody, I'll bet."

"But I can't get it until Joey's old enough to have his wishes heard in court. Right now, it's Mama's show, all the way." He said nothing more, but she could feel his mood darken, and she drove on silently.

As they rolled toward the sun, Jeanne donned her rose-colored sunglasses. "I'd be glad to take it the rest of the way in," she said, "if you'll give me directions."

"Okay, I'll just sit up here with you," he replied.

The number of churches kept pace with the number of teetering old barns with shiny tin roofs. Pink and gray rocks rose out of green pastures. The western sky was going orange, like fruit punch, over the dark green plains and valleys as they drove into Knoxville.

"Let's drive the course right now," Dick suggested, when he found their location on his map. He drew out of his pocket a much-creased course map and shook it open.

"It starts out near the Univesity of Tennessee campus, on Neyland Drive," he said. "Here."

They had time before dark to cruise the country roads through Strawberry Plains. Jeanne slowed to a crawl, twenty-five miles an hour, or twice the speed of the very best marathoners. Dick, grinning, eager for the race tomorrow, slapped his flat palm on his knee, saying, "Wow, this is really going to be *great*!

The pretty city lying in the arms of the Tennessee River pleased Jeanne, as they looped south and approached the river again. They'd crossed the Holston River and the French Broad, Dick making a ribald crack about that name for a river, and took the John Sevier Highway.

"Boy, look at the hills," he groaned. "I've got to run those and maintain a less than seven-minute pace all the way."

Crossing the Chapman Highway, the marathoners would take Neubert Spring Road paralleling the highway and charge through the twenty-mile wall. They'd hit the Maryville Pike, shut off traffic on Chapman, cross the river where it became Ft. Loudoun Lake and turn West down Cumberland Avenue through the University to the finish back on Neyland Drive where they began.

"Okay. I've got an idea of the course now," he said. "I'm preprogrammed. Let's take a rest."

They dined out in her first southern cafeteria, a large room with golden wood paneling, metal chandeliers that gleamed like brass and carpeting, thick to the step. Waiters lugged trays; waitresses hovered to refill coffee cups. They had their fill of sweet potatoes, ham and greens. Dick stared at Jeanne with suppressed excitement—not all of it, she knew, for tomorrow's race.

"I want you to stay in the van with me," he said softly, once they were outside in the bracing chill of the early November night.

Jeanne hid a small burp and said, "It'll be too cold."

"Not on your life. Not with my down comforter. Not for two."

"Dick—"

"It's your friend, the unnamed lover, that I hypothesized, right?"

She nodded.

"I knew you were already spoken for," he said. "But you're safe. Do you think I'm going to burn up all the glucose I've loaded onto these scrawny bones by making love to you?"

"Well, that puts a different light on—"

He dropped an arm across her shoulders, and wearily they staggered like drunks to his van. "Jeanne, we'll drive to a spot across the river on the south shore off the Cherokee Trail. My brother used to live here, and we fished a lot. I know the shoreline. It'll be nice, with the view of the city at night. I won't push you. Stay with me. You can take a motel room, but it'd be so much nicer if you came and kept me warm. Okay? I'll do the same for you."

So she did. Dick found a spot where he could hide the van off the road behind shrubbery. The shore dipped to the softly murmuring black river, reflecting lights from the opposite shore. A romantic setting, but Jeanne turned her back as Dick struggled out of his jeans and shirt and burrowed into the bed. Slowly she shed her own slacks and shirt, remembering the sauna, examining her own feelings and finding warm affection and sympathy for Dick. It felt good.

She followed him into the bed wearing the long antique cotton gown with an embroidered yoke that Lily had left her, the color of old paper, with faded handmade lace. It was fragile and beautiful, but not especially warm. She stopped shivering when Dick turned over and put his arms around her.

Jeanne remained still and wordless.

"A good-night kiss?" he asked.

She could feel his hands flowing over the delicate gown, as he exhaled in appreciation.

"Jeanne, you are a lovely, lovely lady." He hugged her tightly and leaned his face toward hers, stopping abruptly. "Jeanne, you've made me forget my beer!"

She found herself giggling in the warm circle of his arms, her bare toes resting on his. "You can't do without hydration."

"I can't do a lot of things I'd like to," he said ruefully. "Good thing I don't mind warm beer. Fewer bubbles and belches. Just like England."

"I didn't know you'd been abroad."

"I haven't been abroad. But you have. A broad? Excuse me. Terrible pun."

The beer can opened with a noisy pop, and Jeanne felt a fine spray on her face. Laughing, she wiped her face clean with the back of her hand.

"Want some more?" Dick asked.

"Thanks, I've had plenty already."

They sat in silence as Dick downed two beers and crushed the cans. "I'm done. That's enough. Shorter may be able to down a six-pack the night before a marathon, but I sure can't. It's been a good day, Jeanne. I'm glad we met. I've never felt so relaxed before a race before."

He took her face lightly in his hands and brushed her lips with his. "Good night, Jeanne-with-the-light-brown-hair," he crooned.

"Good night, Dick. Sleep well." The light of a million stars twinkled through the wide windshield. Counting them, Jeanne fell asleep, a smile on her face.

Chapter Nine

DAWN WOKE HER before his travel alarm sounded, but she found Dick was awake, too. He kissed her on the lips and pulled her closer, smiling. She embraced him.

"Did you get enough rest?" she asked.

"I'd like to sleep with you every night, Jeanne."

"Thank you," she said, meaning it.

"Hope I didn't thrash around. I know I slept twice as well as I would've without you. You are, Jeanne, when you're asleep, a dead ringer for Audrey Hepburn."

He started to sit up, but groaned. "I'll have to do a lot of stretching. You were right. All day in a car ties you in knots, even without being the driver. Brother, I'm stiff."

She didn't say, "So I noticed," but she smiled, and he read her thoughts. Groggy, well-rested, protected, Jeanne wanted to give more than she had, and take more in her turn. She pulled his head down and kissed his mouth. Surprised, he began to stroke her through the old-fashioned gown.

"You are some sensuous woman," he noted. "How many dates add up to the hours we've spent together? We've really made contact. Maybe that other guy doesn't mean as much to you as you think."

"I don't know. Can any person—"

"Love two people at the same time? Sure. It's a proven fact. Take your two brothers. You don't love them one at a time, like, say, Harry from January to June, and Barry from July to December, or whatever they're called."

Her laugh broke the tension. Dick got out of bed and pulled on a T-shirt from his overnight bag.

"What's it say? Your shirt?"

"My son got it for me last Father's day," he said, holding it up for her to read.

My Dad Runs Faster said the front, and on the back were the words Than Your Dad.

"Joey's idea. Sylvia probably hated forking over for all those press-on letters."

"She's not a very friendly lady?"

"Running helped break us up. She didn't run."

Jeanne wished Joey could see his dad run today. She would be his only supporter, and her own work would demand much of her time and attention.

He sat on the comforter in T-shirt and red running shorts, trying to bend forward to clasp his bare feet. He couldn't.

"Here, let me massage your legs," she offered, and amazed herself by telling him she was good at massage. She'd had practice only on girlfriends' sore necks—no backs, no legs. No men, ever.

Dick was already lying flat on his stomach with his runner's tight hamstrings and Achilles' tendons wait-

ing. She began to work on his left leg, an impromptu
performance she hoped would help him.

Dick sighed. Grunted with satisfaction and sighed
again.

She massaged in her own invented pattern and felt
the muscles seem to ease up. This was fun, working
her fingertips and the heels of her hands into the firm,
beautifully shaped legs under their floss of curly hair.
She wished she could do this for Erkki before or after
running.

She amazed herself. Here she was in this van, massaging Dick's legs after spending the night with him.
At the same time she was thinking of Erkki. Where
was she headed? What was she doing? She felt a little
bit drunk, drunk on her own power, so long held in
check by those superfluous eighty pounds.

"My back, too, please."

"You'll be too relaxed to run. Like after a sauna."

"Do you sauna?" he asked.

"Once."

He was quiet for a moment. "I'm in heaven," he
sighed finally. "Honest. I've never had a massage."

"I've never given one."

"Honest? You're too much." He reared up one elbow to look over his shoulder at her. The sunrise shone
through her gown as she knelt, both hands still busy.
He fell back, groaning, tugging his shirt up over his
ribs.

She had to straddle him to massage his back, that
lovely structure of cables and pulleys over a framework
of bones. From his shoulders to his waist she squeezed
and pressed and pounded her fists, making him grunt
with pleasure and tighten his buttocks under her. She
tried to kneel so she wouldn't sit on them, but that got
tiring.

"Jeanne," he murmured, "this time I'll break three hours. In your honor."

"You'll win the darned race," she said, karate chopping gently over his shoulder blades, listening to him snort at her praise.

"How about the old gluteus maximus?" he murmured.

"Nope."

"What d'you mean, 'nope'?"

"No go. I'm staying away from them."

"The hell you are. You're *sitting* on them."

"I am quite aware of that."

"Let me turn over."

"The front of a runner doesn't need massage, it's the backs of the legs that—"

"I need it," he said, turning over. "Oh, but I need you."

He held onto her so that she ended up lying on top of him.

"I adore you, Jeanne Lathrop. Be worth giving up running today to make love to you. Properly."

"You'll do neither," she said, pulling away from him.

"Let me please you."

"There's no time."

"Stop pretending you're not as excited as I am."

"Dick, I am *not* promiscuous."

He glared up into her face. Then he said, "Nobody said you were. I thought we were friends. Loving friends."

He let her go and sat up. "I'll take a workout. You get dressed." He was up and gone in a flurry of cotton flannel sweats, socks and shoelaces, the door slamming behind him.

Jeanne lay face down, embracing a pillow. She had

wanted him, but the need had peaked and gone, leaving her breathless. Her body, her heart and her head were all telling her different-things. At least when she was fat, she hadn't had to make these kinds of decisions. She wanted a chocolate donut, a dozen chocolate donuts, in the worst way. No, no, no. As confused as she was at this moment, she knew she didn't want to go back to being the old Jeanne.

Shakily she got into gray wool slacks, a turquoise sweater and a pair of running shoes. She brushed her hair and applied color to her pale cheeks and lips. After a few deep breaths she gathered her work tools and stepped outside the van.

It was early when they arrived at the starting line. Race officials were busy at tables on the sidewalk by the road, but the crowd had not yet begun to gather. Dick would drink nothing but some orange juice he had in the van, using it to wash down a vitamin pill. He had let her drive to Neyland Drive, calling out directions to the University and where to park. The city streets were deserted, a Sunday, and the only strollers seemed to be aiming for the wide, thinly traveled Drive between the University and the river.

Jeanne exulted in the display of colorful T-shirts, shorts and tricolor shoes on finely trained, tanned bodies. It was surprisingly warm for early November, and most of the entrants were already out of their sweats and windbreakers, leaning against posts to stretch calves, arms stiff as if trying to push them over. Or seated on patches of grass stretching hamstrings and thighs.

Jeanne had brought a Nikon and a Yashika, one loaded with color film, the other with black and white, both strung around her neck. She had stuffed a pant pocket with film and tapes for the hand tape recorder she could palm and whisper into, like a cop's walkie-talkie. There was hardly room in the other pocket for notepad, pen and wallet.

University students stood in clots, watching the sign-in and joking among themselves. Crowds would swell, she knew, about two hours after the start, when the arrival of the frontrunners was imminent. While Dick lined up for his packet of number and pins, she watched orange-shorted race officials stringing bright plastic flags on ropes between stanchions to make the chute. Off to one side stood uprights with a banner hanging between them saying on one side Start and the other side Finish. Finnish, she thought, shaking the thought away. Dick had infected her with his punmaking.

Jeanne roamed in wider and wider arcs, studying the array of regional T-shirts. The varied accents were further proof that the stretching, meditating or jogging entrants were not Tennesseans all.

She murmured observations into the tiny tape recorder, overhearing women entrants relating anecdotes that might make good copy for *Fancy Free*.

". . . in July, I ran a marathon at eighty-five degrees, if you can believe it. I carried an extra tampon, just to be safe, in my pocket. When they sprayed us with water at the aid stations, the thing puffed up and exploded!"

"Talk about lugging things," responded her companion, "I ran one twenty-miler behind two kids with a Frisbee. They kept it in the air the whole way, going back and forth between them, but darned if I could pass those crazies. No way!"

She saw Dick approaching with his number, 747, holding it by one corner and offering her four safety pins. Knowing he was fully capable of pinning a number to the front of his shirt, she understood that he needed to belong to somebody. She handed him the tape recorder and did the job of pinning for him. It covered part of the legend Joey had composed.

"I'll be yelling for you when you come in, so you'd better have a real kick left in you."

"I hope I'll be close behind someone else. That competitive edge brings out the last shred of strength in me. I'll kick out hard."

"Three hours, right?"

"Under three. They've got a few hot shots running, so they expect a 2:20 finish. A 2:40 for the first woman," he quickly added. He put Vaseline on his waist and nipples and between his legs, then gave the jar to someone who'd forgotten to bring any. In the hazy cool he'd run hatless with a white sweatband.

"Fly like the 747 you are," she joked, and then she had to leave him, to walk along the grassy bank of the Agriculture campus. She used half a roll of film on the crowd massing behind the starting line. She thought she recognized a couple of faces right at the front, so she moved in and took zoom shots. The registration list would tell her who they were, the men and women likely to set a course record.

The winding route she'd driven last evening with Dick had seemed endless. And *she* hoped to do this a year from now or even in the spring? She couldn't wait.

A race director in a Nike official's shirt used a bullhorn to draw the late registrants from the tables. The restless crowd cheered when this last flurry of numbers joined the other runners who were hopping from foot to foot in place like children waiting to go to the toilet. Everyone was eager for distance. And speed. Dick waved at her from midpack, where the three-hour people rightfully belonged. Other photographers and two videotapers were busy, as were reporters with mikes. A brass band struck up a tune to raise everyone's adrenalin level a little higher.

The starter's gun startled her, though right on time, and the lead runners sprinted as if they'd come off starting blocks.

The rest of the pack howled a toneless shout like a battle cry, but when the band began playing the familiar theme for the Olympic telecasts, the runners roared spontaneously, louder and louder. Jeanne almost cried out, tears rushing to her eyes. It was impossible to explain. She couldn't have been more excited at the Olympics.

The end of this mob of runners had to dance in place as slowly, slowly, the entire one thousand began to move.

She knew that out there on the country roads local trackmen, students and runners' spouses would be filling cups with drinks, and split callers with stop watches would be racing to their stations at the crucial mile markers—one, five, ten and so on in increments of five—to announce the runners' times. Tape recorders and cameras, too, would record every runner at each check point.

She grinned. And all this cost a runner not one cent beyond the six-dollar entry fee. For a finisher, the rewards would last a lifetime. And perhaps make that lifetime longer. Terrific.

Chapter Ten

JEANNE CHECKED HER watch every ten minutes. There wasn't too much for her to do until the runners began to cross the finish line. Sitting cross-legged on the grass, she surveyed the corps of race officials stringing flags, setting up timers' chairs on platforms and rehearsing stick handling to establish the order of finish. A tongue depressor's number told whether the runner came in eighth, eightieth or eight hundred and eighty-eighth. You wouldn't see any tongue depressors at Boston or New York. Time and place were tabulated by computer at those races. Things were certainly a lot simpler here in Knoxville.

Photographers set up shop for finish line photos, and the huge digital clocks spun their ten-inch numerals. The runners had been on the road for an hour and a half, and it was ten thirty-four a.m. The crowd swelled. Jeanne decided to talk to some of the spectators. Did they have friends or relatives in the race? Was this the first marathon they'd witnessed? Were they from

Knoxville or had they come some distance to watch the race?

When it got too crowded to make her way through the crowd, Jeanne took a stroll up Neyland. She'd be back in time for the finish to get photos of the winners, male and female, and of Dick. He would love to have a shot of himself crossing the finish line wearing Joey's T-shirt. On her stroll she encountered plenty of gas guzzlers on wheels; she preferred the carbohydrate guzzlers on foot. It wasn't right to let cars on the course this close to a race. Give the runners some air, for heaven's sake. Exasperated, Jeanne hurried back to the finish line.

Half an hour later, plus a little, the winner was proclaimed even before he neared the Alcoa Highway bridge. He was well ahead of number two. She could hear the applause and shouts, at first faint and then louder as he drew closer.

She sprinted, cameras bouncing on ribs, straps crossed over chest. Behind the roped-in spectators, she got to the finish line in time to focus on the narrow ribbon.

The exultant winner leaped through the tape, both hands held high. His feet hardly seemed to touch the ground. After moving through the chute he strolled in circles, head bent, panting only moderately. Number two came in a minute and a half behind him. Here was a man over thirty, she was sure. It was not a sport at which teenagers excelled.

"Won in 2:21:11!" She confided to her recorder, and the first woman, a diminutive, pig-tailed imp, appeared. Lo and behold, here came Dick, number 747, looking strong, sailing in the woman's tracks, a grin of pure astonishment on his face when he spotted the clock.

Jeanne snapped him, ran to catch up and touched his icy fingertips, "You're just incredible!" she screamed, and then, hugging a camera under each arm, dashed toward the incoming mobs of runners. There was a bus crossing the bridge now, and fewer spectators back near the junction of West Cumberland and Neyland. Everyone wanted to be near the finish, to see the times and the joy the runners found as they reached their hard-won goal.

The view of the bridge was splendid. Jeanne jerked one camera around to her front, found the light setting and put it on infinity. A half-naked young athlete came loping down the grass from the bus stop on the Alcoa Highway, a number clearly visible on his shorts. She got two zoom shots of him before he reached her, but he didn't join the stream of runners. She expected him to, but he approached her directly, clapping and shouting, "You're lookin' great! Go for it!" to the racers.

"Hey, don't you dare jump in, 233," she yelled at him, only half kidding. "I've got a picture of you getting off that bus!"

He laughed aloud. "Me? Ma'am, I'm just headin' for the finish to see who won. Who won?"

"I dunno, but his time was 2:21:11."

"Terrific! I pulled a hamstring, so I thumbed a ride on the bus—free ride for a runner. I don't wonder you thought—"

He ceased speaking and squinted back the way he came, shading his eyes.

Jeanne lifted her camera. Finishers, well strung out but increasing in numbers, padded past them toward the left. Toward the right, a car left the highway and dropped slowly down into the Ag campus parking lot, disappearing behind other cars. The brown Lincoln turned toward the course now, and Jeanne hopped higher up the bank to watch it. Silly. Everyone driving today was slowing to honk plaudits or just to stare at the spectacle. But the Lincoln stopped, its door opened. Jeanne snapped a distance shot, and out stepped a numbered runner. Another injured man? Gray-haired, tall, handsome. She almost turned back to speak to the bus rider, but he was limping toward the finish line. The Lincoln geared up, roaring into the Ag campus, and the middle-aged runner moved toward her as Jeanne quickly crouched behind a car like a cop in a shootout, snapping and snapping, praying her roll of film would last. He'd run right onto the course, and there was no orange-shirted official in sight. She shot him falling in behind a tall black runner, then shoved her camera under her arm and sprinted along the edge of the road, so fresh that she was able to outdistance runners behind that fraud numbered 1503. She was fueled by furious indignation.

"Hey, No-Number! Get off the course, gal!" yelled a man on the sidelines.

He meant her, but she had a job to do.

"Cheater!" she screamed, and speeded up, pointing.

Soon someone was going to dart out and jerk her unceremoniously off the course. Unregistered runners could screw up the order of finish. Crowds grew thick on the sidelines now behind beflagged ropes. The band was playing, and 1503 must not have heard her scream. Laughter and cheers marked her progress. The man she pursued was stiff; after riding in a car he did not run smoothly. Her bouncing pair of cameras got in her way, but she wanted them for a very important picture.

She gained on 1503. Devoting herself to speed, trying to accelerate without proper running gear above shoe level, she found she was flagging. No man his age seemed near. Was he after a division win? Over fifty? The forty-year-olds would have been in long ago. The rotter could take the trophy if it wasn't won already! Maybe he was sixty and much too early at the line. He'd even qualify for Boston!

Furious, she put on a kick like none she'd ever managed before, and reached out and grasped the man's elbow. He turned to her with a horrified expression.

"Stop, cheater!" she screamed and dug in her heels, nearly toppling him, holding onto his arms now with both hands. "Cheater!"

Then he did a foolish thing. He flung out his other arm, missed her, and swung again. This time he connected, clipping her across the side of the head. Other runners passing were only blurred legs as Jeanne fell, feet flying, cameras swinging. Onlookers were darting under the ropes, eyes wide, mouths gaping open. The man she'd caught was being embraced by two spectators, protesting loudly.

On her knees, Jeanne came up snapping pictures.

An official came dashing in, examining the man's number and his relatively dry T-shirt and face. No salt, no flush. Jeanne fingered her mouth for loose teeth, nodded her thanks to those who lifted her from her knees and pointed her mike in the cheater's face.

"As a fellow runner, I would like know why you want to cheat like this. It's a disgrace to the sport."

"Young lady, you are making some very serious accusations. It would behoove you to choose your words carefully."

His coolness was infuriating. Considering the number of still, movie and videotape cameras around, number 1503's cheating attempt was well documented. She could prove it with the film in her own camera.

Runners streamed by, heads turned to watch the fracas. A policeman burrowed through the crowd.

"I know what I saw. You are a fraud!" Jeanne looked up at him. He was a tall man, in good shape. "You didn't run the whole course. You rode it in a brown Lincoln." She spun around to the cop. "Officer, I have photos in here to prove that." She tapped her camera.

"He hasn't run any twenty-six miles," said the official. "Look at his skin. He's dry; hair's half dried."

"I most certainly did run every inch of the course." He placed his hand on the arm of the official who was holding on to him. "If you will unhand me, sir," he said imperiously. "I suggest you consult the records at the checkpoints. You will see that I have passed through each and every one."

The race official looked incredulous. "Some, maybe. Not all."

"Now if you will excuse me, I would like to rest after this tiring effort." Number 1503 turned to Jeanne. "Were I you, young lady, I would burn the film in that camera." With that he strode off, head held high.

"You want to press charges, ma'am?" asked the policeman gently.

"For what?"

"Assault. He hit you. Knocked you down."

"No, I don't think so," she said in a daze. "It's not important."

Slowly she realized she was sitting on one heck of a story. Why had the man done it? And who was he anyway? She flipped through her mimeographed marathon program. Number 1503. Arthur Beale. Charlottësville, Virginia. Age 58. Best previous marathon time 3:26. Just six minutes less to qualify for Boston. It was something to go on but not much.

Suddenly Dick was there beside her. "Agent Invincible!" he crowed. "You're amazing. They ought to have had you up at Boston when Rosie ran. That guy would have clinched the fifties class for sure. The clock's just gone to 2:51 now."

"I want to know everything there is to know about him, Dick. His reasons, his profession. I wonder what he does. He looks so well-manicured. And he's so cool. That's what really makes me mad. Probably fifty people have his exit from that Lincoln on film, and he just stands there and insists he ran the whole race. Whew!"

"Calm down, my little muckraker. You sound a little overheated to me," Dick said, putting his hands on her shoulders.

Jeanne removed them. "I'm going over to talk to him some more. Coming?"

Dick shrugged. "If you can't beat 'em . . ."

Reporters wouldn't let the man escape. The name Rosie . . . Rosie, hung in the air. The race director was directing a tirade at Beale that made Jeanne pale. Beale looked at the ranting director as if he were no more than a pesty mosquito.

"He looks a little bit like my father," Dick marveled.

"I trust," Beale was saying, "the Knoxville Road Runners Club and the Knoxville Chamber of Commerce will be able to raise the funds to pay damages from the libel suit I intend to bring against this contemptible little race. Someone from my law firm will contact you tomorrow."

"An attorney! That's incredible," Jeanne whispered to Dick.

"Remember Watergate," someone murmured behind her.

Jeanne made her way through the maze of reporters, photographers and spectators. "Mr. Beale . . ."

"Well, if it isn't Lois Lane again. The persistent girl reporter."

"The name is Lathrop. Jeanne Lathrop. I'm with *Fancy Free*. What does a professional like you get out of cheating in a local marathon?"

"If you do not leave me alone, Miss Lathrop, I will sue you and your footloose magazine for every penny—and I'm sure there are few enough—you have. I do not make idle threats."

With that, he pushed Jeanne aside and made his way through the crowd, refusing to say anything further to anyone. Jeanne switched off her tape recorder. Beale was a tough customer, but that made Jeanne all the more determined to get his story.

"Hey, Jeanne, there's Melton Dickensen, the real winner of the over-fifties division. Shouldn't you interview him?"

Jeanne knew Dick was trying to distract her, but he was right. As Dickensen sauntered over, she hastened to photograph him and stick her mike in his face. He was pulling on a green Knoxville Marathon T-shirt, just like the one Dick wore. First place or last place, the T-shirts were the same. Dickensen was a professor at U. Tenn. He was especially glad to have won this hometown event, and he thanked Jeanne for preventing Beale from crossing the finish line before him.

"My pleasure, Professor." She had never meant anything more.

Dick thought a picture of the two of them together would be good and snapped them grinning and shaking hands. "All you two need are a couple of white hats," he whooped.

Dickensen was spirited away by other well-wishers, and Jeanne had her first chance to look at Dick after all the excitement. The toll his effort had taken was evident. He looked gaunt, salt was caked on his forehead and at the sides of his mouth. Dear Dick.

"How about splurging on a motel tonight?" he asked softly. "Long hot baths for us both, another massage for me and one for you in return?"

"I'll think seriously about that," she replied. "But I have some more things to do here. Why don't you go off, shower and get some rest, and I'll meet you later?"

"You're still thinking about that Beale character, aren't you?" Dick frowned at her.

"Dick, he hit me. He threatened me. I need to know why."

"*Hit* you?"

"He knocked me over when I stopped him from getting back on the course. It didn't hurt. I was more shocked than anything else. Look, I've just got to talk to someone who knows him. His wife, his family, someone. He didn't come here alone. Someone drove that Lincoln." Jeanne felt herself getting more and more excited.

"Well, just take it easy, will you? I didn't much like the looks of him. He seems slippery to me. And he didn't murder a child, Jeanne, he cheated in a race. Keep your perspective, okay?" Dick sounded concerned, and she was touched.

"He's devalued something that is important to me. I want to follow up on it. That's all. Now I think you should head for the showers or you'll be stiff as a board tomorrow." She kissed him lightly on the cheek and tousled his curls.

When he was gone, she took a slow look around her.

The focus of her article began to shift in her mind. Melton Dickensen was the real winner here today, as Jacqueline Gareau had been the real winner in Boston, despite Rosie. Beale deserved no free publicity; Dickensen did. Whatever she found out and wrote about Beale, the professor should get the cover story.

Chapter Eleven

JEANNE CONDUCTED MORE interviews while Dick drove off with some runners to shower at the house of a race volunteer. The most inspiring talk was with a seventy-one-year-old woman who had finished in 4:42. She had more energy at seventy-one than most people had at seventeen.

"Big switch," said the woman's sub-vet (ages thirty through thirty-nine) winner. "Remember when Jock Semple tried to rip off Katherine Switzer's number at Boston in 1967? 'No women allowed.' He was knocked over by her boyfriend. Now you've pulled a *man* from a marathon for cheating. Things have changed a lot in the past few years. I understand Jock and Kathy are very good friends now."

Jeanne winced. No way that she and Beale would ever speak civilly to each other, much less be friends.

She had just about used up all her film and tape when Dick returned. "Now I'm someone you might like to hug," he said, glowing, wearing jeans and the green marathon T-shirt, and scented with after-shave.

"Let's head out now," Jeanne said. "Not stay the night in Knoxville. There won't be a free motel room in miles, I'll bet, not after an event like this. Let's leave Interstate 81 a little earlier and swing up through Charlottesville."

"Sure," he said. "You got relatives or something there?"

"You can come in a little late for work Monday?" she asked, avoiding his question.

"Uh huh," he said, narrowing his eyes slyly. "Sure. Priorities can be somewhat shifted, Jeanne."

"I'm hungry."

"You oughta be," he said. "No breakfast, and you've been here all day. Let's eat. Let's shove off."

They drove out of town the way they'd come and stopped at a family style restaurant. Food put her back into shape, though with her thoughts churning she hardly remembered what she ate. She was outlining in her head an article with photos for *Fancy Free*. It might bump the article on Erkki's research out of first place in her schedule. Well, she'd get back to that. Dick gazed at her, shaking his head in wry amusement. "Must be fun to be a reporter. Newshound. And a little dangerous. If I'd seen that guy hit you, I'd have floored him, even in the shape I was in," Dick said, looking no more tired now than she did after a few miles' jog.

She drove to the Virginia line while he stretched out on the bed in back, and then he took the wheel. In Roanoke she called Charlottesville, and found out from long-distance information the number for an Arthur Beale, Attorney. Scary, but she doubted he would be home this soon.

"Mrs. Beale?" Jeanne drawled. "Is Mr. Beale at home?"

The woman sounded very sweet. Jeanne almost lost her nerve. No news had reached Mrs. Beale. Her husband, she said, was out of town. "He is a marathon racer," she said with evident pride. "And he's fifty-eight years old."

Such candor further disarmed Jeanne, who implied that she was a client of his. No, no message. The slight southern accent she'd acquired during her years in Washington and could draw on for occasions like these should convince the woman. She'd sound different in person, when she dropped in on Mrs. Arthur Beale. Planning as she went. Hit the road—fast.

She took the wheel again for a speedy trip up to Interstate 64 East to Charlottesville. Dick was sleeping peacefully behind her, and she pressed the accelerator hard. A hundred miles to go. What time did Mrs. Beale turn in?

In the sleepy southern town well after dark, she had trouble locating the neighborhood, but found it as exclusive as she had expected. The Beale house was large, set back in a grove of sheltering trees. No lights. Darn! It was after ten; Mrs. Beale had retired for the night.

Jeanne pulled out of the driveway and drove back to a motel she'd spotted on the way. She woke Dick, telling him they'd arrived in Charlottesville.

"I want my hot bath, Dick. You promised."

Dick moved willingly from the van's bed to a motel bed in a double room with gold-flecked wallpaper, two hanging lamps and a deep shag rug. She let him bathe first, while she paced, chewing her thumbnail, trying to decide how to approach Beale's wife.

When she got her chance in the bathroom, she ran

scalding water in the tub, adding a generous dollop of baby oil. As she sank back into the hot water, she realized how tired she was. Too tired to think about Beale or work any longer. The water drew the aches and tension from her body, and her mind emptied of thoughts. She felt herself drifting, becoming drowsy.

"Jeanne? You all right in there?"

She sat up with a start. Dick. "Huh? I guess I dozed off. Be right out."

Dick was lying in bed waiting for her to join him. What would it be like to make love with him? For that was certainly what would happen. Would he be different than Erkki? Erkki. A few days ago she had thought she was in love with him. But Dick was so attractive, so warm, so friendly. Why should she deny herself a night with Dick? She had denied herself too long. Far too long. Do not think of Erkki. Not now.

In her lacy gown she slid through the door into the bedroom and found Dick lying face down, nude on the bed, the covers neatly turned back. Written in her lipstick were small words on each thigh and calf. Rub me. Me, too.

Jeanne smiled. He didn't move a muscle, his strong, narrow bottom as enticing as a woman's bosom must be to a man. She climbed on the bed and clamped a hand over each muscular calf. This time he didn't sigh with pleasure but whooped with pain.

"Sorry. They *told* me to!"

"They hurt tonight."

She smiled, settling down for the pleasant labor of very gentle massage.

"My thighs need it, too. In front."

"Then turn over," Jeanne said bravely.

He did, keeping a corner of the sheet over himself,

which, as he must have known, was far more tantalizing than total nudity. He kept his eyes closed.

The adductor muscles were so tight that she could read every sensation on Dick's grimacing face as she explored tan thighs hot and thick with muscle.

"Relax," she commanded.

"I am. Wow! That extra speed really takes it out of you. You realize that my 2:49 was a six point three pace? Can you do a seven-minute mile yet, Jeanne?"

"Nope. I still hover just below eight. I'm an LSD person—long, slow distance." She touched him more gently, warmed with admiration for his achievement. Over hills, too.

She studied the narrow waist, the rising and falling ribcage, the furry chest so unlike Erkki's wider, hairless chest, but dear to her, regardless. The sheet moved. She ceased massaging.

"Come lie down beside me," he said without opening his eyes.

"You're all worn out."

"I slept in the van, remember? While you drove all those miles. You're the one who needs a rest."

She lay down beside him and pulled the covers over them both, flipping off the bedside lamp after she did so. His arm slid around her and his hand cupped her breast.

"Jeanne, I think I'm falling for you. What are we gonna do about that?"

She stiffened. "Please don't complicate things, Dick."

"When you want me," he said, "*if* you want me, you know what to do."

She didn't know what to do. Just whistle? So she lay still, her eyelids sagging. He smelled of soap and toothpaste and shampoo, and his compact body was

as warm as an electric blanket. Good runner. His pace
was far from the world record of four minutes fifty-
some seconds, but this was no Derek Clayton. This
was a thirty-year-old divorced father who worked at
the Bureau of Land Management and loved her. Was
falling in love with her.

My cup runneth over, she thought. Inside, she was
still fat Jeanne, who might have gone to her grave
without experiencing a single man. Now she had two
and didn't know what to do about it.

"Can't stand success, can you, Jeanne?" said Lily,
floating disembodied above the bed. "Enjoy yourself
fully. Don't do harm by depriving yourself or him.
Dick's a very nice boy."

Suddenly she wanted to make him happy and make
herself happy too. They'd become too close to hang
back. Almost indecent that she'd had to relive her own
tensions through fantasy, leaving Dick to do the same
for himself. There were two of them, good friends,
loving friends, and it was time to end their pain.

Jeanne whistled softly in his ear. She felt him grin
in the dark as he wrapped both arms about her and put
his mouth gently on hers. It began slowly, he being as
careful of her precious body as she was with his. They
found how to make each other respond, move closer,
move in rhythm, link legs and arms, touch toes and
tongues, until Jeanne began to gasp with pleasure.

"Little champ," he breathed, and she did the same
to him, and slid over him until he turned with her and
pressed her down into the mattress. "Jeanne, Jeanne,"
he said, "I wanted, wanted, wanted you." He ended
on a groan.

She held him to her, trying to give him maximum
joy, and receiving more than she'd dreamed, as if her
efforts ricocheted back upon herself.

They did not sleep much. When she awoke, he was dressed and seated, watching her. The sun was glaring through the curtains and the maid was pounding on the door.

"Not yet," Dick called out.

"Whatever time is it?" gasped Jeanne.

"Eleven-fifteen. You needed rest, sweetheart. I didn't give you much rest last night, as you recall."

His eyes were full of love. Love, not lust.

"I slept through your getting up and dressing?" she cried, the business of today rushing back upon her. "What's checkout time?"

"Noon. Don't worry."

"I'm going to see Mrs. Beale."

"You have to be kidding!"

"I'm not, Dick. Beale's from Charlottesville. I looked it up in the marathon program. I telephoned his wife from Roanoke, and Beale spent last night in Knoxville. I've got to scoot over there and talk to her before he shows up."

"So that's why you wanted to stop in Charlottesville. You're headed for trouble, Jeanne. What are you going to say to her?"

"I don't know. She sounded so proud of him."

She sprang out of bed; he sprang, too, catching her in his arms, kissing her. He was supposed to be so sore today that he couldn't move to bathe and dress.

"I love you," he said.

Jeanne just stared. Like a starveling who gorges on food, too much, too soon, she feared she would lose what she had so greedily taken.

"I've loaded the van. Let's get breakfast."

When she was seated beside him in the motel's restaurant, she drank down one cup of coffee and excused herself. Time was short. Beale was coming home to-day; she had to hurry.

Dick ran after her, grabbing her arm. "I'm coming with you."

"I want to do this on my own, Dick. Please let me go. You're hurting me."

Dick shook his head. "Just what is in this for you, Jeanne?" He released her from his grasp, and she stumbled slightly.

She couldn't answer for a moment. "I don't like cheaters. And I don't like anyone who gives runners a bad name."

"So write an editorial. Drop this thing with Beale. You're not personally responsible for public opinion about runners."

"Maybe not. But he threatened me. He threatened the Knoxville marathon sponsors. He threatened the magazine. And he stole Melton Dickensen's limelight. I don't like any of that. And I'm going to get to the bottom of this."

"You're really bucking for the Purple Heart, aren't you, Jeanne? Well, good luck."

He whirled around and hurried out of the restaurant. Maybe she *was* too gung-ho about this, but she had an obligation—to running and to *Fancy Free*—to make sense out of cheaters like Beale. And if Dick Kilmer was too fainthearted to see that, there was nothing she could do about it.

Chapter Twelve

JEANNE HEADED STRAIGHT for the bank of pay phones at the front of the restaurant. Mrs. Beale was at home and would be glad to be interviewed by Miss Lathrop. She was always happy to talk about her husband.

The big house on Mockingbird Lane featured a welcome mat that said The Arthur Beales. Mrs. Beale was gray-haired like her husband, but rounded and comfortably padded, rather like Jeanne's mother. Unlike Jeanne's mother, however, she wore not a flowered housedress but a gray tweed wool skirt, a tailored white linen shirt and a black cashmere cardigan sweater. She went to a good beautician, Jeanne noted, and to a manicurist. Her makeup was tasteful and subdued. She wore no jewelry other than her wedding band, a circlet of tiny diamonds.

"Please come in, Miss Lathrop." Mrs. Beale extended her hand. "If you will come this way, please. I thought it would be pleasant to sit on the sun porch.

It gets the morning sun and has a lovely view of the woods."

What a gracious lady, Jeanne thought. How did she come to be married to someone like Arthur Beale? Mrs. Beale led her to a glass-enclosed porch filled with beautifully tended house plants of countless varieties. The room was comfortably furnished with a natural-toned rattan sofa and chairs, their cushions upholstered in flowered cottons. Mrs. Beale suggested coffee and left the room to prepare it.

Looking around, Jeanne saw the Charlottesville local newspaper. She picked it up and turned to the sports section. There was a picture of her tackling Beale! UPI had picked it up! The paper ran no story with it, just the caption: Woman Reporter Nabs Marathon Cheater. The brief explanation that accompanied the caption named her as a reporter for *Fancy Free*.

Jeanne heard Mrs. Beale returning from the kitchen and hurried to put the paper back in the magazine rack where she had found it.

"You needn't hide that from me, Miss Lathrop. While waiting for you, I sat down to read the paper and came across it myself."

Jeanne wanted to crawl under the sofa but recovered quickly. "In that case, I am very grateful you didn't slam the door in my face, Mrs. Beale. If you prefer, I can go right now. But I would like to hear what you have to say about what's happened."

"Actually, it's good to have someone to talk with. I am quite shocked and surprised, to say the least."

Jeanne asked if she could turn her tape recorder on and set it up while Mrs. Beale poured them each a cup of coffee.

"I don't know where to begin, Miss Lathrop. Perhaps if you asked some questions, it would be easier."

Jeanne smiled, hoping to put Mrs. Beale at ease. She had come here quite prepared to dislike anyone married to Arthur Beale, but found it hard not to be sympathetic to this quietly charming woman. "Why don't you start by telling me how Mr. Beale got interested in running."

"That's easy. About four or five years ago, Art went for his annual physical, and his doctor told him it was time to stop smoking, lose some weight and get some regular exercise. The doctor suggested a class given at the local YMCA. The instructor was a devotee of running and included it in the program. Art was so enthusiastic about the results he took it up as a sport. Now he runs ten miles a day, and I must say he is a changed man. He supports the local running club and participates in many of the local races. And I just cannot understand why he would do something like this. Are you sure of what you saw, Miss Lathrop?"

Jeanne had to tell the truth, not soften it for Mrs. Beale. "I'm not only sure of what I saw, I have it on film."

Mrs. Beale lowered her head. "I see."

"Has your husband been under any particular stress lately? Any physical or other problems? Trouble at his law firm?"

Mrs. Beale was silent as she reviewed her husband's behavior. "Why, no. He's a very healthy man and he has a wonderful practice. And he's very proud of our children. Our oldest son, Bill, was visiting from Washington last week. He's an attorney, too, and was recently appointed a federal prosecutor. My husband was thrilled. He'd always wanted a position like that, but it never materialized. Private practice is much more lucrative, and Art always wanted the best for me and the children. Sometimes I think he's worked far too hard, done some things he would have preferred not to have done."

"That's very interesting. About your son, that is. Does Bill run also?" Jeanne's mind was clicking. Middle-aged man, threatened by his son's success, wants to get public recognition for something. Good copy.

"No, he doesn't. And *he* is the nervous one. He needs exercise badly. The whole time he was here, Art kept urging him to take up running, or some form of regular exercise, before he puts on too much weight."

"And how did Bill respond to that, Mrs. Beale?"

Mrs. Beale sighed. "Not very well, I'm afraid. In fact, Bill and his father had an argument about it. Arthur can be quite stubborn when he sets his mind to it."

Jeanne picked up her coffee cup and swallowed some of the now lukewarm brew. She waited a moment, giving Mrs. Beale some time to collect herself, before asking her next question.

"How many marathons has your husband run?"

"Why, this was his first, Miss Lathrop. You look very surprised. May I ask why?"

Jeanne *was* puzzled. "It's just that the marathon program listed his best marathon time as three hours, sixteen minutes. Unlike some marathons, the one in Knoxville required no previous marathoning in order to qualify for the race." Jeanne explained how anyone entering the New York City Marathon had to have run in at least one official marathon before running in New York, and how the Boston race had stringent qualifying times for its participants. "Why would he say he'd run a marathon before if he hadn't, plus list a very respectable time?"

"I don't know, Miss Lathrop. I just don't know."

Mrs. Beale looked worn out, and Jeanne switched

off her tape recorder and prepared to leave. She thanked Mrs. Beale for her time and hospitality and gave her a business card, asking her to phone if she thought of anything else that could shed some light on the situation. Jeanne wanted to ask if Beale was always so cold and hard, as he had been yesterday, but she didn't have the heart to question Mrs. Beale on that score.

As she was leaving, though, she had one last thought. "Did he go to Knoxville alone, Mrs. Beale? Or did he take someone along to cheer him on?"

"He drove over by himself, but he has friends there; he grew up in Knoxville. I was unable to go with him because of an important fundraising dinner for the local hospital. I chair the fundraising committee, so it was imperative I attend."

Impulsively, Jeanne gave Mrs. Beale a little hug. "Your husband gave me quite a scare yesterday, Mrs. Beale. But I feel much better about things now. And I think I can write a good article, thanks to your candor and courage."

"You're quite welcome, my dear. It is going to be hard enough to face Arthur, but I have my thoughts sorted out now. I will call you if I think of anything else that might be helpful."

Jeanne trotted down the flagstone walk, pressing pocketbook to chest, chin down, thinking furiously. Could she really write this story when it might hurt Mrs. Beale so much? Although she couldn't say she liked Arthur Beale much more than she had an hour ago, she at least had some sympathy for him. And wasn't it important to show Beale's cheating for what it was? A sad attempt by an aging man to be a star. No, she had to write the story. You get back from running what you put into it. If you put in dishonesty, you get back trouble. Everyone, including myself, Jeanne thought, needs to be reminded of that. She would run an honest race.

Jeanne had driven Dick's van a quarter mile down the exclusive drive away from the Beale house and was heading back toward the motel when a car moved quietly up beside her, and a hand rising above its roof motioned her over. She pulled over to the curb, and the Buick stopped close in front of her. Arthur Beale leaped out. He wore a tan V-necked cashmere pullover. The collar of his tattersall shirt was crisp and open, his hair lay in silver waves. He resembled a model or an aging film star.

"I saw you leaving my home, Miss Lathrop. Have you no decency? Do you know the laws against harassment?"

"I'm sure you know all the laws better than I do, Mr. Beale. I simply wanted to know why you did it, and your wife was gracious enough to speak with me. Which is more than I can say for you." Jeanne was amazed at how cool she sounded, despite her rapidly beating heart and queasy stomach.

"I am warning you for the last time, stay away from me and my family. Or you will be a very sorry young woman."

With that he returned to his car and drove off. Maybe he was a different man with his wife and children. How else could Mrs. Beale love him as she so obviously did? How did he manage to make her feel like she was the one who had done something wrong? She knew she was in over her head on this one, but she was determined to see it through.

Chapter Thirteen

SHE FOUND DICK on a sofa in the lobby of the motel, surrounded by newspapers.

"Well, I guess you survived without my help. You're famous. You know your mug's in the Atlanta *Constitution*, Charlottesville paper, Richmond papers, Washington *Post* and *Star*. I would have gotten more, but these were all the newsstand had."

"Somebody at UPI must have thought it was a real cute shot," Jeanne said as she riffled through the pile of papers. There was no turning back now. Everyone would have seen the picture by the time she got back to Washington. The *Fancy Free* staff, Erkki, even her parents in Elmton. "The cat is certainly out of the bag, isn't it?"

Jeanne filled Dick in on her talk with Mrs. Beale and her unexpected meeting with Mr. Beale. Dick looked at her with concern. "He didn't try to hurt you, did he?"

"No, he was the perfect gentleman. Just delivered

his ultimatum and drove off. He gives me the creeps. I don't want to talk about it any more. Let's hit the road. We've got a long way to go."

Jeanne and Dick arrived in Washington at four that afternoon after a strained drive back. Dick was still miffed over her insistence on handling the Beale story in her own way. And she knew he had different feelings about the night they had spent together than she had. In order to avoid a difficult good-bye scene, she asked him to drop her at the office.

When she stepped out of the elevator, she noticed that the doors at the end of the office hall were closed. Unusual. *Fancy Free* never closed on Monday. She had lugged her cameras and suitcase, and no one was here at only four-twenty? No one to give her a lift home?

She knocked, and was glad to hear a chair squeak and footsteps approach the locked door. What was going on?

Nancy's merry face appeared around the doorframe. "You're back! Hey, all *right!*" Yelling over her shoulder, "Hey, it's Jeanne. She's finally home!"

"About time," came a reply.

"Well, let me in, for Pete's sake!"

Jeanne tramped past Nancy's neatened desk with its arrangement of dried autumn blooms, set her suitcase down by the coat closet, shrugged both cameras off and dropped them outside the darkroom. She plodded around a corner toward the bullpen.

Nancy had preceded her, blonde head vanishing at a trot.

"Tat-ta-ta-TAH!" trumpeted Kerry and Ron. Hands clapped, and Jeanne stood blinking at hand-lettered signs, a punchbowl, champagne bottles and, on her desk, a huge vase of purple chrysanthemums.

Our Hero! said one sign. Welcome Home, Reporter of Note!

Nancy's yellow curls, Kerry's flying dark locks, Ron's round, grinning face below sleek black hair—all blurred as the three of them converged on her, glasses in hand, hands reaching to pat her back, pull her into more hugs, kiss her.

"Lady spy," muttered Kerry. "Did you get hurt? Let me see—yeah, there's maybe a hint of a bruise on that cheek. Got any more scars? Can we get a color photo of your rear end for our next issue? That must have *hurt!*"

"Damn it, we went to press two days ago. This story has to wait a whole month," Ron mourned.

"That's okay," said the ambivalent lady spy–police–woman–publicity hound. Tears came to her eyes, and she couldn't manage a grin. What a crowd to work with. Nancy offered a cutout paper heart with ribbon attached.

"It's a long time until Valentine's Day," said Jeanne.

"This is your Purple Heart for valor. Injured in the pursuit of your duties." Jeanne winced, remembering Dick's words in the restaurant.

"What sort of pictures did you get?" Ron asked. "I can't believe we were talking about cheating just before you left. Fantastic!"

"Have you got the shots to prove what he did? I mean before you tackled him?" asked Nancy.

"Sure. I caught him getting out of the car, coming down to Neyland Drive and jumping into the race. Closeups too."

"Now the interesting angle as I see it," said Ron,

"is just what we were tossing back and forth before you left, Jeanne. Why did he do it? What's his motive?"

"Tremendous angle," echoed Kerry. "Did you tape record anything he said?"

"He swore his innocence. Told me off. Threatened me and the magazine with libel, but there's no question that he cheated."

"Wow," said Nancy. "I'll bet you wanted to interview his friends or family. He have anyone there with him you could talk to?"

"Nope. He came alone. From Charlottesville. An attorney. His son's a federal prosecutor." Jeanne closed her mouth firmly, reconsidered and opened it again. "I heard he went to school in Knoxville. It's his home town. So you see some sort of motive there. Maybe he was a ninety-pound weakling as a kid. Triumphant return. At least he didn't attempt to stage a win much under three hours."

"That really stinks," Kerry muttered. "Imagine. Not only cheating, but hitting a woman your size— Here, we got you a chocolate cake to celebrate."

Over champagne and cake, Jeanne told the whole story. No one made a move to leave, even long after five o'clock. They wanted to hear everything. But she couldn't bring herself to reveal everything she had learned from Mrs. Beale.

"We've been fielding calls all day. You've really put *Fancy Free* on the map," offered Nancy.

"If we'd been called something mundane like *Woman Runner*, I don't think we would have had so big a response from just one little caption," noted Ron. "I sure am sorry I held out against the name for so long."

There was a round of *ahas* at Ron's admission, long an office joke.

Jeanne stood up with some difficulty, feeling the effects of the champagne. "Lemme go develop my film, before I'm too blotto to see straight." Half exultant, half anxious, she headed for the darkroom. She wondered what everyone would say if they knew the whole story. And how serious was Beale with his threats? She had mentioned them, but no one had picked up on it.

Through the door of the darkroom, Ron's voice pursued her. "You want to imagine our next issue's cover? Hope you got some good color shots. Maybe a collage of the UPI shot plus whatever else you have. A big shot of Beale in the center. Mug shot. Hang his race number around his neck like a criminal—"

"Stop it, Ron!"

He fell silent immediately.

"I'm sorry," she relented. "I'm worn out. It's a human interest story, yes, but it's a human tragedy, too. Who knows what effect all the publicity this morning will have on his career, his family—"

"You sure can be broad-minded," Ron mused. "Turn the other cheek and all that. I'm really interested to see what you come up with on film. Maybe I ought to write the accompanying story."

"Fine. You do it. I'd like that." She meant it.

"Not on your life. You're the one who was there."

She made contact prints and came out to find Ron seated at his desk, alone in the office. It was almost seven.

"Kerry took your color rolls with her to the fastest processor in town," he said. "Let's see what you have."

"Ron," she said, "if you absolutely must feature this Beale thing—"

"*Must?* Jeanne, who has a better right to the story?

You belong to *us*. It's *your* story. What's going on here? He asked for everything he got, and has to get. It's public domain. There's no problem with libel, with these pictures and what you've told us. What's the problem?''

"We aren't a scandal sheet, and I have the feeling we should take Beale's libel threats seriously.''

"If it makes you feel better, I'll call our lawyer in the morning. But I don't understand your reluctance. These are just great!'' he cried, spreading the prints out before him, sheet after sheet. "Boy, I wish your *Playgirl* piece weren't scheduled for summer. They'd have a field day on the ex-fat girl who really's the gorgeous woman who just hit the wire service.''

This was getting out of hand. She, who'd dreamed so long of being pretty and then popular and then successful, was having too much of all three. A fat, ugly Jeanne could have caught Arthur Beale. Sat on him, flattening him to the road.

When he finished gazing at the contact prints, Ron slammed her on the back enthusiastically.

"How can you say you're just an amateur photographer, Jeanne? Look at these! By God, Jeanne, you learn faster on the job than anyone I've ever worked with. You want my job next?''

That drew from her an incredulous smile of appreciation, but he wasn't entirely joking.

"I'm serious,'' he said. "My title ought to belong to a woman pretty soon. I'm an initiator, not a sustainer.''

"Last hired is the first fired, not the first promoted,'' she said cagily.

"Best qualified,'' he retorted, "is the first promoted around here.''

Then he turned back to the photographs. "Look at

this guy's facial expression. He could chew tenpenny nails. No remorse here, is there? Look at the cop's face. And this man is the real winner of that division?''

"Yep. I want to see *him* on the cover, Ron. That's what was important, not Beale. His time was terrific, and he's a sweet man. A professor."

"We'll . . . think about it," he hedged.

She knew as well as he the bigger drawing card for a popular magazine. Not the saint but the sinner.

"You're overreacting to this, Jeanne. In this field you have to be hard-nosed. Beale's a crook. He pulled a lousy trick, for which he'll get no fine, no jail sentence, nothing but notoriety. Maybe the publicity will help his practice. God knows. Printing this story will make other cheaters think twice. You want to see the sport corrupted? You can't patrol every inch of every twenty-six-mile course. People have to hop into the bushes to take a leak and come back out again. When a guy like Beale cheats—an intelligent, middle-aged solid citizen—he deserves everything he gets, even if it's only bad press."

She stood with her chin tucked down, like a child being lectured. He came over to her and put his hands on her shoulders, staring straight into her eyes. "Look, this is the biggest publicity boost we've ever had. I know that. But I do have principles. I wouldn't feature a true victim in a humiliating posture. Starving Cambodians deserve privacy, but this is different. The Beale thing involves no war, no class or ethnic conflict. No accident, no negligence and, worst of all, no remorse."

"I see."

"We'll tell the Beale story, and let our readers draw their own conclusions."

Jeanne stared down at the photos. Beale's face, cold

as ice, contrasted sharply with the beaming fifty-six-year-old professor who had just put twenty-six miles under his belt. Dickensen's hair hung in his eyes; he was changing his Ancient Marathoner shirt, transparent with sweat, for the new green Knoxville one. The lenses of his glasses were steamy. Nice man. Almost as fast as Dick Kilmer, at twice Dick's age—almost.

She'd fight to get Melton Dickensen on the cover. With the professor's permission, of course.

"Come on, Jeanne. I'll drop you at home. You're taking this much too seriously. We love you here, and the magazine—and I—will stand behind you all the way." Ron put a comforting arm around her shoulder.

"Thanks," she said. "I needed that."

Chapter Fourteen

THE PHONE RANG at ten that night, an hour after she got home. It was Erkki.

"You are not in some Tennessee hospital for injuries?" he asked.

"No, I'm okay. You must have seen the wire service picture."

"That is correct."

His voice brought the old chills down her back. Had the episode with Dick been a dream? She almost wished that were so. How could two men so different both want her? Dick, waiting for her to come to him, charming her with affection and humor, making her want to give to him and then take in return. Erkki swept her away, gave her little choice.

"I don't want you to come over," she said shakily. "I'm too tired. I worked at the magazine until eight—"

"Did you find your traveling companion interesting?"

Dear God! "He was pleasant company," she rushed on. "The cheater's story is really big, but it's gotten out of all proportion. I'll have to work on it all week. And then argue with people on how to feature it for January."

"So you made love with *him* as well?" probed Erkki bitterly. "You do not deceive, Jeanne."

"I said nothing of the kind. Besides, it's really none of your business," she said angrily.

"It is my business. I'm in love with your body."

Well, that was certainly blunt—and precise.

"You'll soon be going back to Finland, Erkki. There's no future for us."

"And you shall be going to Finland, too, I think. Your magazine may send you. To cover the ultramarathon. I discussed this with your boss."

"He didn't tell me that."

"He allowed me the pleasure of telling you. I made to him a proposal, that you examine the ultramarathon for your magazine. The Institute—for you shall help us—will share costs."

"That's wonderful!"

"In June," he continued, "you go. Before then, you must work very hard, for the magazine and the Institute." He fell silent, then said, "So you see, to involve yourself with a boy here is not very practical."

She could almost agree. All those hours in the office just now and Ron hadn't said a word! She almost wished he had told her. Then they would really have had something to celebrate.

"I can hardly believe all this," she said overwhelmed, lying back on the sofa, phone on her shoulder.

His voice might have had hands, it so pervaded the space around her.

"I shall arrive there in half an hour."

"Please, no. I have to get to bed."

"Excellent. Exactly. Get to bed. I join you." Then he hung up.

Jeanne groaned. Her reactions were too tumultuous to catalog. She drank the tea she'd made, showered, got dressed again reluctantly, in a royal-blue long-sleeved jumpsuit. She pulled its long zipper to the top.

Aunt Lily, she knew, would prefer Erkki to Dick. Not because of the rich man–poor man contrast. Erkki might need her, but Dick needed her more, needed her company, her wit, her courage. Erkki had said only, and carefully, "I love your body."

Never choose a man who can't live without you, Jeanne remembered Lily saying. *He's weak.*

Erkki came exactly as promised; he must have been nearby when he telephoned. Perhaps he'd been on business in the city. He did not explain. He stood looking at her, one brow sharply arched. He took off his pearl gray suit jacket, and with the other hand loosened a teal blue silk tie, never ceasing to gaze over her body. She wished the jumpsuit didn't cling so closely; she'd chosen it for comfort and coverage. She kept one hand over the large metal ring at her throat.

"You look tantalizing. Is that something also new from Tennessee?"

"It's something I made."

He walked slowly toward her. "What sort of amusement do you prefer tonight, Jeanne?"

Because she knew that he knew, she caught the faint taunt in his voice, the cover for hurt feelings. She wasn't shocked when he murmured, "Was he excellent? Did he deserve you?"

She bristled but did not answer. Instead she walked

away and poured him a cup of spiced orange tea. He glared at it, glancing quickly up at her, with his narrow lips pressed tightly together. The silence was painful. Unlike Dick he was no talker. His face alone said more than she wanted to hear.

"Tell me about this plan for me to go all the way to Finland."

Balancing his cup and saucer in one hand, he drew the other arm around her and sat down, pulling her onto his lap. She couldn't move, or she'd spill his tea. She didn't move.

"Mr. Liu and I discussed a joint project. The Institute needs a woman to recruit females for the tests and the race. We propose to send you throughout the United States to find suitable women. You can then write about them for *Fancy Free*. In Finland you continue duties for the Institute and write about the ultramarathon. Mr. Liu continues to pay your salary. The Institute pays all your expenses. This is agreeable to you, Jeanne?"

She looked at the pale, shining hair combed back from his hollow temples and down across his forehead. An awful lethargy was seizing her, as if she were drugged. Erkki and Ron certainly had worked things out. It might have been nice of them to consult her beforehand. But to travel all over the country interviewing women ultramarathoners and then spend June in Finland. How could she turn it down? Let them do with her what they would. Let Erkki do with her what he would.

Erkki's finger was hooked through the metal loop of her zipper, pulling it down, down. She looked into the narrowed gray eyes with the pupils dilating now, saw the teacup set aside, felt his hand slide down from her shoulder to her waist to her hip and thigh and then rise to repeat the motion. The zipper moved lower, and he saw that she was nude underneath.

He stood, picked her up, carried her into the bedroom and put her on the bed while he disrobed. "We see who gives you more pleasure," he said huskily.

As he slipped her arms and legs out of the jumpsuit, he caught sight of the bruise on her hip. He switched quickly from lover to doctor.

"That is where you fell, when the cheating runner knocked you down?"

"Yes."

"You have no bruises elsewhere?" He did not wait for her answer but put both hands over one breast at a time and palpated each very thoroughly, examining not just the skin but the inner structure. It was not a romantic thing to do and hardly called for.

"I already have a doctor," she said. "Why are you doing this, Erkki?"

He gave no answer but continued to examine her. Something known to him alone had compelled him to do this, and he would keep his own counsel. He seemed almost fierce in his determination to continue, and Jeanne could not summon the strength to oppose him.

"You are faithful with the Pill?" he asked abruptly.

"Yes, I am."

He nodded. "That is good." Then he sat on the edge of the bed and leaned over her, bringing his face very close to hers. "Jeanne, I need you. I want all of you, and only you. Can you feel the same?" Now the hands that had explored her were lifting locks of hair off her forehead as he kissed her face, fitting their bodies together as if they were made to be joined.

"I don't know if I can," she murmured. "When I am with you I want no one else, but the world is still so tempting to me. I need time. Please . . ."

He cut off the flow of words with a kiss, and they sank deeper and deeper into each other. She could not flee him or even slow the progress of his conquest of her. It was a heady experience, giving herself up to him. He saved himself for the time she was nearly frantic, and then he launched her and went with her, the pilot of their boat, the captain setting out to sea.

Chapter Fifteen

SOMEWHERE IN THE distance a bell was ringing. Jeanne struggled out of a deep sleep. The phone. It's the phone. She groped on the night table and picked up the receiver.

"Hello?" she croaked, her throat dry. She covered the receiver and coughed. No response. "Hello? Is anyone there?" Now she could hear shallow breathing at the other end of the line. "Who is this?" Her heart began to speed up, thumping so loudly she could hear it. She opened her mouth again, but no words came out. With a shaking hand she replaced the receiver in the cradle.

Jeanne raised herself slowly to a sitting position, blinking her eyes and shaking her head. Trying to wake up. Dammit. She hated obscene phone calls in the middle of the night—or was it almost dawn? It's bad enough that the phone rings at all, usually bringing bad news. But then to hear nothing but ominous breathing at the other end. Ugh! Jeanne shuddered and pulled the bedclothes snugly around her.

Why would anyone do something like that? What pleasure was there in waking a person, catching them when vulnerable and scaring them? She knew the caller was a man, testing his power over women in this devious, cowardly way. Men tested their power in many ways, she was discovering. Just hours ago Erkki had drawn her to him with his lovemaking, his plans for her to work on the ultramarathon and go to Finland.

And now he was gone. He must have slipped out while she slept. Like a thief in the night, he had taken her body and soul and gone off, without so much as a word. She loved what he did to her body, but she knew so little about him. He was so silent, so mysterious, so demanding. She had just begun to find herself, and now she was slipping away under Erkki's spell.

Jeanne plumped her pillows and slid back down into her bed. She tossed and turned, unable to find a comfortable position. Each tiny noise or ripling shadow made her start. For company, she switched on her radio and dialed to the classical music station. It was three a.m. The joyous, invigorating opening strains of Vivaldi's *The Four Seasons* filled the air. "La Primavera," the spring. Jeanne hummed along with the familiar music, and it restored her spirit. Being thin and attractive doesn't mean you don't have any problems, she was learning. It was the spring of Jeanne Lathrop, too, and no obscene phone callers or enigmatic Finnish doctors or middle-aged cheating runners were going to keep her from enjoying it.

In the morning Jeanne was groggy from losing so much sleep. She ran to the office hoping to shake off the effects of the previous night. She wanted to get the blood flowing, get some oxygen to her brain so that she could think clearly about all that she was facing.

She hit the shower as soon as she arrived and dressed in the designer jeans and cranberry velour sweater she had left at the office. There was a note on her desk from Ron. See me, it said, so she grabbed a mug of coffee and threaded her way through the maze of cubicles to Ron's cluttered cubbyhole.

"What's up, chief?"

Ron offered her some of the nuts and raisins mix he was munching. She took a handful, her stomach reminding her that she had eaten cake and champagne for dinner last night and skipped breakfast this morning. Not great for the blood sugar.

"Your friend Beale wasn't kidding. I got a call from his office this morning telling me that Beale would sue us from here to kingdom come if we ran the story. The caller was one of Beale's partners, Brinks was the name, and he was about as cordial as a rattlesnake." Ron leaned back in his chair, waiting for her to make the next move.

"Why don't we just drop it then. It's not important enough to make all this trouble over. I have mixed feelings about the story anyway." Jeanne went on to tell Ron about her interview with Amanda Beale.

"All the more reason to go on with it," Ron countered after he'd heard her story. "Look, Jeanne, controversy sells magazines, and that's what we're all about here. It's good copy, good human interest. I want you to follow it up. Talk to Mrs. Beale again, try to locate the son, the prosecutor. Find out about Beale's law practice, try to find out who drove that Lincoln in Knoxville. Don't worry about the lawsuit. I'll take care of it."

Jeanne knew Ron was right, but there was still a knot in her stomach. "I don't know," she stammered. "Something about this just doesn't feel right."

Ron looked her square in the eye. "Hey, kid, you think Woodward and Bernstein were scared off by a nasty phone call or two from some two-bit lawyer?"

She had to laugh at the comparison. "Okay, boss, you're on." Before she returned to her desk, she talked with Ron about the ultramarathon assignment, discussing arrangements for being away from the office for several months, tossing around angles for covering the story. By the time she left Ron's office, her mind was going a mile a minute. There was work to be done.

Thursday afternoon Dick phoned from his office at the Bureau of Land Management. He proposed a run after work that day. Since the night of her return from Knoxville, Jeanne had heard nothing from Erkki. She restrained herself, many times each day, from picking up the phone and calling him. It would be good to talk to Dick, good to be with someone who cared about her and was not afraid to show it. She agreed to meet him at her apartment at six.

Jeanne made it a point to be dressed and ready to go when he arrived. Instead of buzzing him into the building, she hurried down as soon as he rang. Dick was standing in the doorway, bare-legged and shivering. He gave her a quick peck on the cheek. "Looks like you're all set, so let's make tracks."

They ran together to the National Cathedral and around it. Jeanne stared up at the soaring gothic tower rising so majestically above her, making her personal problems seem so small and mundane. Dick took her hand, but dropped it when she didn't respond.

"Is he a runner, too?"

"Who?"

"The other guy. My competition."

"Yep," she nodded, pained.

"Well, first come, first served."

Jeanne flinched. On the farm, service meant the mating of livestock.

"Friends?" she asked Dick a mile later, and touched his arm, wishing they could be more than that. But how could they?

"Friends as a bare minimum," he responded instantly.

They circled Dumbarton Oaks, the lovely estate with galleries, mosaic terraces and lawns. Jeanne looked at it with longing. She had once believed that if you lived in a place like this you had to be happy. But those days were gone. Not even the splendor and elegance of Dumbarton Oaks can keep the problems of the world from your door.

Back in front of her apartment building Jeanne and Dick stood panting after their mile run. "How about we go upstairs for a quick stretch and shower and then grab a bite to eat?" Dick asked. "I've got my work clothes in the van; we can splurge, go someplace nice."

Jeanne looked at his face, full of affection and longing. She couldn't, she just couldn't. "Let's call it a night, Dick. I've been working hard and I'm tired."

"I know that's not the reason you don't want to be with me."

It was impossible to lie to him. She reached out and touched his cheek. "Dick, you're very dear to me, but I need some time to sort out my feelings. You know this is all new to me. I'm not comfortable hopping from bed to bed. And 'your competition' has some powerful medicine. You want a wife, someone to live with you and Joey, take care of you. I don't think I'm the right person for that. At least not now."

Dick shook his angel's halo of curls. "I'm only asking you to give me a chance, spend some time with me, get to know me and let me get to know you. We don't have to be lovers."

"You are too much, Kilmer. Okay, you're on for dinner." She couldn't know if she was making a mistake or not. Could she be friends with Dick after having slept with him? How would this affect her relationship with Erkki? Did she even have a relationship with Erkki? He hadn't called since the night he slipped out of her apartment under cover of darkness. "Only let's keep it simple. We can walk over to Mr. Smith's on M Street."

"Sounds good to me."

Upstairs, Jeanne got clean towels from the linen closet and sent Dick to take his shower first. Thirsty from the run, she went into the kitchen for a drink. The phone rang. When Jeanne picked it up, there was silence. Oh, no, not again, she thought. "Whoever this is, it isn't funny, so stop it," she shouted into the phone.

"Don't hang up," a muffled voice replied. Jeanne heard a click and then a torrent of demonic laughter reached her ears. It sent chills up and down her spine, like being alone in the funhouse.

"You are really sick!" Jeanne cried as she slammed the receiver down. Shaking, she sat down on a stool, her head in her hands. What was going on here anyway?

"Bathroom's all yours," she heard Dick call. Drying his hair with a towel, he stuck his head into the kitchen. "Are you okay? What's the matter?"

She told him about the phone call and about the one she had received Monday night.

Dick knelt down in front of the stool and took her hands. "There's a special number at the phone company you can call to report obscene or annoying calls. I think you should at least report this. Then we'll take the phone off the hook and go have a relaxing dinner. A couple of glasses of wine wouldn't hurt either."

Dick's face, all pink from the shower and full of concern, was almost irresistible. Jeanne kissed him lightly on the forehead. "I'm glad you're here right now."

"So am I," he said in a whisper. "Now, let's call the phone company and get you in the shower and get out of here."

Thirty minutes later Jeanne and Dick were seated at a small table in the back of Mr. Smith's. It looked out over the garden, now closed for the winter. Most of the after-work drinking crowd had left, leaving the dark, homey restaurant quiet, good for relaxing.

Over white wine and fluffy mushroom omelets Dick spoke about his son. Joey would be spending the Thanksgiving holiday with him, and he was excited as he could be about it. "I thought we'd drive to my sister's place in Philadelphia after I pick Joey up in Wilmington. We'll have our turkey there and return to Washington on Friday. I'd really like you to meet Joey. How about going to the zoo with us on Saturday to see the pandas? It'll be a lot of fun."

"I'd like that," Jeanne replied. "I haven't visited the pandas in a long time."

They walked back to Jeanne's apartment hand in hand, swinging their arms back and forth, like children on the way to school. Jeanne had never had a special friend to hold hands with on the way to school. Being with Dick was so comfortable, so easy. She had never had a friend who was a male before, and she found she liked it a great deal.

As they approached her apartment building, Jeanne noticed that her low-slung Porsche, parked a couple of doors away from her townhouse, looked even lower than usual. "Is it the wine, or does my car look shorter than usual?" she asked Dick. She let go of his hand and quickened her pace to reach the car. "Oh, nooooo!" Her mouth fell open. "Someone's let the air out of my tires. That is really mean and rotten."

Dick ran to catch up with her. "Jeanne, is something going on that you're not telling me about? I don't like this one bit. First the phone calls and now this. It looks like somebody has it in for you. Do you think it's your friend Beale?"

The thought struck Jeanne like a ton of bricks. Beale was cold and unpleasant and had threatened Ron with a libel suit against the magazine, but these kind of pranks were childish, warped. "It doesn't seem like his style. He's harassed Ron at the office but he hasn't approached me with any legal suits. And why pick on me? I know I was the one who stopped him at the finish line, but fifty other people must have snapped his picture, too, including the UPI photographer. A lot more people saw that picture than are going to read my article in *Fancy Free*, that's for sure."

"People do strange things under stress, Jeanne. I'd be careful if I were you. I hate to say I told you so, but back in Charlottesville . . ."

Jeanne cut him off. "That's enough, Dick. I'm going ahead with the story. Ron is backing me all the way and that's good enough for me. I didn't lose eighty pounds to keep on being a cream puff."

Dick's face had a hard look on it, one she'd never seen before.

Best to drop the subject. "I'd better get upstairs and phone the AAA, see if they can get a service truck out here to help. 'Now see what you've got us into, Stan,'" she said in her best Oliver Hardy imitation.

Dick cracked up. "That's the worst Oliver Hardy I've ever heard."

It was nearly eleven before the AAA truck had arrived and put Jeanne's Porsche back on its feet. Dick offered to sleep on the couch, but Jeanne insisted he go home. She really was worn out and feeling vulnerable. She would end up inviting Dick into her bedroom, and that wouldn't do at all. Better to head them off at the pass. That's what her father always said. Funny she should be thinking of her parents right now. She had a hunch she was feeling much more guilty about sex than she had let herself consciously acknowledge. Maybe an appointment with Dr. Tinsley was in order.

She thanked Dick for being around when she needed him, for being so patient and supportive. He held her close for a moment and kissed her softly on the lips. "My pleasure, friend," he said. "Take good care of yourself. If you want me, you know what to do."

Jeanne closed the door behind him and locked it, double, to make certain everything was secure. She slid the night chain into place and leaned against the door for a moment. She had just said goodbye to a man who wanted to give her everything—love, security, a home, children. Dick was willing to give all of that and freely. But he didn't speak to her heart the way Erkki did, despite Erkki's brooding, his brusqueness, his unpredictability. But Erkki had a power, a strength that Dick would never have.

Leaving a light on in the livingroom, Jeanne got

ready for bed. She needed company and flipped the radio to late night jazz, drifting off to sleep as Art Tatum improvised on the ivories with Cole Porter's "At Long Last Love." The final words of the song ran around in her brain: Is it a fancy, not worth thinking of, or is it, at long last, love? Was she in love with Erkki or was she just succumbing to the power of the flesh? He was bringing more problems to her life than joy. Maybe she could take the power and strength of Erkki and roll it up with the kindness and caring of Dick and create her own Mr. Right. In her mind's eye she imagined Erkki's lean body topped by Dick's helter skelter curls. She laughed out loud at the funny combination and snuggled down under the covers. Like Scarlet O'Hara, she would worry about that tomorrow.

Erkki was the first person to reach her in the office on Friday morning. As usual he got right down to business.

"On Sunday there is a fundraising outing on the yacht of Mr. and Mrs. Nehmann. We are to raise money for the ultramarathon research. I want to be there with you. This is agreeable?"

Jeanne asked for more information and learned she needed formal clothes for the evening dinner. She wanted to ask Erkki why he had sneaked out on Monday night. She wanted to tell him about the phone calls and the tires, but as soon as he had made arrangements to meet her on Sunday he rang off. Jeanne wished she knew some other Finns so she could find out if this was a national characteristic or something that Erkki alone did. Why, he was barely civil! Exasperated, Jeanne got up from her desk and walked over to the office's only window. She paced back and forth, looking out at the traffic.

"Phone for you, Jeanne," she heard Kerry sing out. "William Beale returning your call."

She had tracked the younger Beale down through the Justice Department phone listings and left several messages for him. She suspected he would not be too eager to speak with her. This was a surprise. The Beale children must take after Amanda, not Arthur. Jeanne hurried back to her cubicle.

"Jeanne Lathrop here, Mr. Beale. Thanks for calling back."

"I hoped by calling you myself, Ms. Lathrop, I could get you to stop annoying my secretary with all your messages. She is a busy woman."

Uh oh. Like father, like son.

The clipped voice continued. "You have already forced yourself on my mother, who is too gracious to have thrown you out, as I would have done."

"Just a minute," Jeanne interrupted. "Your mother knew who I was before she opened the door."

"That is beside the point. What I want to say is that if you don't stop harassing me and my family, I will join my father in a lawsuit against you. My father and I have our differences, but one thing we agree upon is the right of our family to privacy."

"I would hardly call a few phone calls and one visit harassing. And speaking of phone calls, I have had two very disturbing calls at my home, and last night someone let the air out of the tires of my car. Not to mention that my employer has been threatened with a lawsuit by one of your father's partners. If anyone is doing any harassing, it isn't me."

"I fail to see, Ms. Lathrop, what your being the victim of some Halloween pranks has to do with me and my family."

"I can't think of anyone else who would be interested in causing me trouble, Mr. Beale."

"You, you," Beale sputtered, "can't possibly be intimating that you think my father is behind these pranks." Beale began to laugh. "That is the most unlikely thing I've ever heard. Excuse me for laughing, but if you knew my father as well as I do, you would find this quite funny."

"People do strange things under stress," she said, echoing Dick's words to her.

"That may be true, but the picture of my father letting the air out of your tires is a very funny one. Excuse me." Beale coughed, regaining his composure. "In all seriousness, though, I warn you to stay away from this story for your own good. You may think my father is just some crank lawyer from little old Charlottesville, but he is a powerful man. He has some very strong political connections in Washington. I wouldn't fool with him, if I were you."

"I have no intentions of 'fooling with him,' as you say. I only intend to write a story about why a man like your father would cheat in a local marathon. Thank you for calling. It's been very informative talking with you." Jeanne hung up without letting him say anything else.

This story was taking on a lot of dimensions; the actual cheating was just one of them. Here was a man trying to deny something that was well-documented, acting as if he were the injured party. He may or may not be trying to scare Jeanne off—she couldn't prove anything on that score. He was at least well off, if not wealthy, as Jeanne knew from seeing his home, his car, the way he dressed. And by his son's admission, he was not a small town lawyer, but had friends in Washington, unless Bill Beale was just bluffing.

Jeanne picked up the pad she had used to make notes on her conversation with Bill Beale and went off to Ron's office. She had finished bringing him up to date when Nancy rapped on the partition. She carried a manila envelope. "A messenger left this for you. I thought it might be important."

The package carried no return address. Her name was typed neatly on the front, along with the name and address of the magazine. It was thin and light. Jeanne turned it over a few times.

"It's not ticking, Jeanne, so open it and get on with the Beale story," Ron said impatiently. "I've got a lot to do."

"Sorry, it's just that I wasn't expecting anything. I can't imagine what it is."

Jeanne undid the clasp and lifted the flap. She reached her hand inside and felt two thick pieces of paper, rougher on one side than on the other. She pulled them out and looked down. It's me, a picture of me before I lost all the weight. Looking at it closer, she saw that the eyes had been gouged out of the picture. Jeanne's stomach turned over, and she fought to keep her breakfast down. The other was a picture of her as she looked now, wearing running shorts and a *Fancy Free* T-shirt. In this one, her left breast had been gouged out, just where her heart would be. These were two of the pictures that were supposed to run with the *Playgirl* article. Jeanne threw the pictures on Ron's desk and raced to the bathroom.

Nancy and Kerry arrived a moment later, picked her up off the cold tile floor, helped her wash her face and put a paper cup of water into her trembling hand. Kerry held her hand as she lifted the cup to her parched lips. She took a few swallows.

"Thanks. I think I'll be okay now."

The two women led her back to Ron's cubicle. They brought in an extra chair and made Jeanne put her feet up.

"I'm awfully sorry about all this, Jeanne," Ron said tensely. "Kerry can take you home as soon as you feel like it. She can stay with you the rest of the day if you like. I don't think there's much we can do about any of this, but I'm going to put in a call to the lawyer anyway. I feel responsible because of my insistence on going ahead with this story."

"You're not going to pull me off it now, Ron, are you? I really want to get to the bottom of this thing now."

"We'll see, Jeanne. Just go home and rest for now. Don't think about it for a couple of days. Enjoy the weekend. Do you have plans?"

She told him about Sunday on the yacht.

"I suspect the good doctor has more than a professional interest in you," he grinned. "Sounds very romantic. Now get out of here. Take a cab and put it on your expense report."

Feeling much better, Jeanne decided to go home alone, saying she would call if she wanted company. Kerry went downstairs with her and saw that she got a cab.

Jeanne settled back for the short ride home. When she was fat, she had hated being the butt of cruel jokes about her girth. And here she was, as thin and trim as could be, again the butt of a cruel prankster. At least as a child she could stick out her tongue. But what could she do now? She had thought herself such a heroine for stopping Beale from crossing the Knoxville finish line. But she wasn't getting a lot of glory out of it. Life in the fast lane was not all it was cracked up to be.

What was she going to do for the rest of the day? She didn't want to stay home alone all day. Nor did she want Kerry to come over and hold her hand. Aunt Lily's voice came to mind, as it so often did in times of trouble. When in doubt, shop. It does wonders, even if you don't buy anything. She would shower and nap and run off to Garfinkel's. There were still a few dollars left in the Aunt Lily fund, and a new gown might be just the thing for Sunday's shipboard dinner. Her first time on a yacht. Lily, Jeanne said to herself, I hope you're right.

Chapter Sixteen

JEANNE WAS BEAUTIFUL. The fact that she didn't know it made the beauty more entrancing, Erkki decided from his vantage point at the rail, just watching her smile. It was a warm day for the end of November, the last day to take the *Mitzi* from its harbor at Fair Haven. It now loafed along the eastern shore of the Chesapeake Bay.

He and Jeanne had driven down earlier in the day with the Nehmanns in their Mercedes. The foursome had spent a quiet afternoon on the boat, going for a brief sail before returning to the harbor to allow the caterers on board to prepare for the rest of the guests who would be arriving at six for cocktails and formal dining. Both couples had retired to staterooms to change into formal attire. He had wanted to change with Jeanne, but propriety dictated that he use a separate room.

The urbane American girl had taken well to the sea, thought Erkki, and the color it brought to her cheeks was delightful. She had confessed to him in a brief moment alone that she had never been on a boat before, much less a yacht. There wasn't "much ocean" in South Dakota, she told him with a nervous giggle.

Standing on the gently rocking deck in his tuxedo, crisp white pleated-front shirt and black velvet bow tie, he could not take his eyes off Jeanne. Her gown was off-white satin, the bodice draped in wide folds that offered a tantalizing hint of the firm breasts beneath it. The skirt clung to her lithe form, covering her legs but allowing the viewer to see the outline of her limbs. When she moved, the dress moved softly with her. Against the chill of the November evening she wrapped herself in the black silk shawl she had worn on their first night together. In this costume, she could have been the star of a 1930's film.

Beautiful Jeanne. He had taught her from the beginning. Now his apt student glowed with her talents, like a pianist fluttering nimble fingers while she spoke, or an artist calling on her familiarity with the palette to name the colors in a sunset.

Any man would see that this woman thrilled to the act of love. Any man would be drawn to her, her childish small nose and the Dutch bob and the uneven sunburn from running so much.

He could not keep his mind in these channels, or he would sweep her off the deck, down to the lounge of the yacht. He would ease her onto the couch and drive her with him to their inevitable cataclysm. How marvelous, that moment when she had wanted him, said yes, yes, and drawn him into her, while her body had barred his way. They had conquered the stubborn barrier, he and she, laboring together, and the experience came back to him again and again undiminished. He sensed the rich fantasy life that had sustained her and that now promised unending variety and excitement. For them both. Good for a lifetime.

It would be a joy to show her Finland in June. He wanted Jeanne in Helsinki with him, but with the realization that she was actually coming, a chill shook him. Jeanne would learn of his past, of Kristina. He must find the time and place to tell her himself, in his own way.

Albert Moore, a colleague from the Institute, was talking to Jeanne now, his hand resting casually on her shoulder as they looked across the bay to Annapolis. Erkki felt a stab of jealousy unworthy of his relationship with Al. No matter that Al was considered devastatingly handsome, with his square jaw, penetrating eyes and prematurely silver gray hair. He could trust Al. It was Jeanne he could not trust. Her need to test her wings was too large. He did not want to scare this emerging butterfly away.

Jeanne must have sensed his eyes on her for she turned, catching his eye across the deck. She excused herself and came directly to him, not dropping her social mask even when she was inches from him.

"Can I do something for you, Dr. Haukkamaa? You seemed to be calling me."

"I simply wished to tell you that you look very beautiful tonight."

Jeanne smiled up at him and took his arm. "Perhaps we can discuss this in private."

It sounded like a wonderful idea. He had yearned for the same thing on this fine yacht, much larger than his own sailboat docked in the marina near Helsinki. He wanted to make love to her. He kissed her and took her hand, leading her down the steps to the lower deck and then down more steps into the central lounge between a pair of cabins and the galley.

"Let us not talk of anything but our happiness," he said. "Let me hold you; no one will come."

Jeanne's marvelous readiness did not fail him. She kissed him passionately, clinging very tight, giving way to sleepy-eyed passion. It had been a week since she had come to him, or he to her.

He drew her into one of the cabins and shut the door. He put Jeanne up against the wall, panting, both of them gasping now, and he slid his hands under her gown.

He knew how to ease her troubles and set about it quickly. Her strong, runner's legs wound around him. Standing, he took her without talking, only kissing.

The impact seemed to take away his very skeleton, leaving him hanging on the wall, pinning Jeanne there in midair, boneless and smothering the groans that others might hear. She clasped onto him, clung, said, "Oh, I need you, Erkki, Erkki, take care of me, Erkki!"

Once before he had taken care of someone. He released Jeanne and led her to the small hard bed built into the cabin. As he lay there with her pressed to him, feeling her breasts dig into his chest, he remembered Kristina's breasts, he remembered finding that harbinger of doom, remembered its feel beneath his fingertips.

"Like a broken bit of tooth," said his medical professors. "Hard, painless, often in the upper outside quadrant."

He'd dug into her armpit for the lymph nodes and found what terrified him. Enlarged. One of them enlarged. She'd objected, but still he pressed on, finding more, like a boy going for hidden treasure, but this treasure was a time bomb.

"Kuhmua," he'd said. *"Mita hoitoa olette saa-neet?"*

"What treatment have you been taking?"

Stina Svensen's father was a Swedish manufacturer, her mother a foreign correspondent. She was born late in their lives, and suffered all the attentions of an only and beautiful offspring. By the time he met her, Erkki was a resident physician in a reputable hospital, looking for a wife, able at last to support one.

He sighed. Mistaking his sigh for one of contentment, Jeanne ran her hands up and down his back. So much had happened since then; Jeanne's presence reminded him. Was it only two years ago?

Erkki remembered the first time he and Stina had made love, remembered his first sight of the magnificent bosom she displayed teasingly in her low-necked dresses. She was a Swede, with a face and a body she was proud of—not shy and modest like most Finnish girls.

Stina's skin was honey gold. Her hair, perfectly straight and long, was darker than his and filled with red highlights. Her facial bones gave her a hollow-cheeked look and would wear well. Her mother, beyond sixty, was still beautiful.

It was on their second night together that he found it.

She jerked away from his hands, frowned into his horror-filled face. "I take many vitamins," she said. "That is my cure."

"You might die, and vitamins will not cure you," he said, shaking her, becoming savage.

"I will live. My horoscope says that," she announced very firmly and moved away from him.

"You are only twenty-two years old!" he cried, himself thirty-two and totally appalled. "It's clear that there is nodal involvement already. This lump is not likely to be benign. Stina, for God's sake, you need surgery—right now. How long have you known?"

She shrugged. "A few months. I will never have surgery. I would rather die than be deformed. Mutilated." She was an infant, she with her college degree and her three languages, including Finnish. "I wish for a cure, and I will have it without mutilation."

He said she must go off the Pill immediately. The Pill would aggravate the cancer. She said, "Maybe." If only he'd stopped then, all this agony would never have begun. She might have had a chance. But he didn't stop. He imagined that as her lover he could overwhelm her with statistics, convince her that she'd still be beautiful, not maimed, that things could be done, implants, anything, anything. Get radiation at least. Chemotherapy preferably.

He wasn't sure he loved her. He desired her and disapproved of her superstititons. It was infuriating enough when patients said, "God will take care of me." Stina didn't even mention God. She depended on soothsaying and vitamins.

She refused all the standard treatments. And yet, he had convinced her she was doomed without them. That conviction had shifted her goal from mere survival to immortality. And he had helped her, totally unwitting, totally unaware of what she wanted from him.

He was a new clinician, a star graduate, and the world was open for him. "You will give a good inheritance," she said, which he didn't understand for three months. Then he did.

"Olen raskaana," she said. I am going to have a baby.

"How on earth, how?" he screamed at her. "You wouldn't even go off the Pill!"

"Oh, yes I did. When you first told me to."

He remembered holding his head in his hands and reeling around the room. Everything doomed here: denial, delay, hormone pills. And now a pregnancy. His child.

"You must get help. You must abort the child and have surgery. Pregnant, you can't have chemotherapy. Pregnancy makes cancer go wild."

"You know I shall die. Well, then I will have a baby before I die to continue living for me. With my face and my mind—"

"God help us, not *your* mind!"

"That's cruel!"

"You're cruel. To yourself, to me, your parents—"

"You haven't told them, have you? You *promised*."

He hadn't. Being a doctor, he was accustomed to keeping patients' secrets. But with a child coming, and the beginning of discomfort in her breast and arm, Stina relented a little. She'd go up to Oulu for radiation treatments. She wanted to live to have her baby. His baby.

Though they both knew he did not love her and she did not love him, he had little choice. He married her, though she never asked him to.

"Erkki. Erkki." Jeanne was shaking him, and he came back to the present with a start. "We'd better clean up and go upstairs. Dinner will be served soon and people will miss us."

"So you wish to erase the signs of your passions, Jeanne. That is impossible, you know. I think you try to make a conquest with the other gentlemen this evening. You wish to see how many men will desire you.

None will give you what I can; you will come to know that."

Color rose to Jeanne's cheeks. "You are impossibly arrogant." She pulled away from him and started toward the bathroom at the far end of the cabin.

Erkki followed her, stopping her progress by clasping his strong arm tightly around her wrist. "I can give you everything. You will see. You will want no one else. That I promise."

Jeanne broke free of his grasp and went into the bathroom, shutting the door. Just what did he want from her? She felt like she was being killed with love. After a hasty toilette, she reentered the stateroom. Erkki sat on the bed with his back to her, his head in his hands. But even seeing him in this defenseless posture could not soften the way she felt. "I am going upstairs now. I think it's best we go up separately."

Erkki watched her leave. I say too much, he thought. I want too much from her. I want too much for her.

Chapter Seventeen

IT WAS THREE in the morning when the Nehmanns dropped Jeanne off at her apartment. The evening had been interminable after her encounter with Erkki. Somehow she had smiled and chatted her way through it. Exhausted, she tumbled into bed, without even removing her makeup.

Monday morning the alarm went off, and there was the whole day to be faced. Would it be full of dirty tricks? Setting aside such worries, Jeanne took a long, cleansing shower, brewed some strong coffee and left for the office, where there was much work to be done— too much work to have time for any distractions.

She would be leaving on her recruiting and interviewing trip right after the New Year holiday. She had to plan her itinerary, make her contacts, familiarize herself with the Institute's tests and procedures and do a lot of background reading and research on ultramarathoning.

In order to prepare for her long absence from the

office, she had promised Ron to leave a backlog of articles to be run during the months she was away, so that Kerry and Nancy would not be totally overwhelmed. There just wasn't enough money to hire another staffer and continue to pay Jeanne's salary.

The Beale article would run in the January issue, which would be put to bed the end of next week. So that had to be finished off. There was simply no time for mooning over Erkki, trying to figure out his moods and attitudes. It was enough that she would have to see him frequently while preparing for her trip on behalf of the Institute and *Fancy Free*. He had acted last night as if he were the only man in the world. The old Jeanne had despaired of finding even one man to want her, but now there was Erkki and Dick and who knew who else waiting in the wings.

At the office Jeanne worked quietly and steadily all morning. The quiet was shattered slightly before noon by a phone call from Arthur Beale himself.

"You just don't quit, do you, Miss Lathrop? You seem to have some notion that this is a comic strip world and you are working for the *Daily Planet*, with a nice Perry White to protect you and Superman to come to your rescue should you need it."

Jeanne could hardly believe the man had phoned her directly. So far his attacks on her had been furtive and backhanded. They had also been relatively harmless. She did not wish to antagonize him, but she did want to keep him talking, see what would slip out. Beale would be too smart to give himself away deliberately.

"Some pranks have been played on me recently," Jeanne said cautiously, "and so far I haven't needed Superman to help me out. Just the AAA."

"My son and I had quite a chuckle when he told me

about the phone conversation he had with you. Imagine a man of my standing letting the air out of someone's tires, like a juvenile delinquent. We found it very amusing, Miss Lathrop."

This guy was too much. "I'm glad you did, Mr. Beale, because I found it annoying. But not nearly as annoying as the nuisance calls I have been receiving."

"Yes, my son mentioned those as well. It is a pity that people don't use the telephone for its intended purpose."

Jeanne was silent, waiting for him to go on. He obliged.

"Which brings me to the purpose of this phone call. Since you have made your intention to publish an article about me quite clear, despite phone calls on my behalf by my partner and my son, I find it necessary to apply more direct pressure. I find you are a most popular young woman, Miss Lathrop. In my day well-bred young women did not make liaisons in the way they are made today. I take it you have some degree of affection for both Mr. Kilmer and Dr. Haukkamaa. Although it is hard to tell about these matters in these loose times."

Jeanne drew a sharp breath. Beale really had been keeping her under surveillance. He had invaded the most private area of her life. Jeanne drew a tissue from the box on her desk and wiped her forehead and upper lip. She was sweating as if she had run six miles. "And what have my friends got to do with this, Mr. Beale?"

"Nothing really. but you seem a hard young woman to convince. However, I suggest you query Dr. Hauk-kamaa about the status of his visa renewal and Mr. Kilmer about his visiting privileges with young Joseph."

She hoped Beale was bluffing. His son had said something about his having powerful connections. Given everything else that had happened, he might make good on his threats, if those connections did indeed exist.

"We're talking about the freedom of the press here, Mr. Beale. I am going to write this story and Ron Liu is going to run it, no matter what." Jeanne was angry now and her voice rose in pitch and loudness. "I think you are a very disturbed man and I hope you will get some help. You did something dishonest and you got caught. Why don't you stop trying to pretend that it didn't happen?"

Beale's voice didn't alter a single decibel. It slid over the phone wires in the same condescending waves. "Because it didn't happen, Miss Lathrop. I passed every checkpoint in Knoxville. The race officials are now admitting that."

"But I have pictures of you getting out of a brown Lincoln, wearing running clothes and a Knoxville marathon number."

"Photographers have been known to fake pictures, Miss Lathrop."

"I'm not the only photographer who snapped you that day. UPI ran a picture of you in papers all over the country."

"They ran a picture of you tackling me, not of me getting out of a—Lincoln, did you say it was?"

"There must be fifty pictures of you getting out of that Lincoln."

"That is where you are wrong, Miss Lathrop. I have combed Knoxville and have not been able to find a single one. I suggest you think about what I've said."

Before Jeanne could say anything else, the phone went dead. She sat motionless, staring into the receiver for several moments, before she pressed down the receiver button to get another dial tone. She punched the push buttons to get through to Erkki.

"Haukkamaa here."

"Hi, this is Jeanne. I just got a . . ."

Erkki interrupted her. "I cannot talk with you now. I wait for a call from the immigration service. There is some trouble about the renewal of my visa. I will call you later in the day. You will be in your office?"

"Yes, ah, yes, I will," she stammered.

"Good. Until later."

Again the phone went dead, and Jeanne held the lifeless receiver in her hand. Heart pounding, she punched the buttons that connected her to Dick.

"I'm glad you called, babe. I may have to cancel the zoo trip on Saturday."

"Is Joey sick?" she said, hoping against hope.

"No, I just got a call from some crazy Wilmington lawyer telling me that Sylvia thought I had been mistreating Joey during my visits with him and that I had better not try to take the boy this weekend. He was taking out a court order to prevent me from seeing Joey. Jeane, I'm just sick about this. My lawyer is talking to Sylvia's guy right now."

Jeanne hesitated. How could Beale have arranged something like this? With enough money and determination anything is possible. Should she tell Dick about her phone call from Beale? No, that wouldn't do any good. "I'm so sorry Dick. I know how much this visit means to you. Let me know if I can do anything for you."

"I just need to know you're there rooting for me."

"I always wanted to be a cheerleader, but that was out of the question in high school. Looks like I'm getting my chance now."

Jeanne rang off and sat at her desk for a few moments, wondering what to do. Her head was fuzzy and her heart was heavy. She needed to lighten up and think, so she headed for the bathroom where she changed into running clothes.

The cold November air hit Jeanne like a slap in the face. As she hit her stride and her heart and pulse rates accelerated, her head began to clear a bit. She didn't have the power or know-how to challenge Beale directly, so she had to get to him some other way. Suddenly, the face of Amanda Beale entered her mind's eye. She would call and ask for Amanda's help, see if she could reason with her husband, get him to drop his pressure tactics. It was the only way she could think of.

Back at the office, after a quick shower and a conference with Ron, Jeanne phoned Amanda Beale. Phrasing her words as kindly as possible, Jeanne told Amanda all that had happened in the last couple of weeks. Mrs. Beale was shocked and dismayed, but did reveal that her husband had been acting oddly since he returned from Knoxville. He was jumpy and short with her and often disappeared from home and office without letting anyone know where he was going. After Knoxville he had stopped running, and Mrs. Beale attributed the change in behavior to that and to the pressure of having been caught at the finish line. She told Jeanne she would try to find out what was behind her husband's behavior and would phone if she had any information for Jeanne. Jeanne apologized for calling with such difficult news, but Mrs. Beale said she needed all the information she could get if she was to help her husband.

By this time it was late afternoon and Jeanne was exhausted. On her way home she stopped for a visit at the National Cathedral, hoping the inspiring structure would help her put all that had happened into perspective. She sat quietly for a while, letting the hush and the glow of the day's last rays of sun passing through the stained glass windows restore her spirits.

Jeanne spent a quiet Thanksgiving with Ron and his wife, who had invited all three *Fancy Free* staffers for dinner. There had been many jokes beforehand about having Sweet and Sour Turkey or Moo Goo Gai Turkey for dinner, but Helen Liu served all the traditional American foods. Kerry contributed a sweet potato pie, Nancy brought a broccoli casserole and Jeanne, no whiz in the kitchen, supplied the wine.

The office was closed on Friday. Jeanne spent the day at home reading and thinking. She had not heard from Erkki, despite his promise to call her on Monday afternoon. He promised her everything but gave her nothing to hold on to.

Around eight that evening the phone rang. It was Dick.

"Still want to say hi to those pandas tomorrow? I got a little guy here who just can't wait to see them."

"Oh, Dick, you're with Joey! How wonderful! What happened?" Jeanne felt a release of some of the tension she had been carrying around since Monday.

"My lawyer got tough and told them they couldn't prove any of the crazy things they said I had done, and Sylvia relented. Apparently Sylvia got a call from some woman who said she had dated me a couple of times and that when Joey was with me I didn't feed him, kept him up until all hours of the night and that I abused him, but only in ways that wouldn't ever show. Sylvia questioned Joey, but he denied everything. She figured the kid was just scared or loyal or something. The lawyers fought until Wednesday, and then I got the word that everything was okay. By that time it was late and I just rushed off to Wilmington to get Joey and then on to my sister's in Philly. We had a great time, only Joey ate too much pumpkin pie and turkey and had a tummy ache today. I couldn't eat anything; my stomach's just getting back to normal now."

Jeanne told him she'd love to go to the zoo and arranged for Dick and Joey to pick her up at ten the next morning. Pandas first, then lunch.

Dick sounded so happy, Jeanne found herself crying after she hung up. Maybe everything would work out all right. She was tempted to call Mrs. Beale to see if things were any different in Charlottesville, but decided against it. If Amanda Beale had anything to say to her, Jeanne knew she would call.

Jeanne dried her eyes, suddenly tired. She fixed herself a cup of warm milk and climbed into bed. She wanted to be alert and awake for the outing the next day. Six-year-olds took a lot of energy.

When Jeanne opened the door to her apartment at ten the next morning, she saw two Dicks standing there, one standard size, the other miniature. Jeanne stifled a grin as the little boy shyly shook her hand, looking up at his father to see if he was doing okay. Joey was so serious about performing his introductions correctly that she dared not let him know she was not equally serious.

Joey was shy at first and spent a lot of time holding Dick's hand and hiding behind his legs, but with some gentle coaching from his father and lots of smiles from Jeanne he warmed up to her. By the time they left the zoo in late afternoon they were old pals, Joey eagerly

chattering away about school and friends and how
much turkey he ate at Aunt Betsy's.

As much as she enjoyed Dick and Joey's company,
Jeanne began to notice things which disturbed her.
Dick beamed at her once too often. He kept asking his
son if Jeanne wasn't great and wouldn't she be a fun
mommy to have. Jeanne wanted to say something to
him, but Joey was always right there.

When they stopped in front of the glass-enclosed
cage where Ling-Ling and Hsing-Hsing lived, Dick put
his arm around Jeanne and gave her a big squeeze. The
giant black and white bears were playing, rolling up
and down the man-made hills in their enclave. The
children laughed and crowed at their antics. "They
make quite a team," Dick whispered in her ear. "And
so would you and me and Joey. Think about it,
Jeanne."

"Not now, Dick. Not today. Can't we just enjoy the
pandas and Joey and each other without putting any
labels on it?" She turned back to the pandas. *Dick
wants to put me in a cage just like they are. They're
well fed and well taken care of, but they're still in a
cage.*

By four o'clock, Joey was exhausted, full of hotdogs
and popcorn, and they headed back to the van. Joey
fell asleep in the back before they'd left the parking
lot.

"The kid's all full of junk food. I'll have to make
sure he gets a decent dinner." Dick was silent for a
moment. "Here I am worried that he eats right and
Sylvia has the nerve, on some stranger's say-so, to
think I'm mistreating my own kid. That burns me up.
I guess she's anxious. I've been talking about having
more time with him, maybe six months a year, one of
those co-parenting deals. That doesn't sit so well with

Sylvia so she grabs onto anything to make me look bad. I just don't want the kid to get stuck in the middle."

Why bring up Beale now? It would only upset Dick more. "Anyone can see you're a great father, Dick," was all she could manage.

"It would be a lot easier for me, Jeanne, if I had someone. A single father doesn't get too much support, but if I were married. . . ."

Jeanne sighed. Did spending a few days and going to bed with someone once entitle them to a whole lifetime with you?

"Dick, if you're this serious about me, maybe we shouldn't see each other anymore. I couldn't help but notice the way you looked at me all afternoon. I'm not ready to be a wife or a mother. There's another man in my life. I'm leaving town in a month for I don't know how long. It's been nice to know you and to know Joey, but I don't think we're right for each other right now. Maybe you should just drop me off at home and see to getting some green vegetables into your son."

"You don't really mean that, do you, Jeanne? I won't say anything else about marriage if it'll make you feel better."

"Maybe you won't say anything else tonight but you'll say it tomorrow or next week or next month. I feel too pressured."

When they drove up to her building, Jeanne took Dick's hand. "I'm sorry, but you're rushing me. And I don't want you or Joey to get hurt. And I don't want myself to get hurt." She pressed his hand and leaned over to kiss each cheek, ignoring the tight expression on his face. "One for you, one for Joey."

How could she be so cold, she wondered as she climbed the stairs to her apartment. Where was her heart? For years she had buried it under layers of fat, but now it was exposed, beating close to the surface. Dick gave too much; Erkki too little. Too hot, too cold. Where was the porridge that was "just right?"

Chapter Eighteen

THE MONTH OF December passed swiftly. Jeanne worked hard and ran hard. She heard nothing from Dick. She was tempted to call him, if only to make sure everything was all right with Joey. But she had closed that book and was reluctant to open it again.

She saw Erkki on her frequent visits to the Institute but privately only once. Over dinner she questioned him gently about his visa problems, but he would only say that that it might be better for him to stay in Finland after the ultramarathon in June. Jeanne could get nothing more out of him. He spent the night in her apartment but left early in the morning while Jeanne was still asleep. When she woke, there was only the indent of his head on the pillow to convince her he hadn't been a dream.

At *Fancy Free* she wrote the Beale article, and the January issue was put to bed without further incident. There had been no more dirty tricks, and Jeanne stopped expecting a surprise around every corner. She had heard nothing, nor had Ron, from any member of the Beale family or from any member of the Beale law firm. Could this be the calm before the storm? There was nothing to do now but wait until the magazine hit the stands on December twenty-seventh.

Jeanne had convinced Ron to run Melton Dickensen's picture on the cover and had personally phoned the professor for permission, which he was only too glad to give. Ron had insisted on the collage effect for the photos that accompanied her story: the black and white shots of her tackling Beale, plus her shots of Beale emerging from the car and merging with the runners.

Her article, What Price Victory? featured shots of Rosie, several other disputed finishers in U.S. marathons, and a picture of Beale surrounded by agitated Knoxville race officials.

She had tried to analyze why cheaters cheat, and referred to Mrs. Beale only in passing. Do runners try to regain youth and compete with personal rivals, even with members of their own families? She stressed the heartache caused by unethical shortcuts.

A moderate and balanced article, which passed muster with Fancy Free's lawyer. But the photos and the cover might be enough to send Beale up the wall, across the ceiling and down the other side, even though she made no mention of the pranks or Beale's threats to her, the magazine and her friends.

The itinerary for her trip had been set. She was to fly to California after the first of the year and work her way back East. She would be on the road through March, then would return to Washington until leaving for Helsinki in June. Jeanne was excited, but scared, too. She had never traveled much, had never been overseas. All of a sudden the world was at her feet. She wasn't sure what to do with it.

The holidays were upon her even before she knew it. She shopped and sent gifts out to Elmton and purchased presents for the *Fancy Free* staff. A few days before Christmas she was at the Institute making last-minute arrangements and went to the cafeteria for a bite of lunch. Erkki brought his tray and joined her.

"Soon you shall go to California," he said gloomily. "We have had hardly any time together lately. How I would like to see California this winter, though Washington has so much easier a winter than that to which I am used."

"Is it pitch-black all winter in Finland?"

"It is wet and dark and very depressing in October and November. Many people die then, some from suicide. When the snows come, the moon makes the world very light and strange. You can see again. The jogging paths have electric lights. We run all winter. But it is late in spring before we go to work in daylight or come home without car lights."

"That is so intriguing!"

"And Helsinki is very far south in Finland. In the very north of my land the Lapps live in darkness in winter and in the summer always with light."

"I wasn't even sure where Finland *was* until I met you," she admitted. "My geography is awful. I always picture Scandinavia as a bunch of bananas, but I didn't know Finland was resting right against the banana tree. Russia."

"Did you notice where Leningrad is? Only over the border. The border that lies much closer to Helsinki now than once. My family lived near Ladoga. Now it is Soviet land."

She was eager to see Finland and to meet his family,

and told him so. He did not seem pleased. Something must await him there, and she needed to know what it was. Speak much of Finland, and he'd tighten his face and raise his shoulders slightly.

Jeanne changed the subject. The cafeteria had been decorated for the holiday. A small artificial Christmas tree stood in one corner, and a cardboard cutout Merry Christmas sign was strung across the doorway. Jeanne asked if he was looking forward to his first Christmas in the United States.

"Christmas is very hectic here in the United States. So many gifts and parties. My head is swimming."

"It has gotten overdone. I feel it more here in Washington. Christmas was much quieter in Elmton. Do you mind being so far from home on Christmas?" Jeanne asked, hoping he would say something about his family life.

"In Finland it is a day for family and for church. Can you come to my home on Christmas Eve and I will show you how beautiful a Finnish Christmas can be?"

Jeanne was thrilled at the unexpected invitation. "That would be lovely, Erkki." She had made no plans yet for Christmas. In years past she had spent it with Aunt Lily if she couldn't get home to Elmton, but this year there was no one close. She hoped this intimate holiday celebration would bring her closer to Erkki. There was so much she did not understand about him and about herself. On this special night, alone together, they would have time to explore.

On Christmas Eve Jeanne drove her Porsche to Erkki's Bethesda home, passing houses dressed in their Christmas finery. There were few cars on the street, and Jeanne felt the peace that had finally descended tonight. The night was so silent you could almost hear the electricity flowing into the tiny colored bulbs that adorned the houses and trees she passed. She and Erkki would enjoy this same silence together, to be broken only by soft sighs and words of peace and joy and new understanding. Her heart blossomed with hope.

Erkki met her at the door, crisp and handsome in gray tweed trousers and a pale blue shirt open at the collar. He held her close for a moment and then guided her into the livingroom. A fire crackled in the fireplace, and an end table held a decanter of cranberry liqueur and a tray of cheeses and dark Finnish flatbread crackers.

They sat before the fire and toasted the holiday season. "I have so much to give you," Erkki said as he disappeared from the room. A few moments later he stood at the threshhold of the room, his arms laden with packages. Jeanne opened one large but weightless box to find two Finnish lampshades made of paper-thin strips of natural pine, so flexible that they were wound around in a circle and stacked. One was large, the other smaller. Erkki had furnished cords and bulbs and even the hooks to be fitted into her ceiling. When lit, the lamps would give off a golden glow lovely in its softness.

"They're so beautiful!" she exclaimed, but he wasn't finished. Next he gave her Finnish glasswear, thick and sparkly like pillars of cracked ice, and a tablecloth whose pattern was surrealistic reindeer under a midnight sun.

Her mother, informed in a weekly letter that Jeanne was dating a Finnish doctor, had responded, "I've heard the Finns called the most artistic people on earth."

Jeanne hadn't heard that, but now she saw the truth of it.

Similar instincts had led Jeanne to give Erkki something essentially North American. She had turned to the only nonimported culture—Amerindian. She found soft deerskin moccasins with tiny beadwork, but such a gift seemed paltry compared to what he'd had sent over for her from the great Helsinki store, Sokos.

But he appeared to know her intentions, and her last-minute bonus gift of a large book of national park scenes did seem to delight him.

"I shall have much to take away with me from America," he said.

She didn't say, "like my heart."

Packages unwrapped, Erkki wrapped his arms around Jeanne. "You are the present I most want to open tonight."

Ever so slowly he undressed her, his long thin fingers making her body sing. It was like a concert pianist playing Christmas carols up and down her spine, and she wanted to burst into song. Joy to the world! She was naked in front of the fire, warmed by its flames and by the flames inside her. There was fire, too, in Erkki's eyes as he removed his own clothing, never taking his eyes off Jeanne.

He lay down and pulled her on top of him. She was ready to receive him and cried out as his flesh leapt into hers. Jeanne felt his strength inside her and reached deep and hard for it. He taunted her with it, teased her, withheld it until he no longer could. Gasping her own pleasure, she felt his juices flow into her in long shuddering waves.

Many moments later, Erkki rolled away from her. Propped on one elbow, he looked into her eyes. "You take as much as I give, my Giini. Do not fear it. It is good."

"You give everything in lovemaking, Erkki, but in other matters you are secretive and difficult to understand. You make me want you and not want you at the same time."

He took her small hand in his larger one and kissed each finger and the palm. "Come, I have another surprise for you."

Not wanting to break the spell, Jeanne followed him obediently. He will tell me when he is ready, her heart said. The surprise was the luxury of a heated swimming pool. In the cold night they played in the sapphire water, submerged to their noses, tangling and disentangling. Finally they made love again, underwater, on the wide steps at the shallow end of the pool. It was an experience Jeanne would long remember.

Erkki lit a fire in the sauna, and they scrubbed each other with birch branches until their skin shone pink. Another dip in the pool to rinse off and they glided up the stairs to Erkki's bedroom. Jeanne felt like she was made of rubber, without a bone in her body, so relaxed and satiated was she.

Jeanne stretched out on the bed, her mind somewhere between twilight and reality. She heard Erkki's voice, asking her not to fall asleep yet. He had a bedtime story to tell her. She sat up but did not open her eyes until she heard the word wife. This was the story she most wanted to hear.

He spoke of meeting Kristina and finding the cancerous growth in her breast. Jeanne's mind flashed back to his strange impromptu examination of her. He told of Kristina's pregnancy, her reluctant decision to go to Oulu for treatment.

"She lost the baby at Oulu but responded well to

the treatment. When Kristina returned to Helsinki, we resumed living together as man and wife. I fitted her myself with the diaphragm and saw to it that she used it, but she was able to deceive me and became pregnant once more. Now the cancer was more advanced. I insisted on abortion, so she left me and went to live with her parents. After that she refused to see me. I have a daughter, Impi she is called. Never have I seen her. She lives with the Svensons. Although they do not need it, I send to the Svensons every month money for her support."

So this was the deep, dark secret that Erkki had kept locked up for so long! A beautiful young wife dead of cancer, a child conceived in deceit. Erkki must be consumed with guilt.

"I want to claim my daughter," he continued. "The Svensons speak no Finnish. She grows up speaking only Swedish. This is not good for a Haukkamaa. Stina's parents bear me no love, I am sure. After Stina left me, her parents did all they could to keep me from her. They tried even to keep me from the funeral."

Erkki paused and lifted her chin with his hands. She could not help but look into his eyes. "Alone I cannot do it. I came to America to get away from the past. But it haunts me. Please come with me, Jeanne. Stay with me in Finland after June, after the race. Be mother to Impi. I am afraid to claim her alone, so great is my bitterness. Be wife to me. A real wife this time, with love on both sides."

Jeanne could do nothing but sob. At last she knew! But did Erkki know what he asked of her? With a great effort she stemmed her tears and collected her thoughts.

"You ask so much, Erkki. You ask me to leave my job, my friends, my family and go to a strange place where I do not speak the language, where I know no one but you. You ask me to be a mother to a child I have never seen, that you have never seen, who speaks only a language neither of us speaks. What would I do in Finland? Maybe I could send a magazine article back to the States once in a while, but that is not enough for me."

"Jeanne, I have much love for you. It will warm you, even through the Finnish winter. Please come with me."

Silent tears ran down Jeanne's throat. So this was love. Leaving a life she had just found for one completely different. At least Dick would not have taken her out of the country.

"Give me time, Erkki. I will think about it. I love you. I can't make you any promises, but I will think about it. I'm glad you were finally able to tell me, though. Thank you."

"You are welcome, Jeanne. To everything I possess, you are welcome. Since I know you I have wanted to tell you. On the yacht I almost did, but only my bitterness and jealousy came out. It is Christmas. We start over."

Cradled in his arms, Jeanne slept deeply. Today had been full enough. She needed to forget tomorrow.

Chapter Nineteen

BUT TOMORROW ALWAYS comes. *Fancy Free* came out two days after Christmas. Jeanne's stomach lurched every time the phone rang in the office, but the entire day of publication passed without an unsettling incident.

It was a hectic day. The staff was still high from Christmas, and Ron was floating about six inches off the ground because his wife was pregnant. Helen had told him the good news by hanging a third stocking over the mantel on Christmas morning. Ron had brought the tiny red and green knitted stocking to the office, and it hung on the partition of his cubicle. At lunchtime Nancy had sent out for sandwiches and beer for an impromptu celebration.

"Here's to the new Liu," Kerry had quipped, beer bottle raised high.

Jeanne had joined in the merriment, glad to have something to distract her, but a part of her could only sit back and watch the festivities. In the past few weeks she had been offered two chances at motherhood—instant motherhood—and her response had been far from joyful. The difference is all in the wanting, she thought.

She left the office about six and walked home slowly. She had run six miles before work that morning, and with the tension of the day and all that had happened with Erkki on Christmas Eve and Christmas, Jeanne was drained. As she walked the two miles from office to home, her thoughts drifted far afield. Memories of childhood Christmases swirled in her brain, pictures of the old Jeanne eating her way through mountains of Christmas cakes and cookies. Vacation days spent stuffing her face and reading instead of playing outdoors with other children. Jeanne alone with her food, her only solace. Being alone felt normal to her. It was being with others, being close to them, that was alien to her. The kind of closeness Dick and now Erkki wanted to press on her was frightening, more than she could handle.

A few doors from her house she fumbled in her bag for her keys and jumped when she heard someone call her name. Jeanne looked up to see Arthur Beale standing in front of her townhouse.

"I suppose you're happy now, Lois Lane has gotten her big scoop."

Beale was wearing a business suit and a camel hair overcoat. He wore no hat; a Black Watch plaid woolen scarf was draped around his neck. His words came out in puffs of smoke as his warm breath collided with the cold December air. What was this well-dressed man doing at her doorstep? What did he want from her?

"What are you doing here, Mr. Beale?" Jeanne asked, trying to maintain her composure.

"I came to personally bring you to your senses."

"There's nothing wrong with my senses. You've proved your point. You've caused trouble for me and my friends and my magazine. The article we printed was timid, to say the least. Why don't you just drop it?"

Jeanne pushed past Beale and jammed her key into the lock of the outer door. She tried to slam it shut, but Beale had his foot wedged in the door before she could close it securely.

"Aren't you going to ask me in?"

"I most certainly am not, and if you don't leave this instant I'll begin screaming. You've already brought yourself enough trouble, Mr. Beale. Can't you see you're just making things worse for yourself?"

A low-pitched, insidious chuckle escaped Beale's lips. "That's where you're wrong, Miss Lathrop. I'm not the one who caused the trouble. You are the troublemaker. I've tried to show you what happens to little girls who make mischief, but you don't seem to understand."

With that Beale pushed harder on the door, forcing himself into the entryway. His arms shot out, and he grabbed Jeanne, shaking her like a rag doll. The sudden attack threw Jeanne off balance, but she recovered in a moment.

Beale released her and raised his right hand as if to strike. Jeanne was still holding onto her keys. She grasped the key she had used to open the front door between her thumb and forefinger and lashed out at Beale's face with its jagged edge. She caught him by surprise and left a gash in his left cheek.

An astounded Beale brought his hand to his wounded face, giving Jeanne a chance to dash up the stairs, three at a time, and get safely behind the door of her own apartment.

Trembling, her back against the door, she felt her legs give way and she crumpled in a heap on the floor. This isn't fair, her brain screamed. Why is he picking on me like this? She knew she had to do something. In Knoxville she had waived her right to press charges on Beale. She would call the police right away. But what would they do? Given Beale's connections, the incident would be hushed up in a minute.

I am not going to take this anymore. No way! Jeanne stumbled into the kitchen and took her notebook from her purse. She had Amanda Beale's number in there. One ring, two, three. Please be home, pick up the phone, Mrs. Beale. On the fifth ring she heard Amanda Beale's cultivated voice.

"This is Jeanne Lathrop, I'm calling from Washington. You've got to help me, Mrs. Beale. I don't know what else to do."

Jeanne told Mrs. Beale what had happened. She could hear the tightness in the older woman's reply.

"I'm so sorry, my dear. I have been trying to get Arthur to see someone to talk about this cheating incident and his inability to let it pass and be forgiven and forgotten. I don't think he can forgive himself, not so much for doing it, but for getting caught. Thank you for not calling the police, although it is strictly what you ought to have done. I will phone my son Bill and make sure he takes care of his father tonight. You have my word I will do everything possible to see that this doesn't happen again."

Jeanne sobbed her relief into the phone. She had done more crying in the past few days than she had done in her whole life. But sometimes only tears can wash away the hurt.

"Is there any friend you can call, Jeanne? I don't think you should be alone tonight."

"One of the women from the magazine lives only a few blocks from here. I'll give her a call. Just between you and me, Mrs. Beale, why do you stay with him? I guess I've only seen one side of your husband, but it's not an especially pleasant one."

"We have three children, Jeanne, and five grandchildren. We married very young, when Arthur was working his way through college. You don't throw all those years away because someone gets into trouble. Arthur has stuck by me through some hard times, and now it is my turn to stand by him. I know you young women find that hard to understand, but that's the way I choose to live my life."

Jeanne thanked Mrs. Beale softly and put down the phone. She had a lot of respect for Amanda Beale. A lot of women would have crumpled under such pressure, become defensive or angry. But Amanda Beale was a gem. If anything good could come out of this experience, it would have to be getting to know Mrs. Beale.

There was no answer at Nancy's, so Jeanne decided on a hot bath and some herb tea, maybe a light salad after her bath. But before she headed for the bathroom, Jeanne put in a call to Dr. Tinsley. She left word with his service that she would like to speak with Dr. Tinsley tonight. With all that had happened, Jeanne knew she needed the therapist's insights. She couldn't do it all alone.

The next day Jeanne sat in Dr. Tinsley's sun-filled office, looking at him leaning back in his dark brown easy chair as he waited for her to begin the session.

"I didn't expect to be sitting here so soon," she said. "When we terminated, I really thought I could handle it, but everything's happened so fast my head is swimming and I don't know what to do."

Dr. Tinsley nodded. "I don't know what 'everything' is, Jeanne. You sounded very distressed when I returned your call last night. Do you want to start with that?" he asked in his fluid voice.

Jeanne related the incident with Beale and then went on to tell the therapist the story from the beginning at Knoxville. That led to Dick, which led to Erkki. Dr. Tinsley let her spill it all out without saying anything. Occasionally he made a note on the pad on the cluttered end table next to his chair.

"That's quite a sequence of events. Anyone would need help sorting that out. I'm glad you were able to call me without feeling like you'd messed up because you needed to see me today."

"Well, actually," Jeanne admitted, "I had thought of calling you a few weeks ago, but I waited until my circuits got overloaded before I made the call."

"So what can you do to clear the circuits and get the electricity flowing again?"

Jeanne began to speak of her trip, which would start when she flew to California on January 4. The more she spoke about it, the more she realized just how excited she was. Here was a chance to be really independent, to be completely on her own. She had not thought of it in those terms before, but it was the perfect opportunity to put the new Jeanne to the test. Even Washington held a lot of old baggage. She had been fat here while in college, she had made her transition here; then there was Dick and Erkki, both met in Washington. Aunt Lily had lived here. There were as many ghosts here as in Elmton, South Dakota.

"I think I can use this trip," she summed up, "to

start fresh. I don't want to run away from anything, but I need some space and some fresh horizons."

"That's a positive way to think about it. What you must be careful of, though, is inflated expectations," Dr. Tinsley counseled. "You have changed a great deal, but the person you used to be is still with you. Don't expect that you won't run into difficulties on your trip. Expanded horizons can give you new insights, but it will not change things overnight or erase all your problems. But I think you know that."

Jeanne laughed. "I may know it, but it never hurts to be reminded—as often as possible."

"Now what about—Air-key, is it? My Finnish is not what it used to be."

Leave it to Dr. Tinsley to lighten the mood. "My instincts tell me to make a clean break. I can't possibly do what he asks of me. My feelings for him are very strong, but men are new to me and I'm not absolutely sure I'm in love with him. He's also very hard to read, he runs hot and cold. Some of that may be because of his unresolved feelings about his wife and child, but there's no way for me to be sure. As hard as it may be, I need to go off to California with as few loose ends as possible."

"I think your instincts are good ones. Our time is up for today. If you'd like to see me again before you leave, please call and we'll find a time. If I don't see you, have a good trip."

Feeling fortified, Jeanne left the office, closing the door softly behind her. I may have closed some doors today, but there are so many more to open.

Chapter Twenty

ON NEW YEAR'S EVE Jeanne and Erkki attended a party at the home of Dr. Albert Moore, Erkki's colleague at the Institute, whom Jeanne had met the evening of the Nehmann's yacht fundraiser. Most of the guests were Institute employees and knew Jeanne from her many visits to the Institute.

Genevieve Moore was a French woman and a gourmet cook. She had prepared an elaborate buffet, but Jeanne was so nervous that she hardly noticed the food. Even the chocolate torte on the dessert sideboard got only a passing glance. Who could think of food when tonight, after the party, she would tell Erkki that she wished to go off to California free and clear of any loose ends!

Jeanne watched Erkki as he circulated around the room. He seemed never to laugh out loud. If he found something amusing he smiled, but never allowed himself the release of laughter. As usual, he was impeccably dressed. His clothes were of the latest fashion, but his reserve made him seem like he came from another, more formal era. What was a once plain and fat girl from Elmton, South Dakota, doing fancying herself in love with this foreigner?

Since she had spoken her intention to break with Erkki in Dr. Tinsley's office, Jeanne had been wondering how and when to tell him. Should she wait until morning, or should she tell him as soon as they got to his house after the party? The sooner she got it out, the better. On the other hand, why take the chance of ruining what was to be her last evening with Erkki, her first lover, her first love?

Erkki must have sensed Jeanne watching him, because he excused himself from the group he was with and came to her side. "I wish more to be with you than with the others this evening. Your eyes say the same to me. Shall we sneak out, as they say?"

"It's not even midnight yet, Erkki. We'll be missed."

"To me it does not matter."

Jeanne felt his pale blue eyes bore through her like laser beams. "All right. I'll get my coat and bag." She touched his hand lightly. It was warm and dry. "Meet me at the front door."

After apologies and goodbyes, Jeanne and Erkki made the short drive from the Moore's home to Erkki's. Jeanne was silent as they entered the house. She slipped off her coat and went to the closet to hang it up. As she reached for a hanger, she felt tears well into her eyes. Her resolve was weakening. She thought of the idyllic nights she had spent in the house, the sauna, the heated pool, before the fireplace. Could she really walk away from it all? How could she not? It was that or find herself in Finland with a strange child. As Jeanne hung her coat on the hanger, she felt Erkki come up behind her and slip his arms around her. He nuzzled her neck, planting light and tantalizing kisses behind her ears. Desire grew quickly, and Jeanne turned around in his arms. "Last one upstairs is a rotten egg," she whispered in his ear, nibbling on the lobe.

With a giggle, she broke away from him and bounded up the stairs, unbuttoning her blouse as she went, leaving a trail of clothing that Erkki followed to his bedroom. He shed his clothing and joined her on the oversize bed. Neither was in the mood for preliminaries this evening, and he took her quickly and eagerly. A few moments later they lay panting in one another's arms. When her breathing had quieted down enough for her to talk, Jeanne said with a low chuckle, "Do you think we can get into the Guinness Book of Records for that? Fastest-love-making-on-New-Year's-Eve-in-Washington, D.C.-metropolitan-area? I wish I'd had the stopwatch going for that one."

"There is enough of records and statistics for me at the job, Jeanne," Erkki said in all seriousness.

"That was a joke."

Erkki nodded solemnly. "Oh, yes, you make the joke. Now I understand."

Jeanne didn't know if he did or not, but she didn't want to push the issue any further. This was just one more example of how she and Erkki were worlds apart.

Erkki propped himself up on his elbow and looked at the bedside clock. "It is fifteen minutes before midnight. I will go downstairs for a bottle of champagne so that we can toast the new year."

Erkki returned in a few moments with a bottle of Dom Perignon in a silver bucket and two fluted champagne glasses on a tray.

Jeanne raised an eyebrow. "I suppose you just happened to have that lying around the house," she said, indicating the special bottle of sparkling wine.

"I thought we might have other things to celebrate this evening besides the coming of the new year."

Needing to change the subject, Jeanne glanced at the clock. "It's nearly midnight. Why don't you open the champagne? Would you like to watch the ball come down in Times Square? It's on television, a very American custom. You shouldn't miss it."

Jeanne walked over to the television, which was hidden behind louvered doors in the center of a large shelved wall unit that also held books, a stereo system and phonograph records. At least the festivities would buy her a little time.

The room was chilly, and Jeanne felt goose bumps rise all over her. She hurried back to the bed and got in between the covers. Handing her a glass of champagne, Erkki did the same.

"All those people stand out in the cold to watch a lighted ball descend a pole on top of a skyscraper?" Erkki asked in disbelief.

Jeanne herself had never quite understood this particular American ritual and told him she was still trying to figure it out herself. But it was as American as apple pie. The ball descended and the television commentator shouted the countdown. "Five! Four! Three!! Two!!!! *One!!!!! Happy New Year!!!!!*" the set blared. The crowd whooped and cheered, the lyrics of Auld Lang Syne rang out.

Erkki and Jeanne turned to one another. They clinked glasses. Looking deep into one another's eyes, they drank. Droplets of champagne dribbled down Jeanne's chin as she tipped the glass too far back, so disconcerting was Erkki's gaze. Erkki reached behind him and fumbled for the remote-control box on the bedside table. Without ever taking his eyes off Jeanne's, he found the right button and the televised merriment disappeared. No Royal Canadians this year, Jeanne thought. Only peasant Finns.

He put down his glass and took Jeanne's out of her hand. With his tongue he gently licked the champagne from her chin and followed the droplets down over her chest, plucking each one from her. By the time his mouth reached her breasts the nipples were erect, and Jeanne felt shivers of joy as he lifted a final drop of wine from her left breast.

Erkki pulled back the covers and slid Jeanne down in the bed, never stopping his kissing and sucking. With tongue and lips he explored every inch of her soft body, now pliant with desire. He buried his face in her furry triangle, murmuring his passion. When the anticipation was almost unbearable, Jeanne felt his tongue part her lips, and with light flicking motions he brought her perilously close to the precipice. His fingers entered her and Jeanne writhed under him, her hips moving in ever-widening circles. The flood gates opened, delicious moans escaped her lips as Erkki eagerly lapped up her love juices. He slipped his fingers out of her and clasped her breasts, feeling her chest heave up and down as her breathing became real once again.

Jeanne took Erkki's hands and pulled him up close to her. The urge to give him something special was very strong for her. "Lie on your back," she whispered. Reaching over to the bedside table Jeanne wet her fingers with champagne and sprinkled it over his body. Drop by drop she licked it away, missing no spot, working her way slowly downward. When she took him in her mouth, she felt him stiffen. With infinite care and patience she kissed, stroked and fondled him until she tasted the sea.

He pulled her on top of him and they lay quietly together. Time seemed to have stopped.

"In a few days you will be leaving for California. I shall miss you greatly. But we will be in touch because of the work we do. Not only do we love together but we work together. It is only a few months we will be apart. It will go quickly and then we are together forever. After tonight I think I know already your answer."

Jeanne could think of no painless answer. "What you ask of me is impossible, Erkki. When I leave for California, I want to leave with no binding ties. I need to be free to live and experience all the things I've missed. I have been tempted often in the past few days to say yes, to follow you anywhere. But deep inside I know I would resent you, I would worry about what I have missed. It's too much, too soon. I can't do it. I just can't."

He said nothing for the longest time. His face was hard and set, and there was no way for Jeanne to know what he was thinking. "If that is your answer, there is nothing for me to do. You bring me much pain and much disappointment. Now I think I will sleep."

He turned his back to her. Jeanne felt like a steel wall had been built between them. "That's it? You have nothing else to say?"

"If I beg and plead will it change your mind?" came the muffled answer. Erkki spoke more to his pillow than to her. He was right. What could he say to change her mind? Jeanne turned on her side and curled up behind him, stomach and breasts nestled against his back, one arm around him. She thought he would try to push her away, but he didn't. Eventually she slept.

In the dark of the night they reached for each other in sorrow and desperation and made love one last time.

At dawn Jeanne dressed and prepared to leave. She shook Erkki gently to wake him. "I'm leaving now. I think it would be best if we have as little to do with one another as possible. If it is all right with you, I'll transmit my data and reports to Al Moore."

"As you wish." Erkki did not open his eyes.

Jeanne felt the tears stinging her eyes, but she fought them back. I will not cry in front of him. I will not make this any harder than it is. Tentatively she touched his face, his hair, memorizing them with her fingers as well as her eyes. She would have to see him in Finland in June at the ultramarathon. Anything could happen in six months.

"Goodbye." Her words could hardly be heard.

Jeanne walked out unsteadily into the pale blue light of dawn. A new day, a new year, a new life beckoned.

Chapter Twenty-one

BACK IN GEORGETOWN, Jeanne busied herself with preparations for the trip. There was packing to be done, drawers and closets to be emptied for the sublet tenant. She knew she wouldn't be able to do any freelancing until after the ultramarathon. Even though the Institute was paying her expenses and *Fancy Free* would continue paying her salary, she didn't want the added expense of paying for an apartment she wasn't living in. The housing service at her alma mater, George Washington University, had matched her up with a graduate student in need of an apartment for the spring semester.

The following night Jeanne was the guest of honor at a bon voyage party given by the *Fancy Free* staff. They went to a Chinese restaurant, where Ron and Helen ordered a feast. They stuffed themselves on steamed dumplings, minced meat and vegetables wrapped in dough and steamed in a wooden basket; Mu Shu Pork, thin pancakes filled with sliced pork, Chinese mushrooms and other vegetables; a whole fish steamed and smothered in a spicy ginger sauce; beef with sizzling rice, fine slices of fileted beef given a last-minute cooking at the table so that the rice crackled when you ate it. They had soup last, in the Chinese manner, a clear broth swimming with chunks of crab and ears of baby corn. The Lius promised an even better meal at a restaurant they knew in San Francisco, run by distant relatives, and wrote down the name and address, along with special dishes to be ordered. "Go there if you miss me and be sure to tell them I sent you so you'll get special treatment," Ron told her.

"I've eaten so much tonight, I may not eat again until I get to California," Jeanne groaned. "And I can't imagine a meal much better than this one."

Everyone nodded in agreement. Over a final pot of tea and fortune cookies, the staff presented Jeanne with a going away gift, a small knapsack with the *Fancy Free* logo. *You can't leave us behind,* read the card signed by Ron, Kerry and Nancy.

"I'm really going to miss you folks. We've really become a family and it's tough to leave you. But I'll be calling in regularly, probably so often that you'll hardly know I've gone."

With much hugging and wisecracking, the group broke up and everyone went home.

The next morning Jeanne made her final trip to the office. She checked through the articles she had written to be run during her absence, going through them with Nancy and Kerry. She gave everyone a copy of her itinerary, plus phone numbers where she was likely to be reached, although she would phone in any changes. The National Running Data Center had supplied her with names and addresses of likely women ultramarathoners, and she had set up appointments from that list.

At her final conference with Ron, she told him that she and Dr. Haukkamaa had decided it would be easier for her to report to Al Moore, so if he needed anything from the Institute he should talk to Dr. Moore. Ron accepted her explanation without probing.

While she was in with Ron, Kerry called her to the phone. The caller wouldn't identify himself. A streak of fear flashed through her as she picked up the receiver.

"Miss Lathrop, Arthur Beale here."

"What can I do for you, Mr. Beale?" asked Jeanne in her coldest voice.

"I'm calling to apologize for my behavior the other night. I still don't know what got into me, but my wife and son have finally succeeded in talking some sense into me. I wanted to win so badly I was willing to do anything, and then I got so angry at being caught that, well, I just snapped. Mrs. Beale has convinced me to go for some counseling. It's tough for a man like me to grow old and see my powers diminishing."

Jeanne felt a surge of relief. "Thank you, Mr. Beale. I think your wife is a remarkable woman." Jeanne couldn't muster any more warmth than that.

"If you'd like to be our guest at dinner some night, I would be willing to talk to you about anything you like."

Jeanne just wanted to end it. "That's very good of you, but I'm leaving for an extended business trip the day after tomorrow and I'm afraid I won't have time."

"I thought you might want to write a follow-up article." Beale was persistent, if anything.

"I don't really think I do, Mr. Beale." Jeanne looked at Ron who had been following the conversation. "If you like, however, you can write a little piece yourself and send it in to Mr. Liu." Ron nodded his assent.

"If he feels it is of interest to our readers, he may run it. I think Mrs. Beale should write a little piece, too, about her experience as the wife of a runner and how she dealt with what happened in Knoxville and after." Jeanne hated speaking in euphemisms, but she wanted to be careful with Beale. "Please give my regards to Mrs. Beale," Jeanne wanted to end this conversation. "Thank you for calling," she said before he could say anything else. "Goodbye."

"Well, it looks like we wrapped that one up okay," Jeanne said to Ron. "You may even get a couple more articles out of it."

Ron eyed her through his wire-rimmed glasses. "You don't seem very happy about all this."

"I'm just glad it's over with, that's all. It was quite a strain, and I'm still pretty angry about it all. I'll catch you later before I take off."

Everything was falling into place. She was free of Beale, of Dick, of Erkki. She had only herself and her job to worry about. That is enough for anyone, she thought.

After double-checking her desk, she put the files she would need in her briefcase, said her last round of goodbyes and took off for her next stop, the Institute.

She went directly to Al Moore's office, passing Erkki's mercifully closed door as quickly as she could. Al was glad to see her, as usual. He had taken an almost fatherly interest in her and knew of her romance with Erkki, although they never discussed it openly.

"So, Jeanne, all set to take off?" Al smiled as she poked her head into his office.

"I just came by to pick up the questionnaires and check on a few last-minute things." Jeanne paused. "I, um, I also wanted to tell you. Uh, has Erkki spoken to you this morning?"

"No, he hasn't. What is it, Jeanne?"

"Well, we decided it would be easier for everyone if I reported directly to you instead of him." Jeanne lowered her eyes.

"He's a tough customer, I know, but he's the best in the business. And the more I hear from you, the *Moore* happy I am," he added the pun heartily seeing her difficulty and trying to make things easier. He got up from his chair and walked around to Jeanne, putting an arm around her.

"Thanks, Dr. Al. You're a real pal."

When he laughed, Jeanne looked up questioningly. "You're a poet and don't know it," he reminded her. "Let's go down and see if Elizabeth has finished putting the questionnaires together."

One of Jeanne's jobs was to help the runners fill out the sixteen-page form. When she began her association with the Institute she had studied the questionnaire for the male runners: family background and personal medical background—a detailed account of every relative's illnesses, including grandparents and siblings, and each runner's physical characteristics. History of diseases, drinking, smoking, exercise patterns, blood pressure, blood chemistry, urinalysis—the works. It read like an application from a highly suspicious insurance agency covering allergies and asthma through whooping cough. Diet was another important category. Then came running history—the age at which one started to run, distances per month, longest runs and races, injuries, effects on the body when running was stopped for a significant interval.

For the women runners, another page had been added: onset of menses, pregnancies, miscarriages, abortions; effects of running on menses, dysmenorrhea, amenorrhea, estrogen therapy, birth control method.

Besides getting the physical data, for which the runners might need to consult records from hospitals and doctors or quiz family and parents, Jeanne was to interview each runner about the psychological effects of running, especially ultramarathon distances.

Elizabeth, the administrative assistant for the project, had the packet of papers all ready for her. It was bulky and would take up most of the room in her briefcase. Too precious to trust to airline baggage handlers, Jeanne would carry it with her on the plane. Each questionnaire had already been coded, ready for computer analysis when completed.

Realizing she would not want to pass Erkki's office again, Dr. Moore steered her right to the elevator. "Have a good flight, Jeanne. I'll be talking to you soon. Don't worry, I know you'll do a fine job. And everything will work out, you'll see."

As the elevator doors closed, Jeanne waved bravely. Everywhere doors were closing on her. Hopefully, some would open for her in California and beyond.

Chapter Twenty-two

SEEING THE PACIFIC for the first time, Jeanne recalled a line of lyric poetry. How did John Keats put it? For "Stout Cortez and all his men"? Something about "a wild surmise, speechless upon a peak in Darien"?

That's how she felt the whole flight. From Dulles Airport she flew six hours nonstop through two meals, one movie, two sodas, two cocktails and three short hikes down the aisle. If she could have gotten away with it, she would have put on her Nikes and run three miles up and down the aisle.

Her seatmate had given her his window seat and then pointed out the Big Horns, Rockies and Sierras. From the air they were hot fudge sundaes—sheets and clots of dark forests like chocolate poured over ice cream snow. Mono Lake winked like a blue eye near Yosemite, and El Capitan itself was visible. Wonderful, wonderful! Glory like this made the pains of her life petty.

Carla Silver met her at the San Francisco airport.

Hearing that Jeanne had never seen the Pacific, she drove North out of her way to pick up Highway 1, the narrow coastal route down the peninsula.

"I'll do rotten at a hundred miles," chattered Carla, this blonde, bright-faced California woman well past thirty, "but it's such a wonderful idea—his study—the Finnish doctor. Think of it, to do so little for a trip to Europe!"

"Where's the Pacific?" asked Jeanne.

The wife of the basketball coach and mother of four teenagers whipped her car into Gray Whale Cove lookout. "There it lies!" she announced, and pulled up short.

Trees—Monterey pines or Monterey cypress—bordered the sea. Jeanne leaped from the Honda and sprinted to the edge of the grove, looking down upon the most gorgeous expanse of water she'd ever seen. Tears stood in her eyes, and Keats came back to her. There it was, totally different from the navy blue, sluggish, circumscribed Atlantic—which you never look *down* on unless you're on Maine cliffs.

Green, endlessly wide, so misty, with long, lazy swells and white breakers on dark black-silver sand. They climbed down to the water, Jeanne in her khaki pantsuit, wetting her cuffs, feeling that she'd earned the right to be a child for a moment. No shells, just shiny stones of black, green and red. Carla spoke of seals, whales, otters, abalone. Underneath were moray eels. On the silver mirror of the tidal zone, Jeanne bent, touched her fingertips to the foam and raised them to her lips. Salty. Really the Pacific!

With the sighing rush and retreat of the breakers continuous in her ears and her head bobbing constantly to survey everything, Jeanne rode toward Palo Alto, listening to Carla describe her running friends. Lydia

Aspeth, who painted, was the only close friend slated to run the hundred miles. Jeanne was to stay with her.

Carla described the running club and its offshoot, Running Mothers, five women who trained together in all weather. "We'll try to lay on a little quake for you," she bubbled. "We sit between Hollister, the famous epicenter, and San Francisco, with its memories of the Great Quake of 1906. Visitors are disappointed if they don't at least feel a tremor." White teeth sparkled against her rosy winter tan. Sun had dried her skin into fine wrinkles, but her laughter kept them moving so they blurred. She was thirty-eight, she admitted proudly.

Jeanne had tossed her sheepskin coat onto the backseat and pocketed pigskin gloves bought to fend off Washington's icy rain later in the trip. Carla wore jeans and a red pullover with short sleeves. Jeanne enjoyed the warmth of the climate and of the car.

When they arrived at Lydia's, the sound of the car brought her running out. Tight gold designer slacks, turquoise bouclé top, copper earrings, tooled western boots. Lydia was a swinging divorced lady, Carla had said.

And Lydia's house—it sat on the crest of a forested rise, a semicircular building with all the walls on one side just floor-to-ceiling windows. Outside a deck ran around the house, giving a clear view of the Bay.

"Spectacular!" cried Jeanne, gazing up at the high, open-beamed redwood ceiling. The fireplace was a free-standing red lacquered stove. Sheepskin rugs were tossed among statues of copper and marble, seascapes as real as the beach she'd just sampled and wall hangings of rope and shells.

Jeanne raved and raved like a true Midwesterner.

"John got the kids, and I got the house," Lydia

quipped. "He has another house—bigger—and a condo at Mammoth and another in Hawaii."

"He's in oil. Petrodollars," explained Carla.

"I had a divorce, a slipped disk and a drinking problem until I met Carla and started running."

"We ran Bay to Breakers before it was up to twenty-five thousand entrants, and then worked up to the San Francisco marathon, round and round in Golden Gate Park, and then Lydia says, 'I could run farther than this.' So we do. We have. *She* doesn't hit a wall until thirty miles, and then she keeps on going."

They strolled through the rooms of the glass and redwood house, daiquiris in hand. There was a different breathtaking view in every one. There was a waterbed in one of the bedrooms, and Lydia jiggled a fake fur spread to make waves ripple from foot to head.

"Do I get to sleep in here?" Jeanne asked. "On second thought, I think I might be seasick."

"You can sleep anywhere your South Dakota heart desires," said Lydia expansively. "Let me refill your glass."

The rugs were deep and the Spanish tiles ornate. Jeanne felt giddy. Perhaps she was in Arabia, and the draperies would open to show dancing girls in jeweled veils, their bellies undulating like waterbeds, hips slowly revolving—Jeanne stiffened. She must be suffering from jet lag, having lost three hours in flight after a sleepless night.

Now it was nine p.m. at home. She was famished. Carla had gone home to her coach husband and the many children and a spaghetti dinner. Lydia was opening a bottle of Pinot Noir and Jeanne despaired of ever being fed, but Lydia brought in a tray of hors d'oeuvres she had popped frozen into the microwave oven just seconds before.

"See, just two drinks today," said Lydia. "Running saved my liver, just in time, just before good ole AA time. I wonder if I could run on alcohol as fuel, in an emergency, jet propelled?"

Jeanne nodded sleepily.

"My hot tub's out on the deck," she said. "My lover and a friend of his will be over at eight for a dip. And anything else you might feel like."

"Huh?" Jeanne tried to keep her eyebrows out of her bangs as she fingered her wine goblet. "He's bringing along a—"

"Once I saw you were so attractive, I told him to."

"You might at least have asked me first, Lydia. I'm not used to . . ."

Lydia cut her off. "Don't worry, dear. We're very open out here. Do what you like. There's no pressure to join in on anything you're not ready for. I mean, back in the Midwest where I'm from, too, if you don't drink at a party, you have to hide it, pretend to stagger, to be accepted socially. Here you can smoke grass or not, drink liquor or not, make love or just conversation."

"Mmmmm," said Jeanne. No one would make her do anything she didn't want to.

"As for the hot tub, if you wish to, you can. With or without a suit."

She hadn't brought a bathing suit or suntan oil or sunglasses; she thought she was taking a winter trip. Dumb.

They sat on big pillows around the fireplace, Lydia debating whether she should go skiing on the advanced slopes and risk breaking a bone before the ultramarathon.

Suddenly a new friend, youthful for thirty-three,

popped in. "The guys are here, hi, Lydia," Aaron saluted and squirmed out of a jacket.

Her lover turned out to be a salt-and-pepper bearded Stanford professor in a brown leather jacket that smelled like a saddle. A younger companion, another professor, wore denim Levis and jacket, contrasting with a gold velour shirt. Stephen. Dark-haired and pleasantly attentive to Jeanne, he kept the conversation going as they sat around the flames, snacking on open-faced sandwiches featuring prawns and olives on cream cheese.

Lydia checked her watch. "I think the tub's hot enough now, 102° or 104°. Let's take a dip."

Jeanne, relaxed by food, drink and quiet companionship, inhaling secondhand fumes like burnt rope emitted from Aaron's pipe, lay back on her pillow, looking out at the lights of Oakland. Stephen closed his hand over hers.

"Two a.m. in Washington," he said.

"I can feel it," she said.

"You a runner, too? Lydia associates only with runners or potential runners. Or skiers. Want to warm up in the tub?"

Why not, Jeanne thought. I'm here for new experiences. She sleepily stripped in a bedroom, wrapped herself in a towel and went out onto the chilly deck in the midnight wind to find her new friends already neck deep, heads bobbing in a ring around the circular redwood tank.

"Lovely, lovely," said Stephen. Jeanne thought he meant the warm water sending steam toward the stars. She had her feet immersed before she began to shed the towel.

"Ow!"

"You see why they call this a Cannibal Stew?" asked Lydia.

Jeanne wasn't about to be an infant, a party pooper. The sauna had been practice, she told herself. She slid down to stand on the circular bench on which the others sat. Scalding. Not hot air, but thick, clinging water. Scented with sandalwood. No, that fragrance came from fat candles dripping wax on the rim of the tank.

Arching her back, grimacing, Jeanne lifted the towel and submerged herself slowly, while the men watched with interest. Bare breasts do float. Interesting. Down, down into the roiled water.

Lydia was built for running, with breasts that made Jeanne's look bovine in comparison. Stephen was darkly furry from throat to knees, while Aaron wore his hair on his head and chin. Jeanne sat with her chin just above the water.

"You could use a pillow or book to sit on, petite Jeanne," said her male friend. "Too bad we have nothing waterproof."

Jeanne wanted to pay attention to what was being said, but lethargy overcame her. She nearly dozed. Doze, and she'd drown. Stephen slid beside her and put an arm around her waist. She opened heavy lids to find Lydia and Aaron already gone.

"Lovely little import," Stephen said soothingly. "How do you like California . . . men?"

She started to say "just fine," arch her back and cuddle when she found herself being lifted from the water and wrapped snugly in her towel by a solicitious and gentle naked man who murmured endearments and praise of her lovely self. She noted the effect she had on him, but she was too relaxed, boneless, to care.

"Would you like a drink, love?" he asked her.

"No. No thank you."

They stood by the stove where exploding coals still gave off drying heat. He kissed her. She considered that, as if she'd tasted something novel, a fruit never tasted before.

"I like you, Jeanne Lathrop," said the square-faced man with wet black hair and a good tan. "I'd like to please you."

Stephen led her into the dark guest room and put her onto the waterbed. She rocked and rose and fell on the wake from his climbing in. "Oh, golly," she murmured. She really could get seasick on this thing.

Misinterpreting her remark, Stephen embraced her tightly from behind, intent on possession.

"No," she said in sudden panic. "I'm not ready for that. I'm sorry. Please understand."

"No problem," Stephen said. "What would you like?"

"A drink. I'll take that drink now."

"That's not exactly what I meant, Jeanne."

"I'm asking for some time. I'm not used to this instant intimacy."

Stephen shrugged and raised his hands as if to say okay. "That's cool, baby. We can ease into it. I'll see if Lydia has any herb tea in the kitchen. Good for jangled nerves."

Jeanne felt alone, adrift on an alien sea, no oar in her life raft. What was she doing with this stranger? He was nice enough, but not really special for her like Erkki or even like Dick. She hadn't come out here to fall into bed with every stranger who crossed her path. If Lydia or anyone else wanted to do that, it was their business. She was Jeanne Lathrop from Elmton, South Dakota. When Aunt Lily had advised her to taste and touch the world, this wasn't what she had in mind.

She heard Stephen's bare feet pad softly into the

room. He carried a tray with two steaming mugs of tea. She took one and felt some of the soothing liquid warm her throat and insides.

"Thanks for the tea, Stephen. I don't think I want anything else right now."

"Lydia sure has some crazy friends," he murmured under his breath. "So what's going on? You seemed hot enough a few minutes ago."

"I've changed my mind. Nothing else is going on." She wasn't about to tell him her most personal thoughts. She hardly knew him. The thought brought a smile to her lips. A few minutes ago she was going to sleep with him.

Stephen shot her a look of disgust. "Next time Lydia invites me over, I hope she has someone for me who's not so uptight."

Who did this guy think he was? It was her right to refuse. "Good night, Stephen."

"Yeah," he said, "I can take a hint. So long, South Dakota."

Naked as a jaybird he left the room. I may be from South Dakota, but I do know what I want, she thought. I may get off the track every now and then, but I straighten out. Between the jet lag, the booze and the hot tub, Jeanne could not stay awake a moment longer. She drifted off into a dreamless sleep.

Chapter Twenty-three

JET LAG PAST, Jeanne got down to work. She spent the next couple of weeks interviewing the Running Mothers, helping them fill out their medical forms and getting them to local hospitals for tests, the results of which would be sent back to the Institute in Washington and fed into the computer. By the end of the preliminary testing, only Carla and Lydia had agreed to go to Finland. Every time she called to check in at the Institute, she had to bite her tongue to keep from asking about Erkki. Some part of her wanted to hear from him or even about him. She kept pushing that part to the back of her mind.

Living with Lydia was quite an experience. Lydia was the only member of the Running Mothers who didn't have children at home. Every time Jeanne asked about her kids she got a wisecracking evasion from Lydia. As far as Jeanne could figure out, the children lived in Hawaii with their father. When she questioned Carla or any of the other women, she got only a polite evasion. The Running Mothers were loyal, if nothing else. And they were good copy for *Fancy Free*.

The procession of men through the house was dizzying. Lydia kept trying to promote playmates for Jeanne, but after the Stephen episode, Jeanne refused.

She did not refuse, however, Lydia's invitation to join her on a weekend skiing trip to Mammoth Lakes, a forty-five minute flight due East over the Sierras. They left late Thursday afternoon for a long weekend.

Howie Tanner, pilot of the plane he introduced to them as a Beechcraft Barón 58P, was a contributor to the museum where Lydia was an exhibitor and lecturer. The way Lydia hung on to him, Jeanne had to wonder if he were one of Lydia's lovers. He was in computers, he said, in Silicone Valley. He skied avidly, but his wife did not. Nor did Aaron.

The Sierras, southern Yosemite in particular, reared fiercely before the plane, which ascended in air currents, bucked, wagged its tail. They made straight for a soaring peak, wavered, seemed to halt, then rose straight up, passing over it, the tips of giant trees almost brushing the underside of the plane. Then down, down, down the sled of the other side and up again. Snowfields were broken by frozen streams, lakes and falls.

"Flying's the only way to get to Mammoth in winter, since Donner Pass is a helluva way North, and the southern route is through Los Angeles," Howie explained. "Thirteen thousand-foot peaks over there, Jeanne." He pointed.

"Howie's a downhill man," explained Lydia, resplendent in blue bib pants of contoured nylon shaped to her waist, with straps crossed over a red and yellow nylon windshirt. She was a cross between farmer and spacewoman.

Snow dry and blowy can insinuate itself into clothes, to melt unpleasantly later. Tight garments tried to be proof against that uncomfortable event. That dawn, Lydia had supplied Jeanne with windpants and a blue and yellow ski jacket. Also suntan lotion and goggles.

"You're so generous," Jeanne said.

"You didn't know you'd be going skiing, pal." Lydia chaffed.

"I still don't believe it."

People skied in South Dakota, but Jeanne had feared long slats would not be enough to keep her above ground. And padded clothing would have increased her girth, goggles would have accentuated her nose. In the old days.

"Stephen hasn't been around for a while, Jeanne, but he's phoned."

Jeanne did not rise to the bait but kept her own counsel. Do your own thing or don't do it.

Howie took the turboprop into the closest airport, then rented a car to drive North between plowed snow-drifts worthy of South Dakota. Icicles three feet long hung from the eaves of the quaint cabins and chalets of Mammoth.

They'd use a condominium belonging to Lydia's ex-husband. "I'm not sleeping with Howie," Lydia blithely remarked. "He's our transportation; I'm his lodging. You've got a choice, you know. Start learning downhill skiing and spend both days falling down, or learn Nordic. As a runner, you'll be sailing all over the meadow and taking short hills by afternoon today."

"Really? I've never even *been* on skis."

Fifteen minutes later, Jeanne was signed up for a cross-country lesson, and fitted for skis as tall as herself plus her extended arm. Instead of robot boots to keep ankles immobile, she was fitted with leather shoes such as bowlers wore. Her feet would be free to lift and bend. Unlike Lydia's short, wide skis, Jeanne's were as narrow as her shoes and arched under her feet so she stood suspended above the floor. How could she travel on such things? The ski fitter shouted over to a big blond in fitted pants like Lydia's.

"Got a first-timer here. Hap Sanders, Jeanne Lathrop."

Thus did her friendship with Hap begin, her teacher and coach. The men exchanged wide smiles.

The blond buried her small hand in his big one. "Delighted," he said, squinting down at her. "The sun is warm today, Jeanne. Maybe you should shed some clothes."

"Maybe." This guy doesn't waste any time. He had the dark tan, brilliant eyes and the thumping good health of all skiers. The women had the same exuberant looks, plus oiled skin, hairdos resistant to wind and wool caps and figures like movie stars.

She was accustomed to runners at starting lines, eager and muscular, bare bodies featuring bony knees, hairy arms, varicose veins and beginner's flab. They did not compare with the expensively suited, windburnt, privileged sportspeople indulging themselves here on the ski slopes.

"The altitude here is eight thousand feet," Hap noted. "You'll feel light-headed."

"Light-headed brunette," cracked the other man admiringly.

"Well, I do run. Half marathons," Jeanne retorted.

Hap cocked a sandy brow admiringly, clapped her on the back and led her out of the warming shack, skis over her shoulder. Like archery bows, they twisted in her grasp, threatening to clear the counters of caps, gloves and lotion bottles. She climbed to the gathering place and bent to put the skis on, right, then left.

When she forced her shoe onto the pins at the toe, the ski skittered forward, and she sat down hard. No one laughed or even looked. The dozen brightly clad students, men and women, waited while Hap trod upon Jeanne's runaway ski. Then the class watched him demonstrate Nordic skiing, as he flew down a deep track, long-legged, narrow-hipped, in green nylon tights and a black sweater. He'd donned large goggles and a cap.

The sun reflected brilliantly from the crisp snow, so Jeanne put her goggles on, too, a pole swinging from each wrist. Would she ever be able to glide with that enticing lilt of the body Hap displayed? She shed her ski jacket in favor of her thin pullover. Hap's eye fell upon her and lingered.

The first shock was being asked to give up her poles, lest they'd be used as crutches or training wheels.

Her mouth dropped open. She'd stayed upright only by leaning heavily on those twin props. Without them, she'd fall flat. It didn't help to hear that the other students were downhill skiers already.

When she limped on her seven-foot feet to the rows of parallel ski tracks, things looked better. The skis were engineered not to slip backward. Following the tracks made by other skiers, they could not veer to the left or right; they had one choice of movement despite what *she* did. Hap was a good instructor. The class glided up and down the tracks, turning awkwardly at the ends and coming back, leaving star designs in the snow. Even over deep footprints and falls through six-foot snow, she glided without falling.

Skiing was going to be a magnificent sport. Shifting weight from ski to ski, bending forward from hips rather than shoulders, swinging arms as Hap did, she earned his praise. "Push, glide, push, glide; weight on the forward ski, flex knees, head up, lift your heels."

She was catching on. The high altitude was not taming her. "Your balance is excellent, Jeanne," said Hap. "You're a natural."

He led the group to a small slope—herringbone up, determine the fall line and then glide down crouched like racers, knees parallel with abdomen, arms stuck out slightly bent.

The glide was fast and scary. Jeanne was one of the three in the class without a white bottom from falling. Schussing, snowplowing, kick turning—even pole dragging—she absorbed the nomenclature as well as the skills. Her first spill came trying a turn at the end of a schuss—a downhill rush—and crossing her skis instead of veering them gradually together in the snowplow finish.

"Fine, fine!" called Hap. "It doesn't hurt to fall, Jeanne."

Getting up, however, was a hilarious maneuver. Her poles slid on the icy crust, which was like cake frosting, and the skis skittered wide. Still, no one laughed, and she appreciated the display of tact. Later she drove one ski tip through the wedge of the pole and pulling, hung herself up, bent forward, unable to move pole or ski. At that predicament, she laughed aloud.

"Where are you staying?" asked the tall blond when the others had been dismissed to try the beginners' tracks.

She told him blithely, swelling with success at a totally unfamiliar skill on extremely peculiar footwear.

"I teach the afternoon class," he said. "You should

practice. Don't just stick with the meadows; try some hills too. I'll catch you later." Flashing a smile that could have melted snow, he glided off.

She squinted across the bleak expanse of softly rolling rises under the bulk of Mammoth Mountain. For lunch she fed herself some cheese and a breakfast roll she'd stuck in her pocket. No way she would take off the skis and try to get them back on again. To slake her thirst she scooped up snow to suck on.

She picked out a hill twice as steep as the practice slope, and came whizzing down it, remembering only too late that she was lousy at stopping. A lone figure approaching might be skewing in her tracks, or schussing through; she couldn't tell. So she stopped herself the only sure way, by sitting down and skidding. She made a mess of the track, derailing like a train. The skier went past, two tracks to her left, not looking at her tumble. She put down an arm for support, and sank it to the shoulder in confectioner's sugar snow.

Lydia was right. This was fun and easy. She rose, strained her eyes toward Mammoth Mountain, that sleeping mastodon, able to pick out one tiny ski lift meandering up the slope. That's where Lydia and Howie would be, and she didn't need to envy them.

It was nearly five when she raced back to the hut to turn in her rented skis.

Hap stood waiting for her.

"I was about ready to send for the ski patrol."

"Not really!"

"For sure. You could be lost or injured. You're a first-timer. Too new . . . and valuable, to lose."

"Why thank you. But you needn't have worried," she said, getting out of the skis and trying to hoist them. But Hap lifted them off her shoulder.

"You must be starved."

"Sure am. It's tremendous exercise. And I don't even hurt."

"You will."

"I went down hills. Fast," she said like a child.

"*Hills?* Tell Alpine skiers that," he laughed, gesturing toward the mountain. "Thirty thousand ski each day up there, and a hundred and eighty of us teach even more of them."

When she turned in the equipment and paid a small bill, he was still there.

"You gonna ski tomorrow, too?"

"Yes, I want to practice."

"You came with friends?"

"Yes. Alpine skiers."

"Do you have plans for dinner?"

"Not yet," Jeanne admitted.

Hap grinned. "You do now," he said as though there were no question.

He gave her a ride back to the condo. No Lydia or Howie. Hap waited while she changed into soft green-gray tweed pants and a hand-knit Aran Islands pullover. Miraculous! He was changed, too, when she came down. In jeans and a sweater of blue and gray, his eyes looked like bits of sky twinkling under his furry blond eyebrows.

Hap caught her startled expression. "I'm a Boy Scout from way back. Always prepared. I had my stuff in the car, and ducked into the john down here while you were getting even more gorgeous than you were before."

Jeanne smiled her thanks, genuinely pleased at the compliment. As they left the condo, Jeanne's foot slipped on a patch of ice and Hap caught her arm, preventing her from taking a spill. He left his arm on hers until they reached the car. Jeanne found she did not mind it at all.

They went to a rustic steak house a few miles from the condo and got acquainted over lamb chops for Jeanne and sirloin steak, rare, for Hap. The portions were substantial, and Jeanne recalled the days when she could have downed that much food without blinking an eye. Even with the hearty appetite she had acquired on the slopes, Jeanne could not finish her meal. Eyeing her unfinished food eagerly, Hap asked if she were through eating. Without a word, Jeanne exchanged her plate for his empty one and watched as Hap made quick work of the rest of her chops.

"You've got quite an appetite," Jeanne said when he finally came up for air.

"I work hard, ma'am. Tough work ridin' herd in these parts," Hap said in his best Texas accent.

Jeanne had to admit that he worked hard and that he was good at his work. She asked what he did when he wasn't a ski instructor.

"Lifeguard. I go where beautiful women sun themselves. It's the only way to go."

The check came and Hap reached for his wallet. It wasn't there. "I must have left it at the ski hut. Could you pick this up? I'll pay you back tomorrow. This is very embarrassing."

"Don't worry about it," Jeanne said. "It's not fair for the man to pay all the time. I work, too."

"Yeah, but I asked you to dinner."

"So pretend I asked you," countered Jeanne. "I feel like dancing. Is there anyplace I can take you where we can dance off a few of these calories?"

"There's a place with a pretty good band down the road. Skier's hangout." Hap laughed at himself. "As if there's anything else around here."

The band was good, and they danced to the rock music until Jeanne nearly dropped. Hap drove her back to the condo and walked her to the door.

"Are you free tomorrow night, Jeanne? I'd sure like to make up for my goof tonight."

They set a date for the following evening, and Jeanne tiptoed into the dark apartment. As she headed down the hall to her room, Lydia stuck her head outside her door. "You didn't have to come home on my account, Jeanne. There's no curfew here. Didn't things work out with your ski bum?"

"Things worked out just fine, Lydia. We had dinner and went dancing and we're seeing each other tomorrow night. And he's not a bum."

"Who paid for dinner?"

Jeanne did a double take.

"You really *are* from South Dakota, aren't you?"

A sleepy voice echoed from the cavern of Lydia's room. "Come back to bed, honey."

Howie! Lydia did get around. Jeanne wondered how it affected her running and wondered if she could work the question into her psychological profile. She might at least work it into her articles.

"I think you're being paged, Lydia. Do you ever forget who you're in bed with?"

"Honey, I always forget."

Jeanne had never known anyone like Lydia. She hurried to her room to make some notes in the journal she was keeping. She used it to jot down ideas for articles and notes on the project, but for the first time she wanted to keep track of her personal feelings and growth. The old Jeanne had not wanted to leave any permanent record of herself or her observations of the world. But now she was fascinated by what was around her and inside her. Tonight she had lots to put down— skiing, Hap, Lydia—all new, all leading somewhere. She didn't know exactly where, but she knew she was moving.

Chapter Twenty-four

ON SATURDAY JEANNE arrived at the slopes at about eleven. She skied the whole day and got back to the ski hut late in the afternoon. Until she stopped, she didn't realize how tired she was. The achy muscles predicted by Hap had arrived. She'd go back to the condo for a long soak before meeting Hap for dinner.

She got no further than the door when Hap himself appeared. He gave her a friendly bear hug and she groaned, "Muscles I didn't even know I had are sore."

"You need a jacuzzi. I just happen to have one at home."

"No, thanks. I tried a hot tub at Lydia's, and it made me limp as spaghetti."

"This is different, not like a hot tub at all."

Jeanne relented. A few minutes later she found herself in Hap's efficiency apartment, part of his ski instructor's pay. There was a pullman kitchen at one end of the room. Brown wall-to-wall carpeting covered the rest of the floor space. A sofa that folded out into a bed was the principal piece of furniture, and it was folded out but not untidy. His TV set hung on the wall, and two rubber plants provided color. It was far neater than she'd expected a bachelor pad to be. There wasn't much to be neat about, Hap offered, because he spent so little time here.

Hap drew the drapes, and Jeanne gasped at the view. The moonlit mountain seen through a curtain of long crystal icicles reminded her of Finnish glass. Had it been only a few weeks ago that she'd left Erkki's house? She had packed her precious Finnish glass away, not wanting to take a chance that her subletter would break it. She knew the gesture was an attempt to pack Erkki away, but it was a futile one. When she least expected it, he popped up.

"I do have one more room," Hap said, breaking her reverie.

"I should hope so. You promised me a jacuzzi, and I doubt it hooks up to that Mickey Mouse sink over there."

Hap chuckled and pushed open a door to reveal a bathroom almost as large as the other room. On the wall facing the tub there was an enormous portrait.

"Like it?" he asked, studying her face, upturned to his oil painted extravagance.

Upon a dark background reclined a life-sized nude, somewhat in the posture of Goya's "Naked Maja." Jeanne stepped to the foot of the bed, narrowing her eyes. The picture was detailed, yet vague, explicit, yet oddly cool and chaste.

She couldn't say what was so odd about it. Soft white flesh, several square feet of rolling curves, head thrown back, dark hair flowing over the shoulders, large hips, large bosom, very alluring.

She entered the room and put her nose even closer

to the canvas, for canvas indeed it was. This was no print.

"I don't understand," she whispered, and then she did.

The nude so snowy white was made of snow. She was a mountain! The locks of hair were half-buried evergreens; Her beige nipples—exposed rocks. The lines around each breast, twin hills, were ski tracks, tiny, faint double lines.

Extraordinary. Faint tracks delineated her collar bones, her ribs, her hip bones, and converged finally in the patch of woods below . . . below the tiny silhouette of a skier that had at first seemed to be only . . . her navel.

Jeanne turned slowly to Hap standing in the doorway.

"Interesting," she said warmly. "Who painted it?"

"A friend of mine. A woman. Surprised? I get great compliments on it. Pretty clever, huh?"

"I agree. I'd think they'd reproduce it as a postcard to sell at all ski resorts. If it could be sent through the mail! Or as a poster."

"You sound like you're pretty clever, too." Hap reached out and pulled her close. Jeanne gasped involuntarily. He'd hit another sore muscle.

"Okay, no more fooling around until you get whirlpooled."

While he got out towels and set the controls of the jacuzzi, Jeanne asked how such a small apartment rated such a big bathroom, especially with the huge tub and built-in whirlpool.

"This was supposed to be the bath and dressing room of the adjoining condo but the buyer changed his mind at the last minute. So the management turned it into housing for the resident ski instructor. *C'est moi!*"

he skipped. "Everything's set. If you need anything, just call."

Hap left the room, and Jeanne peeled off her ski clothes. She was only in the swirling water a few minutes before the tension and achy feeling began to ebb away. Hap was such a nice guy. Happy-go-lucky. His name was short for Hapgood, a family name, but it suited him to a tee. She liked the fact that he hadn't thrown himself at her, that she was naked in his apartment and he stayed in the other room. Jeanne wondered what he looked like with his clothes off. He would not be lean and pale like Erkki, or dark and compact like Dick, or small and furry like Lydia's friend. She hadn't thought of it that night, but Stephen reminded her of a mole. Jeanne laughed out loud.

"What's going on in there?" Hap sang out.

"I just thought of something funny. Come on in and I'll tell you." Why had she said that? What was she getting herself into?

Before she could tell him not to come in, Hap was standing in the doorway. "You're more beautiful without clothes than you are with them." His eyes stayed on her body, visible in patches through the churning water.

Suddenly Jeanne wanted to be loved. She needed to be held, and she needed the physical closeness of Hap. Without looking up at him, she asked if he would join her.

"My pleasure, ma'am. Anything to oblige a lady."

Cheerfully, Hap removed his clothes. His body was smooth, nearly hairless, and his summer lifeguard tan was only a shade lighter than the skier's tan on his face. A small strip of white skin on his bottom and belly indicated the brief swim trunks he wore on his other job. He was strong and full-fleshed but without a spare ounce of fat. He was all muscle.

Hap climbed into the tub with her. It was so large that it held the two of them easily. They sat face-to-face, legs twined around each other's bodies. Hap took her hands in his. "Feels good, huh?"

Jeanne had to agree. She leaned back and rested her head on the edge of the tub, enjoying the warmth and motion. Hap tugged on her hands.

"Come closer," he said. "I want to hold you."

Jeanne shimmied up to him until they were touching, wrapping her legs around his body as she moved closer. They kissed, tasting each other and the wetness at the same time. Hap caressed her breasts, wet skin on wet skin.

She felt slippery inside and out. Reaching under the water, Jeanne fondled Hap, found him as ready for her as she was for him. "I've never done it in the bathtub. Do you think we can manage?"

"First time for everything," he replied, pulling her up so that she sat on top of his legs, his strong arms supporting her. With another quick motion they were locked together. Hap began to move slowly inside her, and in a few moments Jeanne couldn't tell where she left off and he began, or what was water and what was flesh. She felt like a primordial creature, awash in the swirl of life.

When it was over for them both, Jeanne slid back, turned around and positioned herself against Hap's chest. He put his arms around her, rocking her gently to the rhythm of the water.

"Better than Deborah Kerr and Burt Lancaster in 'From Here to Eternity.' That's a very high rating in my book."

Hap was a film buff. Jeanne thought back to the

scene, the two actors rolling on the surf in Hawaii, the Pacific Ocean washing over them, sea foam and sand surrounding them. It was no coincidence, she thought, that so many of her lovemaking experiences were tied to water and heat.

Hap lifted her out of the tub and they dried each other off with fluffy white towels. "One of my favorite movies is on tonight, Tab Hunter and the troops. How's about we stay in, throw a quick dinner together and cuddle up in front of the TV. I'll drive you home after the movie."

It sounded good, except the part about being driven home after the movie, so Jeanne agreed.

Hap had spaghetti and bottled meat sauce, a few odds and ends of lettuce and vegetables for a salad. They drank beer. Hap insisted on buttered popcorn during the movie. He never watched movies without beer and popcorn swimming in melted butter. They missed parts of the movie, but both had seen it, so neither minded the impromptu interruptions.

True to his word, Hap drove her home after the movie. Jeanne had told him it wasn't necessary, she could go home in the morning. He said he had a couple of hard classes in the morning and would prefer to sleep alone. Jeanne was disappointed but said nothing. At the door of Lydia's condo, Hap kissed her briefly and said he'd see her around. He didn't ask when she was leaving or anything else. Feeling deflated and empty, Jeanne went to her room.

They would be leaving about two the following afternoon. She could have the morning for skiing, then lunch with Lydia and Howie before they boarded the plane for the short ride back to Lydia's. Maybe she would see Hap then, at least to say goodbye.

Her morning on the slopes was good. Cross-country

skiing had a lot of the good things of running. You could do it alone or with someone, you got good, steady exercise. There was more fancy equipment and you needed snow and some open spaces, but it was still a lot less complicated than downhill skiing.

At noon she met Howie and Lydia at the snack bar near the ski hut. Over hamburgers and hot cocoa, Howie and Lydia chattered away while Jeanne swept the room with her eyes, hoping for a glimpse of Hap. When they had nearly finished their meal, he strode in, his arm around a blonde snow bunny in a pale lavender ski suit. Jeanne knew her time with Hap was just a weekend ski resort fling, but she still felt jealous and cheated. Lydia had been right. He was a ski bum. Why had she expected anything else from him? When Erkki and Dick asked for a commitment from her, she had run away as fast as she could. But she hadn't meant to run to the likes of Stephen Alexander and Hap Sanders.

Hap gave her the high sign and smiled, as if she had been only another one of his ski students. That's exactly what their night together had meant to him. She was just one in an endless string of women who were nothing more to him than warm, pliant bodies.

An older but wiser Jeanne Lathrop boarded the Beechcraft Baron 58P for the short flight. How ever did Lydia do it? Why ever did Lydia do it?

Chapter Twenty-five

JEANNE HAD LITTLE more time to ponder the mystery of Lydia because she left for San Francisco on Tuesday morning. In the San Francisco area, she came up with four racers out of fourteen known ultramarathoners. One in Berkeley would take time off from her graduate studies, and another in Oakland had talked her husband into accompanying her. From there Jeanne flew down to Los Angeles and braved a smog blanket to interview a dozen more women.

One was pregnant—very. Scratch her. One was already overseas and unavailable. A third felt she wasn't ready for a hundred-miler, "and there's jet lag to contend with, too. Three hours to the East Coast, six hours to England and where's Helsinki?"

"An hour further east," Jeanne admitted. "Ten hours of lag, total. That is a *lot*. Well, you'd have several days rest before you run." But she didn't try to convince her.

The woman was a complainer better dispensed with.

217

Jeanne struck gold with other women, however, who met with her at the Hilton on Wilshire. She gave an orientation talk and set them to filling out forms. The smog had been blown away by a sea breeze, and snowy peaks were now visible from her high windows. Palm trees along wide, clean streets among skyscrapers in white and black stone, trim as giant dominos, made her think the city had had a bad press. It wasn't San Francisco, but it wasn't Dante's Inferno either.

She had telephoned several women from Santa Barbara, and one had come to her meeting. Now the total number of participants from Southern California was five.

Then Jeanne hopped another jet to fly all the way north to Portland.

Incredible. It was only in 1969 that the first woman ran legally at Boston. Now, in 1980, the woods were full of women who could tackle fifties and one-hundred milers. Because they knew they could.

The flight to Portland was a long one, way beyond San Francisco. "I thought Frisco was in northern California," she remarked to the passenger who told her Portland was 640 miles.

"We don't call it 'Frisco,' and it's in the middle of the state," he had snapped.

No more deserts beneath her. They flew over the miniature Golden Gate Bridge. Over the Napa Valley she drank Napa vintage, and then looked down on the snowy caps of Mt. Lassen and Mt. Shasta. Over on the silvery coastline stood the redwoods.

Portland furnished her three nos and one treasure—wide-shouldered, pig-tailed, blunt and wholesome Mandy Steir, who was delighted about going to Finland. The veteran of a grueling two-mountain, forty-mile race, Mandy was thrilled to hear how flat Finland

was. A college professor, she had free time to travel
and a very supportive husband, also a professor.
Jeanne stayed with the Steirs while interviewing the
Portland candidates. They lived on a small farm, kept
chickens and goats, had a small garden and were nearly
self-sufficient in food. Mandy canned produce from her
garden to last the winter. Her cellar held row upon row
of Mason jars. The goats provided milk and meat, the
chickens eggs and poultry. They ground their own
grain, and every Saturday Mandy baked bread for the
week. It was a long way from the microwave fast food
she had been served at Lydia's.

In a rental car Jeanne drove the couple of hours it
took to get to Eugene, a special place for runners. It
had been the home of Pre—Steve Prefontaine, crushed
to death under his car in the midst of his fast rise to
world renown. Would any Eugene woman run in Finland? Pre had wanted to run against Lasse Viren, the
great Finnish runner.

"I'll sure try," Pat Prince said, limping because of
an injured Achilles' tendon. "Maybe *I'll* be fine by
June, and some of your better bets will be injured. On
the mileage that we'll have to put in—"

"Oregon does need representation. All the U.S. ultradistance record holders among women are Califor-
nians."

Jeanne could see Pat's eyes light up and accept the
challenge. She invited Jeanne to her home for dinner.
In midsentence, a forkful of meatloaf suspended on its
way to her mouth, Pat exclaimed, "Now I know why
you looked so familiar. You're the one who got swatted
by that cheater in Missouri, aren't you?"

"Tennessee, not Missouri."

Pat wanted to hear all about it, but Jeanne cut her
short, saying it had turned out to be very unplea ant

and she really didn't wish to talk about it. *Fancy Free* might be running some follow-up articles if she cared to watch the magazine.

Jeanne turned the conversation back to the ultra-marathon. Besides her injury, Pat mentioned planning a June wedding. "I don't want to calorie load on wedding cake and then take off alone for a Finnish honeymoon without Hal."

"Maybe Hal could come along. All your expenses will be paid. You'd just have to pay for him. Two for the price of one."

Pat said she'd think about it and get back to Jeanne at Mandy Steir's in Portland, where Jeanne would be for a couple more days.

Jeanne got out of Portland with four Oregon women signed up: Mandy, Pat and two others from Portland. She knew she would get most of her runners on the West Coast, but she still had the rest of the country to canvas. January had come and gone. Jeanne decided a side trip to Elmton might be just the thing for a few days rest. Traveling was fun, but living out of a suitcase was hard. She needed to go home, be pampered by her parents and rest her weary bones for a few days. As wonderful as the people she had met were, the old adage still held true, there was no place like home. She would spend Groundhog Day in South Dakota.

In Elmton her mother plied her with food and Jeanne ate heartily. Since she'd been spending so much time with ultramarathoners, running with them as part of her recruiting and interviewing, Jeanne had increased her mileage and her speed. Ten miles was nothing now; her time hovered around eighty minutes. Not bad. It was colder in Elmton than in California or Oregon, but

Jeanne bundled up. Running in the cold burned up even more calories than usual, extra ones expended on keeping the body temperature up.

Her parents still couldn't understand her enthusiasm for going out and running with no destination in mind, but they were glad to see her and to have a chance to get further acquainted with their new daughter.

From Elmton Jeanne stopped off to see the few Midwestern candidates. Then she flew to Texas, traveled through the South, then up the Eastern seaboard to New York and Boston. None of the Midwestern women were available. One Dallas woman signed up. Jeanne found one runner in Atlanta, two in New York and two more in Boston. In three and one half months on the road, she had recruited twenty-one women. The Institute's computers were whirring away. She had ideas for articles that would knock Ron's socks off and a few ideas for some freelance articles that would line the Lathrop coffers. And she had a journal full of thoughts and feelings, a chronicle of her cross-country trip.

Although Jeanne had met lots of men since Hap, no one particularly interested her. She was on the go so much she never had time to get to know someone, and she had learned she was not good at one-night stands.

Erkki had once asked her if she had been in the convent. She had evaded the question, but since her whirlpool romance with Hap she had been celibate. She might as well have been in a convent.

As her plane landed at Dulles Airport Jeanne wished that Erkki would be there to meet her. If she had not refused his offer of marriage he would be. But since her departure she had not heard a word from him. No messages through Dr. Moore, nothing. She was alone.

But then she had chosen to be alone. And she had learned from it. She had also learned from her trip how much of an American she was. Jeanne had loved the people she'd met, diverse but sharing an American drive and openness. Erkki had the drive, but he was reserved and formal. She would not thrive in an atmosphere that was always reserved and formal.

Jeanne took a cab to her Georgetown apartment. Her sublet tenant had left on April 1 and she would not sublet it again for her trip to Europe. Jeanne could unpack her suitcases and refill her drawers and closets with all the things she had packed away, including Erkki's gifts from Finland.

The apartment was absolutely still. In the two weeks between her arrival and the sublet tenant's departure, Nancy had been in to water the plants and check up on things. There was a note on the kitchen counter from Nancy, along with a bouquet of fresh-cut Shasta daisies. Welcome back, the note said, and advised Jeanne to check the refrigerator. Nancy had stocked it with juice, milk, eggs, bread and fruit. It *was* good to be home, and Jeanne was touched by Nancy's thoughtfulness. Someone cared.

The first time Jeanne saw Erkki after returning to Washington was at the Cherry Blossom Ten-Miler. Jeanne ran a respectable 1:14:36 on the flat, well-tended course around the Tidal Basin and past Washington's scenic landmarks. He had finished well before her, and she caught a glimpse of him as she crossed the finish line. He was scowling. Or was the sun too bright for his Finn-gray eyes?

After getting something to drink, Jeanne searched the crowd for him. Because of his height, she had little trouble locating him. Her desire to hear his voice and look into his eyes overcame her fear, and she pushed her way through the crowd to him.

"Erkki?"

He turned, looking neither glad nor surprised to see her. "So we meet again," he said matter-of-factly.

"It's good to see you. You're looking well."

"And you. I watched you finish the race. It is very good, your speed and distance."

"Yes, I've improved a lot, spending so much time with the ultramarathoners." What was she doing chatting with him like he was an acquaintance? She felt the old tug, desire, a melting heart. She stopped herself from reaching out to touch his face and hair. Three and one half months, thousands of miles and hundreds of new faces later, she felt the same. She wanted the man, but not the country and the unknown daughter. An impossible situation.

She heard Erkki compliment her on her work for the Institute. It was the first time he had praised her for it, or even acknowledged it. She thanked him and they spoke for a few more minutes about blood pressures, lipoprotein readings, weekly mileages and the discipline involved in ultramarathon running.

"You must spend some time at the Institute during this last month before the race. We have much need of your services."

Was that just a business invitation, or did he hope to see her personally? Jeanne wondered as Erkki left her side. There was no way of knowing.

May was filled with preparations for the Finnish ultra. Jeanne kept in close contact with her twenty-one runners by phone and by mail. The women were training hard. Jeanne's gradual increase of weekly distance from twenty, then thirty, toward fifty miles was nothing compared with their mileage, which averaged more than one hundred miles per week.

The American runners would arrive in Helsinki several days before the race to give them time to work off their jet lag. Jeanne would coordinate the American women's team, keeping them to their schedule of Institute tests, continuing her psychological profiling for the Institute data and keeping up with their progress for her articles in *Fancy Free*.

The runners had agreed to make rest stops during the race itself to give blood and urine and breath into plastic bags. All runners took rest stops during a hundred-miler, and the test participants wouldn't be hampered by the medical aspects of theirs. Jeanne would be on the course helping with this. It would be hard work.

Erkki would be overseeing the whole operation, and she would have to be in contact with him, since Al Moore was staying behind in Washington to mind the computers there.

By the middle of May, Jeanne realized how tired she was. If she was going to get through the race and perform her duties well, she would have to take a few days off. She would like to fly to Europe a week early and spend some time hiking in the Swiss Alps. Ron had no problem with her leaving a week early nor did Al Moore. But she knew she had to check with Erkki about this. She had been spending a few hours a day at the Institute, and had even consulted him directly when one of her runners had a question or problem. On these occasions he had been correct and helpful. Once or twice his behavior was less than cordial. And each time Jeanne felt less and less fear about seeing him.

It was still with trepidation, however, that she knocked on his door to ask about her week in the Swiss Alps. When he asked her to sit down, her mind flashed to their first meeting. He looked much the same, but she wore no spiked heels to impress him. She was comforable in her pale green spring designer jeans, long-sleeved pullover T-shirt and running shoes. She had lost her need to play the *femme fatale*.

"If you have no large problems with your runners and leave a number where you can be reached, I don't see why you shouldn't have a few days vacation before the race. I wish I could myself go with you. I am very tired from all the work and preparations."

Jeanne had forgotten how hard he was working on his pet project. And he had expressed a desire to go with her. Did that really mean with her, not just to get away for a few days? She could not bring herself to ask so she rose to go. "Thanks a lot, Erkki. I appreciate your understanding."

She was halfway out the door when he called her back.

"Before you go, can we have dinner, for auld lang syne, as you say?"

Tears stung Jeanne's eyes. At least he didn't hate her. She may have lost him as a lover, but perhaps she could make a friend. "That would be lovely." Jeanne's voice caught in her throat.

"Let me know when you leave and we will make the date."

"Yes, I will, let you know, that is. Bye." Jeanne shut the door and went back to the desk she used when she was working at the Institute. Dinner with Erkki. What a lovely surprise. A thaw in the cold war.

Erkki took her again to The Broker, the site of their first date. Over broiled salmon accompanied by dry white wine, Erkki was a charming dinner companion. He told her more about his childhood and life in Finland than he ever had before. Although his life had not been easy, he did not dwell on the hardships, but told of the happy times, the light moments. He hardly stopped talking for the whole meal, which surprised Jeanne no end.

Because she felt so good, Jeanne splurged and ordered chocolate mousse for dessert. As she spooned the creamy confection into her mouth, Erkki asked her how she had ended up in a convent. Jeanne sputtered, nearly losing her mouthful of mousse.

"I never said I was in a convent. You asked and I said I might as well have been."

"If you were not in a convent, where were you that you were virgin at twenty-four? Are there no men in South Dakota?"

Jeanne looked him straight in the eye. "I was fat."

An incredulous look passed over Erkki's face, then he threw his head back and laughed. A real honest to goodness laugh. Jeanne could not help but join in and in a few moments they were giggling uncontrollably, causing amused stares from the other diners.

"How is it that you are so thin and beautiful now?"

Jeanne told him the whole story.

As they left the restaurant, Jeanne felt like she had just met Erkki. He was so much more relaxed and open with her. What had happened? she asked.

"Since I tell you of Stina, I feel a great weight lift from my shoulders. I look forward to Helsinki not only to have the race on which I work so hard, but I want to meet my little Impi. I do not need you for a crutch, Jeanne. I apologize that I did ever ask."

At her door, Erkki kissed her in the European manner, on both cheeks. "Bon voyage. Until Helsinki."

"Thank you for a lovely evening, Erkki. I'm glad we did this. Until Helsinki." She kissed him on the cheek, in the American manner.

Chapter Twenty-six

JEANNE HAD FOUND a bargain flight on an Air France 747, a plane trimmed in passionate pink. For dinner she was fed chicken with asparagus, mineral water, wine and chocolate pastry.

The blue Atlantic wrinkled below her as she flew away from the sun. She'd land in Paris at night, sleep all the next day and take an overnight train to Zurich. She would find a quiet inn or small hotel there, explore the nearby Alps and then fly up to Helsinki in time to meet the runners.

Paris was disappointingly dark, rainy and a test of her college French. After a hair-raising ride to her hotel, she had a bottle of sauterne sent up to her quaint, antique room with its high ceiling, cloudy mirror and noisy plumbing. She slept until afternoon and then took a short jog on the now sunny streets. Someday she would come back to Paris, hopefully not alone.

She had dinner at an open-air cafe, watching young couples hold hands while sad-eyed Frenchmen looked on. The food was delicious, graced by rich sauces, accompanied by good *vin ordinaire*. Jeanne purchased some postcards and an extra sweater for high altitudes and returned to the hotel to pack for her all-night couchette trip to Zurich. She dressed in comfortable jeans and a pullover.

Imagine. Her first view of the storied Alps would come with the morning sun! Lugging her own suitcases, glad for all the upper-body muscles she'd developed as a fringe benefit of running, she made her way along the walk beside her train, searching for her coach.

"*Madame! Vite! Vite!*" called a moustached conductor, leaning out. She hopped on the next coach, and found that the windowed corridor along one side of the train paralleled curtained compartments on the other. Egad! The Orient Express all over again. The train was already beginning to move.

Eventually she found coach ten and compartment eight. Jeanne slammed out of one swaying car, crossed an accordion-pleated juncture that admitted wind and noise and then fought open the door to the next coach. At least her bags had been shelved for her by the last conductor she'd met. She hesitated only a moment before pulling open the sliding door to couchette eight. Inside lay an empty bunk. Jeanne removed her shoes, lifted the blanket and found the sheet was actually a clever bag, sewed together at side and bottom. There was a tiny, linen-covered pillow, and the bed was well padded. Jeanne sank gratefully into the comfortable bed. She fell asleep to the sound of rails clicking beneath her.

The next sound she heard was the *S'il vous plaît?* of the train conductor; it was light out, and she was apparently expected to arise immediately. Groaning, she did, and staggered off down the corridor to brush her teeth in the restroom.

The train rushed on, through the foothills of the Swiss countryside, past old brick buildings. Grapevines trained up poles; dusky red tile roofs graced white stone houses with windows full of pink and red blossoms.

The conductor interrupted her once again at the border to look at her passport and hand her a declaration form. He collected the form and passport and exited down the aisle. Just before the train was due to arrive in Zurich, he returned her passport. Jeanne felt a little thrill of anticipation. Soon she'd be in the Alps!

In the Zurich station, she ordered hot Ovomaltine—Ovaltine in the land of its origins—and a thick cake heavy with wheat. She pulled out her running shoes, stowed her bags in a locker, and took a brisk jog along Zurich's lovely winding river. After a mile it branched into the hazy, sweet-smelling Zurichsee, speckled this morning with sailboats and swans, white on blue. Tall-gabled, steep-roofed medieval buildings fronted the water, alongside Romanesque churches. Twin spires of Grossmunster dominated the skyline. It was eight hundred years old. Wow. She jogged up brick-paved city lanes so narrow that fat Jeanne might not have passed through. Today she had no trouble. Motorbikes buzzed where she expected bicycles.

Flowers cascaded out of windows everywhere, shop signs hung from ornate metal spirals, large medieval paintings hung on plastered houses, statues of knights and kings stood upon cement foundations.

Shivering with delight, she jogged down the Limmat back to the train station. Zurich, standing above the vaults of the notorious Swiss banks, gave her what she expected: towers with clocks, swans, cathedrals and, sprawled across a sidewalk, a huge St. Bernard.

By the station she spotted a tourist announcement: Visit Rigi Kulm.

That sounded interesting so she bought a ticket, retrieved her bags, and hopped the train down the Zurichsee.

At Arth-Goldau she barely made it off the train with her luggage before the air brakes hissed and the train resumed its trip to Italy. Italy? How did she dare? Dash through France, stop in Switzerland, climb an Alp. Next, Finland on the horizon. Two years ago, Washington had seemed the impossible dream.

The blue train stopped on a covered overpass above the railroad tracks must be the funicular. One car. She flew up the long steps and displayed her magic ticket. She was motioned to the car and took her place on one of the hard wooden seats.

Elderly couples dressed in wool britches that buckled below the knee wore heavy boots and backpacks and carried staves. Young men with skiers' alert eagerness sat against fifteen-foot bundles of canvas that rested along the seat-backs against the windows. Tents? Certainly not dozens of skis.

The funicular jerked, rattled and began to crawl—San Francisco cable car fashion—up the mountain at a sharp angle past cliffs, green pastures, and above the lake, which shrunk rapidly as they rose toward the sun.

Then she heard the first cowbells.

Jeanne shook her head in pure delight. Tinny, sweet, an Asian windchime combined with a Caribbean steel band, each bell playing a slightly different note and coming from a different direction, hundreds of them, maybe thousands. Swiss cities have tower bells, and the Alps—cowbells? The music increased as they climbed, rising like heat from the pastures below.

Jeanne leaned out the window, counting snowy peaks, shivering as the car rose and the temperature dropped, but the sun remained warm. The Bernese Alps rose to 14,000 feet, full of glaciers—Jungfrau and its brothers.

The Swiss flag, white cross on red, flew everywhere as they passed small hotels and farms before slowing to a halt. Jeanne left the tiny train station a mile up to climb toward a peak-straddling brown and yellow hotel. A live Alpine band played polkas.

Cows and a pet goat wandered around the hotel where diners sat sunning at tables on a terrace. She had tea and a half-moon cake after nourishing herself with a large shredded salad. It was after four p.m. when she determined that this hotel had no room available.

It is Saturday, *fraulein*, the clerk explained. The rooms are all full. He was very helpful, though, and arranged a room for her at one of the small hotels down the mountain. The last funicular left at eight o'clock and a room would be held for her.

Jeanne thanked him and went back outside. She would take a long hike, have dinner here in Rigi Kulm listening to the polka band and then go down to her room. Excellent. She breathed in the sharp clean air and took off on one of the many hiking paths. Her Leica hung around her neck and she used a roll of film on her walk, capturing the golden light of the late spring afternoon.

She met no one on her hike and was left alone with her thoughts. Erkki was the focus of her afternoon hike. For the first time, the night before she left, she had spent time with him without making love. Both had been able to reveal themselves more than ever before. There had been give and take in the evening, a quality that had been missing from their relationship. Jeanne realized that sometimes you had to close doors before you could open others. She had gone away from Erkki's intensity and had come back from her trip to find a less strained man, to find herself a freer woman. She had been accepted for what she was all over America, with everyone she met. No one knew she had once been overweight and plain. People expected no more than they got from her. Perhaps Erkki would one day accept what she was willing to give. And she would be willing to accept him on those same terms.

Rosy-cheeked and with a parched throat and an empty stomach, Jeanne returned to the little yellow and brown hotel. In the dining room, to the schmaltzy sounds of a polka band, she drank down two glasses of *Apfelsaft,* a delicious, clear apple juice. She dined on *Erbsensuppe*—a thick pea soup—and *Schnitzel*—veal cutlet. For dessert there was cherry strudel covered with whipped cream and accompanied by rich, strong coffee. Tired and satisfied, Jeanne climbed on the funicular for the short trip to the Hotel Edelweiss, where she would be staying.

The Edelweiss proved to be a small, half-timbered hotel with a steeply sloping roof, a railed terrace with tables and a backdrop of dark trees to set it off. Inside Jeanne sniffed the comfortable scent of mothballs and varnish, very faint and homey. She was led down a long, immaculate hall covered with rush matting. The porter opened the door to her room.

The first thing of note was the tall window looking out upon the Bernese Alps. White net curtains, immense pillows on the bed and a folding quilt. The wash basin glistened white in a red stand. She had two deep easy chairs and a vase of wildflowers on the chiffonier. The woodwork and furniture were carved with scrolls and flower designs, as if by an army of elves. A Swiss clock on its shelf chimed softly the hour of nine.

Jeanne was enchanted. After unpacking, she bathed in a gigantic tub among bouquets of wildflowers, and finally climbed into bed, soothed and pleasantly sleepy.

The next morning she had breakfast on the sunlit terrace of the Edelweiss. After breads, rolls, marmalade, raspberry jam and a pot of tea with cream, Jeanne stretched her arms langorously over her head and wondered what to do today.

She decided she would spend the day taking photographs of Rigi Kulm. Perhaps she would stay another night if her room was still available. It was so pleasant here; tomorrow she would take the train back to Zurich, then on to Helsinki.

Jeanne strode purposefully to the lobby desk. To her delight, she was told that her room was available. Camera slung around her neck, she headed for the funicular to take the short ride toward the crest of the mountain.

When she got there she was surprised by a group of young men hang gliding. The gliders were wonderful. They rose like multicolored beach umbrellas while the fliers sat chatting and snacking on the grass among the placid cows, the prams and dogs, the children and grandmothers. Jeanne snapped two rolls of film, catching the gliders first rolled and assembled, and then harnessed onto the backs of young men who stood on the cliffs while companions tossed up handfuls of grass to determine the direction of the wind.

One by one, the men with gliders ran to the cliff's edge, then threw themselves off. Each time, Jeanne was unable to squelch an involuntary scream before the wind caught the triangular wing and cradled the dangling man to let him very slowly sail away and down, down, down.

It didn't take long for Jeanne to notice that there were no women participating in the sport. Only men. She walked over to the spectators and began to look for someone who spoke English. Taking the small notebook she always carried in her pocket, she jotted down notes based on her conversations. She talked to a couple of the hang gliders who knew English. No, they didn't know any women who attempted the sport. It took a lot of upper body strength, something which many women, even good athletes, are short on. By the end of the morning, Jeanne had enough pictures and facts for an article on Swiss Alpine hang gliding. If she sold it, she could pay for part of her vacation. It was one of the great things about being a journalist—you never knew when you were going to stumble onto a story.

She made friends with some of the young people and was invited to share their picnic lunches. They communicated in pidgin English and German and French, with much gesturing and laughing, and lots of translating by the English speakers. By midafternoon her friends loaded up their cars and started their journeys back down the mountain to their homes. Jeanne helped them pack up and waved and shouted as the caravan moved down the mountain.

Left to her own devices, Jeanne picked a different path than the one she had used the day before and went for a hike. She hadn't run in a couple of days, but this terrain was too tough for her to tackle, even though she was in good shape. Walking was a pleasant change. The scenery moved more slowly and she saw things she might have missed had she been moving faster.

Today Jeanne found herself fascinated by the mountain wildflowers and shot roll after roll of color close-ups as she strolled. Her favorite shot was of a single dark pink flower growing out of a crack between two rocks. Even in this hard, shady place the flower had fought its way to the sunlight, and its beauty was testimony to its determination. It's a little like me, Jeanne thought. I grew out of a mountain of fat and years of damage caused by a terrible self-image. And here I am, full of vigor and life. If I can only remember to keep my face turned to the sun.

Jeanne decided to dine at the top of the mountain rather than going right back to the Edelweiss. She sat on the terrace and looked out over the Alps as she ate her dinner of fresh-caught fish, cucumbers in cream, boiled potatoes and fruit under thick cream. She drank a half bottle of white German wine with her meal. It was sweeter than the dry wines Erkki preferred, and she enjoyed the difference. The wine was well-suited to the rich cuisine.

It was amazing what a few days of rest and a change of scenery could do. Jeanne felt invigorated, ready to meet the challenges of Helsinki and of Erkki, whatever happened between them. She returned to the Edelweiss for a night's rest before going on to Zurich in the morning and Helsinki in the late afternoon.

Chapter Twenty-seven

JEANNE'S SEATMATE ON the flight from Zurich to Helsinki was a Swiss businessman who introduced himself as Gustav Schindler. He was going to Helsinki to examine the handicrafts of Marimekko and Arabia Nuutajarvi and Nahkayhtyma, as he often did. He asked if she was a tourist or on business.

"I am helping to organize and report on a hundred-mile road race," she replied.

"Ah. I have much familiarity with the Grand Prix—"

"No. Not cars, people. A foot race."

The question he asked was the same that everyone did, no matter what age, sex or nationality. "Why would anyone run so far? How *could* any person do it?"

"It can be run in under twelve hours. The women's world record is 16:11—sixteen hours, eleven minutes. An American. In 1978 a woman of forty-eight finished in under seventeen hours. The best American man broke thirteen hours."

Herr Schindler's eyes were glazing over. It was sometimes hard for Jeanne to remember that not everyone had the same enthusiasm for running that she had, or the same memory for statistics.

But she hadn't bored him. He asked her about the Helsinki race.

"Fifty-milers are run the entire way, but hundred-milers seldom. There's a lot of walking and resting, and there'll be time for doctors to take blood pressures and collect blood."

"Oh, so it is run for the benefit of science?"

"For the runners we have sponsored, yes. The American and Finnish participants. The race is international in scope, and certified."

They talked further about her job, her own running habits and her marathon hopes. He told her of his business travels, his wife and children.

They were served a cold supper of sliced ham, brown bread and fruit. Herr Schindler insisted on buying Jeanne a Drambuie. They ate and drank at fifty-one thousand feet over the mouth of the Baltic, watching the sun set over the North Sea. As they flew north and the evening progressed, the latitude balanced out the hour. Soon, beyond the Arctic Circle, there would be day all night, the summer solstice drawing near.

"We are approaching Helsinki," Herr Schindler said, pointing at the window. "The city is only a little dry ground in water. It looks, on a clear day, like a hand with fingers spread, lying in the Gulf of Finland. The country has sixty thousand lakes for only five million people."

Jeanne and Herr Schindler shared a taxi from the airport into the city. He was staying at the sumptuous

Palace Hotel. The Institute had booked Jeanne into a smaller, less expensive hotel, but still near the harbor.

From the air she'd counted a dozen parks and inlets, and from the ground she found the streets wide, clean and mostly empty. Half a million people lived here. Where were they?

The architecture ran from heavy, Russian-looking, block-long buildings to wedding-cake, ornate Victoriana. Statues wore overcoats and thick moustaches or nothing at all. Only one iron was mounted on a horse, across from the parliament.

"Mannerheim," Herr Schindler told her in a hushed tone of voice as the taxi drove past. He looked as if he'd have doffed his hat, had he been wearing one. "He was the greatest soldier and statesman Finland has ever known."

Jeanne rememberd the name from a long ago history class, but made a note to read up on Mannerheim. They say travel is broadening and now she could see how. See something, and you wish to know its name, its age and its history. The wide differences in architecture between Paris, Zurich and Helsinki intrigued her the way differences in accents always had. She was looking for national characteristics, surprised to find stereotypes often too true for comfort. No wonder people generalized so; too fast a trip through so many countries would make you do just that. Better to settle down somewhere and study the land and its people. She voiced these thoughts to Herr Schindler, who agreed with her.

The Palace Hotel was an impressive sight. Its dozen rows of long windows overlooked Helsinki harbor like a glass-and-mortar chunk of baklava. Twin cathedrals dominated the horizon on the other side of the boat-filled harbor, with a white dome and a red-and-blue

one. Herr Schindler identified them as the Lutheran
and the Eastern Orthodox.

When the taxi stopped in front of Jeanne's hotel,
Herr Schindler shook her hand as the driver took her
bags out of the trunk. "It has been delightful to meet
you. I will be here for one week. Perhaps we can meet
for lunch one day."

Jeanne had enjoyed the Swiss gentleman's company.
"I don't know exactly what my schedule is going to
be, but I do hope we can arrange a time. Thank you
very much for the taxi ride."

"My pleasure. *Auf Wiedersehen!*"

Jeanne was shown to a spacious double room, which
she would share with one of the runners when they
arrived. The drapes were heavy and dark in color,
necessary in summer when the sun does not set. They
were drawn closed, giving the room a quiet, womblike
feeling. She bathed luxuriously in a giant tub set on a
tiled floor in a spotless common bath down the hall
from her room. Back in her room, although she could
not see the harbor with the drapes drawn closed, the
faint ebb and surge of the water soothed her to sleep.

Early the next morning, English language map in
hand, Jeanne set out for the medical research facility,
which would serve as race headquarters. She would
window-shop along the way. Over breakfast she'd
leafed through some tourist booklets, which had whet-
ted her appetite for carved glass, metal jewelry and
woven rugs, as well as clothing. She would buy a few
elegant fashions to supplement her wardrobe. Today
she wore brown cord pants, a warm orange sweater
and running shoes. June at Hudson Bay latitude is *not*
June in Washington, D.C.

She walked toward the central shopping district, past

a market on the great plaza between boat docks and cathedrals; fish, flowers, vegetables, jewels and hides were laid out under bright red canvas tents. Gypsies in elaborate blouses and aprons sold handfuls of lace; shoppers ate green peas out of the pod, sprinkling pods underfoot like toy green boats. She could not tell which among the strollers were Finns; this was a motley crowd of dark and light, speaking many tongues. But then, behind the displays of scarlet salmon steaks nested in dillweed and the boxes of berries stood kerchiefed, strong-faced women with pale eyes. Finns, surely. And Finnish men sold potatoes from the sterns of moored boats. Jeanne stared hard. Light hair mostly, pale eyes always. They looked indeed like people who fought Russians and, as Erkki had told her, held them off for an entire winter. Silent Finns who knew about work and sacrifice.

Signboards for cruises and tours attracted her attention. Their Finnish hosts would lay out a schedule of diversions for the athletes, a choice of sights to see, and Jeanne would be responsible for supervising the women in such activities and making sure they had what they needed. And that they stayed out of trouble. This was Wednesday. Only today until nine p.m. would she have to herself, and she vowed to use it well. But first she had to check in at headquarters. Perhaps Erkki would be there. Her heart and step quickened.

Etelaesplanadi translated to South Esplanade on her map. Jeanne hurried toward her destination, drooling over the offerings in shop windows. What fabrics! What bowls and chairs, pots and pans! She wished for another surprise inheritance to buy at least one of everything. She hastened past outdoor diners under umbrellas among fountains and statuary, past a bandshell in the esplanade park, turning south to find her way among shops and apartments, parks and churches, and there—there was the modest, modern laboratory she sought.

A receptionist, an ethereal blonde with baby-fine skin and cautious English, seated Jeanne in an alcove on a comfortable, contoured couch. The pretty young receptionist spoke rapidly into an intercom. Her own name was a bit of driftwood tossed up by waves of staccato Finnish. Before the message was completed, Jeanne glanced up to see two long-legged persons striding through the passage she had just left. One almost stepped on her toes.

It was Erkki. He was speaking rapid Finnish to his companion, and walked right past her in his gray suit without word. Then the gray suit halted, and the platinum head whipped around. A dark flush shot up each cheek as he strode back to her.

"Jeanne! You are here!"

He was glad to see her. The sight of him was more exciting than she had anticipated. No words would come at all. She nodded her head and he bent, took her hand and pulled her to her feet. He looked over his shoulder to right and left. Receptionist at right, fellow doctor at left watching Jeanne and Erkki with great interest. Jeanne wanted to cry and didn't know why.

"Come into my office," he said.

Jeanne came, led by the hand. He closed the door behind her and pulled her toward him.

"Welcome to Finland. It is good to see you in my country." He pressed her against him, giving her only a moment to gauge the intensity of his face before he covered her mouth with his. He wanted to engulf her, absorb her.

And she had still said not one word.

Erkki was kissing her deeply now, one hand caressing her hip, the other her back. Tears slid silently down her cheeks.

Suddenly Erkki pulled back. "I apologize. I do not know what came over me. That I should not have done. It is only that I was glad to see you."

Finally Jeanne found her voice. "And I am happy to see you," she said, wiping the tears away with the back of her hand.

He helped her to a lavatory where she washed her face and asked herself what on earth ailed her. It was the latitude, it was the flying. She was fatigued, a stranger in a country where Erkki was completely at home. Rationalizations. She was still afraid of losing her identity if there was genuine closeness between them. Jeanne dried her face and put on fresh lipstick. A fear acknowledged is a fear half-conquered.

"I'm all right," she told him when she came out of the lavatory. "It's just that your intensity frightens me. I feel like I'm getting lost in the crush."

"I think I begin to understand your feelings. But for now let us forget all that. I wish to show you my Helsinki so you will feel more at home here."

Without touching her again, he guided her out of the building and into his Saab, parked on the street. They drove a short distance and Erkki slowed the little car and pointed.

"*Olympiastadion*," he said.

The great circular building of many overlapping, flaglike pillars reminded her of a spectacular airport terminal. Then she remembered it was a Finn, Eero Saarinen, who had designed Washington's Dulles Airport.

"Nurmi," he said, under a statue of a compact, naked Finn running in thin air upon a high pedestal. The

Flying Finn, Paavo Nurmi. Erkki told her that the Olympic stadium had been meant for 1940, but had not been used until 1952. The war intervened.

Erkki drove north, she knew, for the sun was on her right. Now he sharply turned south again, the street sign said *Mechelininkatu*, and he pointed. In a park stood a display of silver organ pipes, enormous in size, that seemed to float in air, bigger than the white-barked birches, the sunlight catching ripples and holes.

"Sibelius," he said.

"Oh." She could not help but be touched by the tour, as Erkki supplied anecdotes for her enlightment and pleasure. She stared out the windows of the car at green parks with white-trunked trees, white-globed lamps on posts along the paths. The joggers reminded her that she hadn't run since her first day in Zurich.

Among the heavy, utilitarian blocks of buildings were gardens, blooming red, white and gold. Streets curved around rugged rocky outcrops twelve feet tall, with shrubbery on top, as if the hard, ancient earth would not be totally paved over. She'd never seen so much greenery in a city of half a million. Its citizens apparently were stacked instead of spread, and the land they did not occupy went for parks and playgrounds and beachfronts.

At the next park further south, with long, white *Silja* line ships docked in view, Erkki stopped the car and opened her door, pulling her out of the seat and leading her with his arm about her.

Against the backdrop of the sea, a statue stood. Heroic in size, high on a stone pedestal with paths radiating from it. A man in black stone, beautifully made, almost nude, raised his left arm to wave a tattered shirt while bracing himself against the broken mast of a ship. She saw the story in the statue before Erkki muttered, "Shipwrecked."

The man's mouth was wide open in a useless cry for help; water lapped below his reaching feet and powerful legs. Alone. Alone with a ship going down beneath him, the last survivor, with no help in sight. Jeanne, staring up at him, felt deeply moved.

Without a word, Erkki pulled her around behind the statue. As Jeanne admired the musculature of the man's shiny back, she saw that the doomed victim was not in the sea alone.

High in his right arm, previously hidden by his head, crouched a little child, completely naked, clinging to his neck. Then Jeanne's gaze fell to the base of the statue above her. Wound about the mast and the man's knees, a woman was curled. To her he could offer no help. The distress banner must be held high aloft, and their child aloft in his other arm.

Jeanne shook her head in pity, and Erkki pressed her against his side without a word.

Tourists sunned themselves on the green grass, chatting, lying back, snacking on ice cream sticks, pointing at the domed cathedrals.

Jeanne walked again around the statue, its subjects frozen in stone a few moments before their deaths, seeing too much for her heart to endure. Why had he brought her here, if not to show her something about himself, reveal some extenuation? The drowning family—man, wife and child were going down unless— unless what?

When she finally lowered her head, ignoring onlookers with cameras and children and noisy, dry, safe babies, she let him guide her back to the car and got in.

"Why?" she asked him.

"Often, after Stina left me, I came to this statue. For hours I would stand and stare. I felt like the man in the statue. What could I do? Nothing but drown in my self-pity. But after I met with you, my feelings became different."

He looked at her. She turned away, unable to meet his gaze. His eyes returned to the road and he was silent for some minutes.

"We now pay respects to Baron Mannerheim."

Off *Hietaniemenkatu* on *Hiekkarannantie* he parked and they got out of the car. The cross was immense, standing over the single tomb.

"He was like your General Grant," said Erkki softly, as if the dead giant could hear him. "Also to us like your Washington and Lincoln and Roosevelt. Also Eisenhower. All the things those men did for you, he did for us. Only one man. He died in 1951 at age 83. Some die not so old."

To make conversation she told of seeing the statue of Mannerheim on her drive in from the airport with Herr Schindler. She babbled on about the plane ride and conversation with the Swiss businessman, but she knew he heard little of what she was saying.

"Jeanne, would you mind if I left you alone for a few moments? Stina is buried in this same cemetery and I wish to pay also my respects to her. I will return in a few moments. In the car it will be more comfortable."

Jeanne swallowed hard and drew in air. Go with him, a voice inside her counseled. Face it with him. You will survive. As Erkki has survived.

"I want to go with you."

He looked at her with surprise. "You are certain?"

Silently she nodded and he took her hand and led her down a series of gravel paths. Only the crunch of gravel under their feet broke the silence. The grave marker was small, simple: Kristina Svenson Haukkamaa; *Toukokuu* 3, 1957—*Heinäkuu* 5, 1980. A bouquet of white roses stood in an urn in front of the marker.

Twenty-three years old. Younger than I am now, thought Jeanne. What would she have done in Stina's circumstances? Jeanne honestly didn't know. In what month did she die? The Finnish words meant nothing to her. It was June 1981 right now. She asked Erkki.

He translated. "July fifth. Last year. *Lokakuu*. October. We met in October," he said, reading her mind.

No wonder he had been so moody. His wife in her grave only four months, a daughter he had never seen living with grandparents who hated him, alone in a strange country. She realized it was her newness that had attracted him, the promise of a fresh start. Jeanne knew about fresh starts.

She had passed this test. She could go further.

"Where is your child, Erkki?" she asked quietly.

His reaction was too swift for him to hide it. Jeanne looked into a face naked with relief.

"Come," he said. "We meet Impi. Impi Haukkamaa."

Chapter Twenty-eight

ERKKI PARKED IN front of a large, pretty house with two towers like squat lighthouses, freshly painted brown and cream and shaded by linden trees. Together, hand in hand, they walked up the flagstone path and through the front door of the house.

In the foyer a matronly woman in a brown jumper took his name. She spoke at first in lilting Swedish, but changed to Finnish when he answered her in his own language. She directed them into a waiting room with a bright red woven rug and white wicker chairs with red and white cotton cushions. Jeanne had time to admire the sunny room before a woman wearing a full apron, replete with ruffles and bows, entered. Holding her hand was a pale-haired, chubby-kneed toddler in a corduroy dress of apple green. Apple-cheeked, too. Born in September 1979, just ten months before her mother's death, Impi was now a few months shy of her second birthday.

The aproned woman pried Impi's small fingers from

her skirt and left the room. The child found herself alone with two strangers. Erkki sat impassive, his elbows resting on his knees, watching the child and waiting.

Impi hesitated, finger on lips, then trotted across the rug. To Jeanne.

Jeanne met her halfway, slid out of her chair, knelt, and embraced the beautiful tot. Jeanne wallowed in a burgeoning maternal surge, cuddling the child, kissing platinum hair not much lighter than Erkki's. She examined each little limb. Impi said not a word or a syllable. She sat now on Jeanne's lap, staring fixedly at Erkki.

Erkki stared back, eyes dry, matching his daughter's silence.

"How do you say father?" Jeanne asked him.

"In what language?"

"Finnish, naturally."

"She does not know Finnish. This is a Swedish nursery."

"Then it is time for her to begin to learn."

"It is *isä*. Eee-sah," he pronounced again slowly.

"Eee-sah," Jeanne said, pointing at him. Impi was not impressed.

"She's too young," Jeanne said, "to understand. Is she here all day? Every day?"

"I presume so. How many days, what hours, I do not know."

Jeanne stopped talking and turned her attention to Impi, who was studying the zipper of her purse and putting the loop of its strap into her mouth to sample American leather.

This childish antic brought the first smile to Erkki's lips. "Impi," he said in a barely audible voice. "Impi." This time the word came out whole and he held out his hands. Jeanne set the child down on her tiny brown oxfords. Facing Erkki for a moment, she grimaced, pivoted and clung to Jeanne's leg.

Moving slowly but with increasing confidence, Erkki bent, reaching for his child, and lifted her onto his own lap. He spoke soft Finnish to her.

Impi leaned away from her father, a finger in her mouth, not sure what or who he was supposed to be. Jeanne felt like crying. Impi began to.

Erkki set her gently on her feet and watched her toddle straight back to Jeanne. Jeanne saw the pain in his face. "The strange words scare her, I think," she said, comforting the little girl with soothing sounds.

"The Svensons cannot keep her. They are old. Sixty-five years and more. Me, they don't want to have her. But I do not allow—what is the term? Adopting of her. Legally she is my daughter."

Impi was quiet now, her fear forgotten in favor of the enticements of Jeanne's dangling hoop earrings. Erkki watched Impi as she laughed and played with the shiny piece of gold in Jeanne's earlobe.

"She is very beautiful," he said proudly. "Like me she looks. Do you not agree?"

"The spittin' image," Jeanne returned laughingly. Only Erkki did not know the idiom and she had to explain it to him. Impi caught the laughter in their voices and giggled and crowed along with them.

Erkki reached out his hand and Impi clasped one of his fingers. "So you think that is funny, do you?" Impi didn't know or care what he was saying. Everything was funny to her now.

Now Impi's nanny reappeared and told Erkki in halting Finnish that it was time for the little girl's lunch. In Swedish she commanded the child to come to her. There was no mistaking what she meant. Jeanne set

Impi down, bestowing one last kiss on her soft chubby cheek. Erkki planted another kiss on the baby's other cheek. It was the first time he had kissed his daughter. Jeanne turned the child around and she walked in her childish rolling gait to the ruffled, beribboned nanny.

Erkki said goodbye in Finnish and waved to the child. Abruptly he got to his feet and hurried out the door, leaving Jeanne to gather her purse and scurry after him. In the time it took to reach for her bag she realized he needed a few minutes alone. She walked slowly out of the building, down the path to the car where Erkki waited, leaning up against the blue Saab.

"I need a good run," she said, making a quick decision. "I'll run back to the lab from here. I haven't run in weeks, and who knows when I'll have time until after the race."

Erkki did not try to discourage her. "What will you do with your things?" he asked, indicating her purse and the sweater she now carried over her arm.

"Take them back to the lab with you. I'll pick them up after my run." She stuffed her wallet into her pants pocket and handed him the rest. "I'll see you later." Then she turned and jogged off, turning once to wave to him as he got into the car.

A good thing that she wore her running shoes this morning. Her slacks didn't bind her much, though she longed for her shorts. But soon she'd forgotten what she wore, engrossed in the rhythm of her feet, the beauty of the city around her.

She ran the first mile slowly. Following so long a layoff, she expected to have no wind at all, but neither her lungs nor her legs threatened to cave in. After the first mile, nine minutes by her watch, she upped her pace and still had leisure to look about. The path followed an inlet of the sea, winding past flowering trees not at all familiar to her, and beds of orange irislike flowers. Always the grass was lush and green. It was hard to imagine this park under snow, or the inlets frozen solid.

On and on Jeanne ran, past ladies washing multihued rag rugs in the water and hanging them on the banisters of docks, over bridges that spanned narrow straits. Birches and firs around her, woodchips underfoot. After two miles her second wind came, and the run became a lark. She was on automatic pilot, flying along. Stopping now would feel unnatural and jarring.

Crossing another bridge, this time a wooden footbridge over a wide inlet where two men fished, not looking up, she ascended a small hill, curved right, then left, and saw a castle.

It was a small castle, standing on a rise, and she could hear highway traffic to her right behind the trees. Cream colored, a crenelated tower stuck up among veils of vines and flowers. Intriguing. She searched for a driveway to take her there. It was obviously modern, in its grove of evergreens, probably a private home, but it was strikingly unusual and she had to see it.

A sign mentioned Akseli Gallen-Kallela, and she climbed a sloping path to the tower.

It was a museum now but had once been the home of the artist Akseli Gallen. She was welcomed inside and given a brochure by a soft-voiced, gentle girl in a woolen dress and clogs.

Behind the tower and connected to it was a steeply pitched shingle roof, topping a traditional country house. This was a castle from only one direction. Sculptures stood on the lawn. She took herself on a tour of the small building, climbing the circular stair up the three stories of the tower with a view. This

Finnish artist, she learned, had designed and created most of the Finnish Pavilion in the 1900 World's Fair, and was an innovator in such disparate arts as weaving, pottery, stained glass, sculpture, print-making and romantic painting. The displays of prints and looms and African-inspired art reminded Jeanne of Picasso. A Nordic Picasso whom she, in her ignorance, had never heard of until today. And she found she preferred his style to Picasso's as she might sometimes prefer a glacier to a Mediterranean cliff.

Gallen's bright, heart-clutching depictions of the *Kalevala*, the national epic, so delighted her that she purchased pocket-sized reproductions. She also found in the gift shop a small stuffed cat made of material reproduced from one of the artist's designs. It was irresistible and practically jumped off the shelf into Jeanne's hand. Jeanne could imagine the apple-cheeked Impi holding and cuddling it. She would buy it for Impi and retrace her steps to the nursery before returning to the lab.

Holding a brightly colored paper bag containing cat and pictures, Jeanne returned to the nursery. The receptionist remembered her and fortunately spoke English. Jeanne told her she had a small gift for Impi and asked if it would be possible to give it to the child personally.

In a few minutes Jeanne was led again into the red and white room. Impi was already there. Jeanne felt delighted that the little girl recognized her and almost released a smile. The stuffed cat did bring one smile, and was clutched to Impi's heart. Suddenly the Swedish words came back, and she stammered them. Impi looked up, and put the cat's ear in her mouth. It had no detachable parts or sharp edges, Jeanne noted. Good.

She sat down on the floor and made up a game of hide-the-cat, passing it behind her, where Impi toddled after it. Jeanne was engrossed in amusing the child when the door opened again, and in walked a tall, gray-haired woman in a dark brown suit set off by beige accessories. Such beautiful clothes. Jeanne would never have taken the woman for Impi's grandmother.

But she was. She must have said so in Swedish, for when Jeanne replied, "I don't speak Swedish. I'm Jeanne Lathrop, from the United States. A . . . friend of Impi's father," the woman switched languages, called herself, "Mrs. Svenson, Impi's grandmother."

Mrs. Svenson was exquisite. Understated makeup, good bones, shiny hair brushed into a swirling French roll. Her appearance belied her sixty-five years.

"I do not know what you are doing here, Miss Lathrop, but it is now time for Impi to come home," the woman said sternly.

Jeanne explained that she was working on the ultramarathon and also writing about it for an American running magazine. While Jeanne was speaking, Mrs. Svenson noticed the cat Impi was playing with.

"Is this a present you have brought to my granddaughter, Miss Lathrop? If so, I do not wish her to keep it." Mrs. Svenson moved over to Impi, bent down and tried to take the stuffed toy away, bringing howls of anger from the child. Impi held on to the little cat fiercely, and her grandmother gave up the struggle.

"Please let her keep it, Mrs. Svenson. I see I have upset you by bringing it, but I don't really understand why."

"It is not the gift, Miss Lathrop, but your presence here that I find distasteful. This is no personal reflection on you, but I do not wish any friend of my son-in-law to have anything to do with Impi. How did you know of her and where to find her?''

Jeanne felt like she'd walked into a lineup, suspect of some terrible crime.

"I was here earlier with Erkki. Dr. Haukkamaa," she admitted.

"So he has come at last to see his daughter. His conscience must be prodding him."

"He has wanted for a long time to see her but has been afraid," Jeanne answered carefully, wanting to keep the conversation going without angering Mrs. Svenson further.

"He ought to be afraid. Afraid of being struck down for his horrible deeds. A colder, more vicious man has never lived on this earth, I am sure. I curse the day he ever met my Kristina."

Mrs. Svenson's words pierced Jeanne like a barrage of poisoned arrows. What had Erkki done to bring such hatred to this woman's heart?

"And what is it that he has done?" asked Jeanne with a dry mouth. Maybe there was more to this story than she knew. "Will you tell me about it? I know only that Kristina died of cancer and that you are raising Impi."

"I do not wish to talk about it here. Since you came here with him, I assume there is a romantic tie between you and . . ." Jeanne nodded as she saw that Mrs. Svenson could not even bear to say Erkki's name.

Mrs. Svenson returned Impi to the care of the nanny. She and Jeanne went to a nearby cafe and ordered coffee. On the short walk Jeanne had learned that Mrs. Svenson had once been a journalist and had spent much time in the United States, which explained her excellent English. Her husband was retired from the directorship of a shipbuilding company.

When the coffee was served and the waiter left their table, Mrs. Svenson gave her version of what had happened between Erkki and Kristina.

"Kristina was our only child, born long after we had given up hope of having children. Her cancer was diagnosed long before Kristina met, uh, my son-in-law. We were not pleased that she had taken up with a Finn, but we thought that a doctor would know how to handle one so young with such a tragic illness. We were wrong."

"First he made her pregnant, which she did not want. Then he forced her to have an abortion so that she could go to Oulu for treatment at the cancer center. The treatment was successful, so he made her pregnant again. When she wished to have another abortion, he forbade it. As her pregnancy advanced and she became sicker and sicker, Kristina could stand it no more and left him while he was at the hospital. Her stories of his treatment of her were appalling. He tried to see her after she came home to us, but of course we would not allow it. Nor would we allow him to see Impi after she was born. He came to the funeral against our wishes. We begged to adopt Impi, but he will not permit it. We wish to return to Sweden but cannot do so because there is no place to keep Impi. We cannot take her out of the country. Every month he sends a check. I want to tear it up, but I put it into an account in Impi's name. My husband and I will fight with all our power to prevent him from raising that child. Had I known he was coming back to Helsinki, I would have forbidden the nursery personnel to let him see the child."

Mrs. Svenson's lilting voice became colder and colder as her tale unfolded. Jeanne listened to the anguish in the woman's voice and did not know what to think. There was no doubt that Mrs. Svenson believed what she was saying. And yet it was hard to believe that the Erkki she knew could have behaved like such a monster. Especially the Erkki who had taken her to dinner at The Broker a couple of weeks ago and the Erkki who had stood with her today by Kristina's grave and the Erkki who had been overcome with emotion at meeting Impi.

"I will not forget, Miss Lathrop. Every week I bring fresh white roses to my daughter's grave. Her memory will live in me for the rest of my days and will live on longer in Impi."

Never underestimate the fierceness of mother love, Jeanne thought. The cultivated woman sitting before her might as well be a tigress protecting her young.

"If you are smart, you will return to America and forget you ever knew this Erkki Haukkamaa." Mrs. Svenson spit out the name as if the words created a foul taste in her mouth.

Jeanne didn't know what to do or say. Was it Kristina's vanity and youth that had led her to become pregnant against Erkki's wishes, as he had told her? Or did Erkki's silence mask evil instead of strength? Would he treat her cruelly if they married? Had Erkki taken on the burden of his people's resentment of the Swedes and acted it out in his marriage to Kristina, without even knowing what he did? In some ways it didn't matter, the result was the same: a young woman dead of cancer, an innocent child caught between elderly, angry and bereaved grandparents and a bitter, guilt-ridden father.

Jeanne knew she had to learn the answers to these questions, but the thought of confronting Erkki with Mrs. Svenson's story made her tremble. They were just beginning to trust one another. Now she had to ask him to answer these charges. The past could only be accepted, not forgotten.

"I know you are earnest in what you say, Mrs. Svenson, but I find it hard to put your story together with the man I know. Erkki has said to me that it was Kristina who insisted on getting pregnant. That he did everything he could to prevent her from conceiving a child."

"Why would a dying woman, in much pain already, want to saddle herself with the additional burden of pregnancy and labor, plus leave behind a half-orphaned child? Does that seem normal to you, Miss Lathrop?"

Mrs. Svenson's voice was strained with anger, and she struggled to keep the low tones required in a public place. Jeanne knew the woman was at the breaking point and ended the meeting with as much graciousness as she could muster.

Before she left the table Mrs. Svenson asked Jeanne to carry a message to Erkki. "Tell him that if he tries to see Impi again I will institute court proceedings to prevent him from doing so, and I will also try to legally adopt the child, despite the disadvantage of my age."

All this because I saw a stuffed cat in a gift shop, Jeanne thought. That's what I get for trying to mother another woman's child. The twists of fate are often strange and incomprehensible. Her relationship with Erkki had never flowed in a straight line, but had been a series of doors opening and closing. Here was another door. Would there be a lady or a tiger behind it?

Chapter Twenty-nine

JEANNE RAN BACK to the lab, hoping to dispel some of her tension, but she was tighter than a piano string when she arrived at the race headquarters. The young receptionist remembered her from the morning. When Jeanne asked for Dr. Haukkamaa, the girl shook her head and said that Dr. Haukkamaa had left for the day. He had left word that her bag and sweater were in his office. He had business and would not be able to see her that evening.

Just like Erkki to leave such a cryptic message. What business did he have that prevented them from being together after what she had gone through with him today? And she needed to tell him what Mrs. Svenson had said. Jeanne asked for and was given Erkki's home telephone number. She collected her things and returned to her hotel. When handed a message slip along with her room key, she hoped it would be from Erkki. It was a request to call Herr Schindler.

In her room Jeanne tried Erkki's number, but there

was no answer. Next she returned Gustav Schindler's call. His business engagement for the evening had been cancelled, and he wanted to know if she was free for dinner.

She told him she had to be at the airport at nine o'clock to meet her runners, but would be happy to have dinner. Could they make it early, about six, to allow her plenty of time to taxi to the airport? Herr Schindler was agreeable and suggested the *ravintola*, or restaurant, of the Palace Hotel which featured *voileipäpöytä*, a fifty-dish buffet, something like a Swedish *smörgasbord*. She was grateful to Herr Schindler for not having to spend the next few hours alone.

The strange foods were appealing, but Jeanne gorged more out of nerves than anything else. Shades of the old Jeanne, she thought, and she did have something to be nervous about. But this food was a far cry from plain old chocolate donuts.

She had the smoked Baltic herring first, then cold reindeer tongue; she sampled a beef and onion casserole; cabbage rolls stuffed with meat and rice and labeled *kaalikääryleet*. There was baked eel and salmon with cream sauce, plus several vegetable dishes and cold salads. For dessert she chose thin pancakes with lingonberry jam, and also tried a berry porridge called *puolukkapuuro*. Cloudberry liqueur sounded so wonderful that she finished off with that toasted-caramel delight.

Over the meal Herr Schindler spoke of his day in Helsinki. He had discovered an unknown designer whose fabrics were so fabulous he was sure she was destined to rival the fame of Marimekko. Herr Schindler was negotiating to be her business representative outside Finland. He showed Jeanne samples, and she agreed they were excellent.

Jeanne described her sightseeing, concentrating on her impressions of the Akseli Gallen museum but leaving out any mention of Erkki or the Svensons. With nearly every sentence she almost blurted out her story.

The conversation waned by the time liqueur was served. Full of too much food and drink and with too much to say, Jeanne fell silent.

"I hesitate to ask a personal question, my American friend, but you seem somewhat preoccupied this evening. It does not seem to have diminished your appetite," Herr Schindler said with a twinkle in his eye, "but I see your mind and eyes wander now and again."

Jeanne looked at her companion and found his round fatherly face full of concern. She thought for a moment before she posed her question. "What would you do, Herr Schindler, if someone you thought you loved had told you a story and then you heard a completely different version of that story from someone else?"

"And who is the someone else?"

"A relative of the person I love." She had said it out loud without thinking about it. Said she loved Erkki. Not thought she loved. Loved.

"It is difficult to say, not knowing the exact circumstances. But I do not wish to pry. I would advise you to trust your loved one. If you question him—I assume it is a male of whom you speak—then you must tell him so and ask him to meet your questions. You should also examine the motives of the person who has placed this doubt in your mind. If you would be comfortable doing so, you might tell me some of the particulars so that I can better advise you."

Jeanne thought about it for a moment and declined, thanking him for his kindness. "I need to work this out for myself."

She glanced at her watch and found it was time to

leave for the airport. "Thank you so much for dinner, Herr Schindler. I have a phone call to make before I leave for the airport."

Gallantly, he kissed her hand. "If you feel the need of some fatherly advice, or even a shoulder to cry on, please do not hesitate to call on me. My shoulder has often been wet with daughterly tears, so I am no stranger to the task."

Jeanne smiled and kissed him on the cheek. "Thank you for everything," she said as she moved toward the bank of telephones in the Palace lobby. Nothing had been resolved in her few hours with Herr Schindler, but at least she did not feel so alone and forlorn. Erkki must be home by now. But again the phone rang in an empty flat.

When the passengers started to deplane from flight 56, she spotted Carla and Lydia together in their bright, California costumes, faces sunburned as evidence of their long training. She ran to her friends, hugging them, looking for Mandy Steir, who herself looked Scandinavian as she came strolling along, talking to another runner. Jeanne counted heads. Twenty-one. Great! All safely arrived.

The athletes were not bothered unduly at customs. "I will bring *home* vodka, not smuggle *in* liquor," Lydia told the uniformed agent. Jeanne knew they'd find a lot more entrancing things to take away from Finland than alcohol. Leading them on a tour of the shops and the monuments would be fun. She would try to keep them away from the colorful dishes. This was not the time for reindeer and salmon and eel, but for pastry and potatoes. Carbohs. Let them spend Monday after the race on fish and meat.

Jeanne thought Erkki might have come out to the

airport to greet the runners, but his "business" must have kept him away.

There was a bus to haul the American women to one hotel, the men to another. There was not enough space to house them all together. Jeanne would share a room with Mandy, her choice; Lydia had Carla as a chaperone. Like an experienced guide, Jeanne drilled them on Finnish pronunciation—stress always on the first syllables—taught them her tiny vocabulary of *kiitos* for thank you, *kippis* for *ciao* or *skoal*, and explained why window draperies were so thick and dark. She had to map out all the room assignments, pass out packets of tourist literature and examination schedules and give them a choice of itineraries to break the monotony of last-minute training. They'd trail over to Erkki's lab, not far from *Runeberginkatu*, for their final physicals tomorrow, then trot around the five-mile race course she hadn't yet seen. Once around in preparation for twenty times around on Sunday.

Runners from other countries were put up at other hotels. "I want to see some Russians," said Pat Prince darkly. "I wonder if any of them will defect."

"Ballet dancers do," Mandy responded. "And ice skaters. And famous writers. Why not runners?"

"Not through Finland," said Jeanne, repeating what she had learned from Erkki. "This country walks a tightrope between East and West. Help escapees, vote against the Soviets in the UN, do anything blatantly anti-Russian, and the USSR can hamstring Finland economically, cancel contracts and throw a lot of people out of work."

"I had no idea anything like that happened. We get so involved in our own lives we forget what goes on in the rest of the world," Mandy lamented.

"You've only been here a day or so, Jeanne. Did

you pick up your information here, or did you study up on Finland before you got here? I wanted to, but with training . . ." Pat's question was interrupted by Lydia's drawl.

"I suspect South Dakota has been getting some extracurricular instruction from our fearless leader, Dr. Haukkamaa."

Jeanne's mouth nearly fell open. Lydia had an uncanny sense where men were concerned. She had never met Erkki, nor had Jeanne mentioned him in any other than a professional capacity.

Lydia continued digging. "Cat got your tongue, Jeanne?"

The other women chimed in, urging Jeanne to own up. She admitted that she had spent some time outside the lab with Dr. Haukkamaa, but said nothing more and changed the subject by drawing her friend's attention to the view as they approached the Helsinki harbor.

At the hotel it took a while to get all twenty-one of the women settled into their rooms. Jeanne managed and returned wearily to her own room, where Mandy was already tucked into bed.

As quietly as she could Jeanne lifted the telephone receiver and asked the hotel operator to try Erkki's number. The endless ringing was the last sound she heard that night.

Jeanne was shaken awake the next morning by an eager roommate recovered from the ten hours' lag and fifteen hours' travel. Mandy was bright-eyed and perky, as if she were back in Oregon.

They met the other women in the dining room for breakfast, taking over a section of the room while Jeanne briefed the women on the race.

Erkki and his associates had the hundred-miler organized to the smallest detail. Each runner would have handlers—local distance runners or upper highschool students. These multilingual helpers would record laps to make sure no one went around the five-mile loop fewer or more than twenty times. Each would furnish his or her assigned runners with refreshments. Tea with sugar, fruit drinks, electrolyte mixes, unfizzed cola, beer—all sorts of concoctions heavy on carbohs would be made available.

The five-mile loop track was the easiest course for an all-night race. This one would begin at ten p.m. and conclude the next day between six and seven p.m. when the slowest runners were expected to pull in. Feeding runners their drinks or solid food every two and a half miles would be easy, as the handlers would merely have to move from one side of the narrow-waisted figure eight to the other.

All handlers spoke the Scandinavian languages plus English or German; a few spoke Russian, Polish and Estonian, Finland's sister tongue. Thanks to Erkki's efforts and her own, the twenty-one American women joined with fifty-one American men to make up the largest foreign contingent by far. The Finns would field eighteen runners, the largest number per capita. The fact that the ultramarathon was not a certified race in Eastern Europe meant there were not many runners from the Eastern bloc countries. A total of three hundred and ten runners would compete.

Each nation had chosen a color: Finland, light blue; Sweden, yellow; Norway, red; Germany, navy blue; England, gold; Russia, brown; United States, green. This way, the handlers could easily locate their runners, first by nation, then by the large number that would appear on the front of each track outfit. Handlers, too, would wear color tags and numbers so each singleminded, heavily stressed racer could immediately find the handler responsible for his or her comfort.

After breakfast the women would join the other runners at the course for a jog around the five-mile course before lunch, which would be served in the stands of a soccer field near the race course. After lunch, they would bus to the lab for physical examinations.

Erkki was at the course when they arrived, wearing track shoes and a warmup suit of dark blue with a small Finnish flag, blue and white, on the pocket. He jogged from group to group on the course, collecting forms, answering questions, instructing, using young people as interpreters.

He greeted Jeanne warmly when he came to her group. But there was nothing in his greeting to indicate she was other than a favored colleague. Jeanne didn't know how to greet him. He didn't know what had happened yesterday. He had made himself unavailable the night before. She tried to speak to him alone but could find no opportunity with the women, overjoyed at finally meeting him, swarming around. When he went on to the next group, she turned her attention to the festivities.

This dress rehearsal proved a colorful affair. It seemed much like the Olympics as Jeanne watched the multinational, multicolored runners studying the route, squinting at the sun, which would be low during most of the race. They scuffed studiously at the sawdust underfoot, a blister-preventing softness she knew they would appreciate. Lights would not be needed, for midnight here was like a hazy pink summer dusk at home. She would love to see at least one of the Americans win a medal here.

She accompanied her friends on their slow, five-mile jog, running alongside Pat and Carla. Lydia chose to chat with a handsome English-speaking Dane on the circuit. Afterward they all ate small meat pies and drank beer. Fruit and ice cream were served for dessert. Jeanne looked around at all the different people—jut-jawed Finns and bony-faced Russians, white-blond Danes and honey-haired Swedes. The Americans came in all colors, reflecting their nation's ethnic diversity.

They piled onto buses to go back to the lab for the ordeal of final physical examinations. Again Jeanne was unsuccessful in finding a private moment with Erkki. That took until late afternoon, when Jeanne and her friends did some touring. By dinnertime Jeanne had discovered Fazer chocolates, and Rocket ice cream sticks with chocolate coating sold at the *Jäätelö* stands. Soon she'd look like *Havis Amanda*, the Rubenesque nude modestly defending herself against sea lions in her fountain by the Helsinki harbor.

When they entered the huge post office hung with modernistic lamps and featuring a striking, larger-than-life nude placed right over the stalls where stamps were sold, Lydia threw up her hands.

"Americans are so damned inhibited!" she admired. "Look how sophisticated the Finns are! All these naked statues and everyone takes them in stride."

Jeanne read aloud from a guidebook. "Nude bathing is common, but men and women use separate beaches."

Lydia threw up her hands again. "I spoke too soon. When is the rest of the world going to catch up with California?"

Lydia was too much at times. It was close to seven by now, and Jeanne suggested they return to the hotel. All agreed. After a dinner of salmon and a rice-filled *piirakka* of rye bread, they retired to the hotel bar for a few drinks before turning in.

Once again, Jeanne tried to phone Erkki at home but got no response. She had no way of knowing what he was doing, nor could she know if the Svensons had taken any action concerning Impi. Jeanne spent a restless night, her sleep punctuated by dreams of statues and monuments coming to life, following her as she ran through the streets of Helsinki. There would be no rest until she came to terms with Erkki and the Svensons and Impi and her own place among these Finns and Swedes.

Chapter Thirty

WHEN JEANNE WOKE she found Mandy stretched out on the floor doing warmup exercises. After a quick trip to the bathroom, she joined her blonde friend in a round of situps and leg stretches.

"How can you do this when you first wake up and still look like you're having a good time? Stretching in the morning is torture for me," Jeanne complained.

"I've always been frisky in the morning. But I can't stay awake past ten o'clock. I have to take a long nap in the afternoon to make it through New Year's Eve," Mandy replied cheerfully.

The phone rang and Mandy was on her feet talking into the receiver before Jeanne could even attempt to stand up.

"It's for you, Jeanne. Dr. Haukkamaa."

Mandy saw the stricken look on Jeanne's face and said something about being starved for breakfast. She picked up the jacket to her warmup suit and left the room.

"Where have you been? I've been trying to talk to you alone now since the day before yesterday," Jeanne said, skipping the preliminaries. This was too important to waste time on chatter.

"Right now I am in the lobby of your hotel. I wish you to join me for breakfast," Erkki's smooth deep voice replied.

"I have to dress but I'll be down in five minutes."

Jeanne hung up and climbed quickly into jeans, a cotton plaid blouse and a navy blue crew neck pullover. Running shoes on her feet. You never know when you'll need to make a quick getaway around here, she thought.

Jeanne spotted Erkki as soon as she stepped off the elevator. He was the only man in the lobby wearing a warmup suit. And he was the tallest. Despite everything she thrilled to the sight of him. He smiled broadly as she approached but did not try to embrace her. No, he would not. This was a public place.

"I would prefer to leave the hotel for breakfast. Too many of the runners are here and will make interruptions. I have matters of much importance to tell you."

They walked a few blocks to a small cafe where they were served thick slices of dark bread with cheese, ham, boiled eggs, butter and lingonberry jam. A small warming tray held coffeee in a blue and white china pot and a pitcher of heated milk.

Erkki dug into his meal, but Jeanne had no appetite this morning. She dug right into the business at hand.

"After we left the nursery I went to the Akseli Gallen museum. In the gift shop I saw a beautiful stuffed cat. I bought it and ran back to the nursery to give it to Impi. I met Mrs. Svenson. Oh, Erkki."

Jeanne's cry was interrupted. "All this I know," said Erkki with his mouth full of bread and ham.

"What?" Jeanne exclaimed. "I've been going around with my stomach in knots for thirty-six hours and you know!"

"Jeanne, we are in public place. Please talk not so loud," Erkki cautioned. "This is Finland, not United States."

Jeanne lowered her voice. "I know very well where I am," she hissed. Before he could say anything else, she lashed out at him. "Mrs. Svenson told me some terrible things about you. She threatened to take legal action to adopt Impi. I've been carrying this around for a day and a half and haven't been able to tell you. I was frantic. It was no easy thing for me to go with you the other day to Kristina's grave and then to the nursery. But you don't appreciate that. All you care about is this race. You've been using your work to avoid your problems for so long you don't even know you do it."

Erkki pushed his plate away as if food had suddenly become distasteful to him. "I have caused much pain for you. I am sorry. I am not used to think of others when I act. Growing up I am an only child. Because my family is Karelian we are treated not so well in Helsinki. I become like a horse whose eyes are covered with black patches. I do not know the word."

"Blinders," Jeanne replied.

"Yes, it is like I am blind. I push ahead and make a path, wide enough for only myself."

"If you don't make room for me, Erkki, we can never be together," Jeanne said sadly.

"This is something I must learn, for soon there will be not only me but Impi too."

Jeanne's face held all the questions she needed to ask. She sat quietly while Erkki told his story.

"As I drove back to laboratory after meeting Impi,

I am amazed at how much love I have for her after so few minutes of meeting her. I telephoned to Mr. Svenson, and he agreed with reluctance to meet with me that evening. I drove to their home outside the city. At first Mrs. Svenson was angry, telling me of her meeting with you, threatening to take Impi away. But her husband is more reasonable and we are able to talk.

"I tell them I do not force pregnancy on Kristina, but she deceived me to become pregnant. I do not force her from our home, but she leaves because she wants to. I tell of my anger and guilt over Impi, but now that I meet her I find much love in my heart for this daughter of me and Kristina. For the first time I cry over Kristina's death. Together husband and parents mourn. Never can we be friends, the Svensons and myself, but our love for Impi makes a bond."

"With all this you never thought to call me or to take me aside to tell me! If I hadn't taken the cat to Impi, I would never have met Mrs. Svenson, she would never have known we visited the nursery, unless the staff mentioned it to her. I am happy you are working things out about your daughter, but it hurts me that you didn't share it with me immediately." Jeanne fought back tears as she made her speech. Damned if she was going to let him see her cry.

Erkki bowed his head, unable to meet her gaze. "I have much to learn about sharing, Jeanne. There is yet more to tell. Will you listen, please?"

Jeanne realized how difficult this was for him. How hard he was trying. "I'd like to hear, Erkki."

He continued.

"Last night I went again to the Svensons. This time early in the evening before Impi was put to bed. With Impi the visit was much easier than the one before. I am never with small baby before. She is much delight. Everything so new. I regret only now you were not with me. But tonight I can fix. I am agreed with the Svensons to pick Impi up at the nursery and go with her to my parents. Will you accompany me, Jeanne?"

She reached across the table and took his hand. "I would be delighted." Jeanne felt him begin to pull his hand away and look around the room, but then he stopped and allowed her to continue touching him. She squeezed his hand and let it go.

"I am sorry I cause you so much worry. I am not fair, am I?"

"No, you were not," Jeanne agreed. "But that doesn't mean you can't change. When we get back to the States I'll show you how much I've changed. A story about my transformation from fat girl to thin woman is going to appear in *Playgirl* in July. You'll see just how far I've come."

Jeanne realized as she spoke that he might not be going back to the States, but she said nothing further on the subject.

"Let's just take one day at a time, Erkki."

"You Americans have an expression for everything."

"We sure do," Jeanne agreed. She checked her watch. "We'd better get going. I've promised the women a final day of sightseeing, and I'm sure you've got a million things to do at the lab."

"Yeah," Erkki said.

It was the first time Jeanne had heard him use American slang. It sounded so funny she burst out laughing.

"Do you know what you just said?"

"Yeah," Erkki repeated and laughed along with her. She agreed to meet him in the hotel lobby at four.

With a light heart she walked back to the hotel. Was this air or solid ground beneath her feet? Jeanne couldn't tell.

In the hotel lobby her friends had just about given up on her. Mandy knew she was with Erkki and had convinced the others to wait for Jeanne.

"Don't you look like the cat who swallowed the cream?" Lydia said in her slinky voice.

They all wanted to know what was going on between Jeanne and the doctor, but she just told them that things were looking up.

Seurasaari, an outdoor museum, left Jeanne with a kaleidoscope of images: peasant huts, manor houses, a small Finnish church with a very steep roof and inside a tiny eighteenth-century sailing ship suspended over the aisle, its purpose to carry the soul to heaven. Even in the charcoal-blackened, low-ceilinged huts transported to this island's collection, Jeanne found Finnish creativity at work. Stools had round holes in the seats for lifting, tables were made of stumps, cradles were artfully built of gnarled dowels. Fireplaces were set on corners, not into walls, so the heat could spread in two directions. The earliest saunas were dark, fragrant, stone and timber rooms with sleeping lofts, each truly the bath and bedroom and focus of the home. "Finns build their saunas first," the guide had said, "and then think about building the house."

The manor house featured clever bunkbeds with stylized ladders, lovely crockery, tile stoves, sculpture, carvings and woven rugs. Even in the old days, when all the movers and doers were the educated Swedish Finns, the Finns without books seemed to be building, shaping, thinking, waiting for their freedom.

The Czars Alexander I and II, said the multilingual

Finnish museum guide, gave the Grand Duchy of Finland almost total independence from 1809 to the turn of the century. Then the two Nicholases tried to subjugate the Finns, losing the country in 1917. Independence Day was December sixth, when Finns celebrate, just as Americans rejoice on the Fourth of July.

There were endless winding stairs at *Seurasaari*. Jeanne cautioned her runners, "Be careful, and quit if you feel tired."

Mandy was taking notes and pictures, her yellow head bobbing; peering into draped beds; bending over a small spiral notebook, scribbling; listening to the guide who was dressed in a magenta Karelian costume: a jumper worn over a blouse, and a stiff high-domed hat.

For lunch they ate *piirakka* pies and thick hot sandwiches made of egg, tomato and herring between slices of dark bread. Jeanne was starving and ate heartily, even though she had no need to carboh load like her friends. But she had been unable to down a bite of the breakfast Erkki had ordered at the cafe.

Then the bus whisked them to the harbor for a launch trip through the chilly, choppy waters to the fortress of *Suomenlinna*, Gibraltar of the North, the largest sea fortress in the world, said the announcements. They debarked from the boat, the *Viapori*, to tour the island's historical museum and a manor house full of silver, china, uniforms and weapons.

Jeanne and her friends wandered over the verdant isle, enjoying an unfenced, open-air sculpture exhibit, and detoured around grassy hills bearing long black cannon. The bravely flying Finnish flag, blue cross on white, inspired Jeanne to feed the others more data on the assaulting Russians who bit off so much—all of Karelia—that they sent refugees streaming into a war-exhausted country that could not feed them. Bombs fell on Helsinki, she said, feeling indignation as if it were her own country. Jeanne was surprised at her own depth of feeling. Finland, she continued, had joined the Germans only to get Karelia back, and took a bit more than had previously been Finnish, thus bringing down upon herself enormous postwar reparations and considerable infamy.

"I read in a book in the hotel," said Mandy gravely, "that it was like the state of Massachusetts holding off the rest of the U.S.A. in a war. For a hundred days. Ten to one odds."

The women were silent for a moment. Even Lydia had no wisecrack to offer.

Pat broke the silence. "Finland is so much like home. In the stores the sales are called *Ale*, as if they just left off the first letter. And the bright colors and all the cars and all the well-fed people. I feel comfortable here."

Everyone agreed that there were many similarities between the two countries, as well as differences. So her friends had noticed it, too, thought Jeanne.

"We better take the next boat," she said. "You've walked miles, and I haven't seen much stretching at all. Remember ten p.m. tomorrow is zero hour. You've got to get some sleep. No partying tonight, please. Eat, drink, and then bed down, okay?" she counseled. "Holy cow, I sound like Knute Rockne. 'Okay men, I want you all to go out there tomorrow and win one for the Gipper,' " Jeanne joked.

Laughter and cheers rose from the group, bringing stares and smiles from the other tourists.

On the way back to the hotel, the talk turned to the race and training. The women exchanged blister cures, argued about diet and the pros and cons of shoe orthotics, the specially molded inner soles that helped prevent injuries. Everyone groaned when the conversation turned to interval training, the grueling spates of alternate sprinting and running designed to increase speed.

Discussion of training regimens bubbled about her. As the boat approached Helsinki Harbor there was a pause to admire and photograph the two imposing cathedrals and the liners taking on passengers. Then the chatter rose around her again: Who among them had met the wonderwoman marathoner of seventy-plus? Who knew Miki and Ruth, Jackie and Gayle—on a first-name basis!—Jeanne would have stood in line for those women's autographs. Who had run the marathon up and down Pikes Peak, or the one encircling Crater Lake, was the topic as they pulled to the wharf now empty of the marketers who had held sway there in the morning.

Jeanne had many invitations for dinner but turned them all down because of her appointment with Erkki. Carla and Lydia were going to a Russian restaurant near the Uspenski Cathedral. Svenska Klubben, the Swedish club, had other takers. Mandy and Pat were going to the Hotel Inter-Continental for the Arctic Salmon Soup, Roast of Reindeer with Wild Rice Sauce and Lingonberry Parfait a brochure had advertised.

When they reached the hotel it was 3:45. Jeanne raced up to the room to wash hastily and put on a dress. She couldn't very well meet Erkki's parents wearing jeans and running shoes.

Her choice of a blue and white jersey print wrap-around with navy blue sandals was a good one. Erkki was wearing a gray suit, a pale blue linen shirt and a dark blue tie patterned with small white crosses. He shook her hand formally, and she noticed how cold her hand was in his warm, dry one. Sensing her nervousness, he leaned down and kissed her on the cheek. She knew it was hard for him to display affection in public, particularly here in Finland, and she appreciated the gesture and told him so with her smile.

They drove to pick up Impi who now came readily to Erkki. She also seemed to remember Jeanne. The three continued on to the Haukkamaa flat, Jeanne holding Impi securely in her lap.

The Toivo Haukkamaas lived in a tall building not far from Helsinki's center. The boxlike white building was set right on the sidewalk with no front yard at all. They rode in an antique open-caged elevator to the sixth floor. Marble stairs wound around the elevator shaft, and Jeanne was dizzy when they emerged on the top floor.

The Haukkamaa flat was neat, refined and immaculate. A stocky, middle-aged woman took Jeanne's hand, studying her closely without a word. Erkki had warned her that his mother spoke little English.

His father was not as tall as Erkki but was as slim and straight, with gray hair, faded gray eyes and a gentle face. He walked with a limp.

There was no physical beauty here, but strength of character and intelligence shone through the lined, weathered face. The Asian fold at the inside of their eyes was there, tying them to their son.

After releasing her hand, Mrs. Haukkamaa took Impi from her father's arms and hugged her, whispering endearments in Finnish. Impi squirmed in the strange embrace, but with a few words of encouragement from Erkki settled down with this new grandmother. She protested vigorously, however, when handed over to Toivo and was set down on the floor to explore her new surroundings under the watchful eyes of four adults.

Mrs. Haukkamaa served cranberry liqueur and the *kaaretorttu* cakes that Erkki had told her about the first night in the sauna. She had never imagined then that she would be sitting in this Helsinki flat eating a plateful made by Erkki's mother.

Mr. Haukkamaa's English was quite good. He asked Jeanne about herself and her life in America and translated her answers to his wife. Although her hosts were formal and reserved, Jeanne felt at ease with them, accepted by them. Before dinner was served she had convinced them to stop calling her Miss Lathrop and start calling her Jeanne. Out of respect she could not do the same, but arrived at the compromise of calling them *isoäiti* and *isoisä*, Finnish for grandmother and grandfather. As Mr. Haukkamaa said, Impi would not speak Finnish well enough to call them that for a long time and Erkki could not very well use those terms, so the task fell to Jeanne to use the new words, so they could get used to them.

For dinner Isoäiti Haukkamaa served a beef and onion casserole similar to the one Jeanne had eaten at the Palace Hotel with Herr Schindler. She learned it was Erkki's favorite dish. For dessert they ate sweet blueberries whipped into a froth thin as a mist.

Erkki had fed Impi before the adults sat down for the meal. His mother had brought out a small quilt under which the baby now slept peacefully.

Although nothing was said about Kristina or the Svensons, Jeanne could see that the elder Haukkamaas were overjoyed about the reconciliation between their son and the granddaughter they might never have seen. They asked nothing about Erkki and Jeanne's relationship, but Jeanne could not help but wonder if they did not wish their son had brought home a Finnish woman instead of another foreigner.

When dinner was finished, Erkki said it was time to bring Impi home. Goodbyes were said. Erkki's mother kissed him on the cheek and kissed the baby, who did not wake when Erkki picked her up. Erkki made a move to return the quilt, but his mother would not permit it. Jeanne shook hands with the new grandparents who beamed as she and Erkki and Impi made their way to the elevator. Only when they had entered the wire cage did the door of the Haukkamaa flat close.

Jeanne waited in the car while Erkki brought the baby into the Svensons' house. She knew it would be embarrassing and trying for both her and Mrs. Svenson if she went inside with Erkki. While he was gone, Jeanne thought about all that had happened since morning. She knew she loved Erkki. The more she learned about him, the better she was able to understand him. But she also knew that she couldn't leave the United States permanently or give up her work, her own family and friends to be wife to Erkki and mother to Impi. Erkki was a Finn. Would he expect her to play the traditional role of wife and mother? Jeanne didn't know, but it was something she needed to find out.

Erkki did not speak on the long drive back to the hotel and Jeanne did not prod him. After he stopped the car, however, she asked if they could take a stroll around the harbor.

"I was about to suggest so myself," he answered.

They had gone only a short way before Erkki spoke. "I think my parents found you very nice. My mother does not speak always so much with strangers."

Jeanne knew this was a compliment and felt flattered. "They were very gracious. It was an evening for family and there I was, a stranger and a foreigner, and I felt comfortable. Of course I was nervous at first, but that went away soon after we arrived." I guess I belong with you, she almost said, but stopped herself.

"You are brave to come with me tonight. Many women would have run away." He drew in a deep breath, as if gathering strength for what was to come next, but he only exhaled slowly and said nothing further.

Jeanne looked out at the harbor, boats bobbing at their moorings, Helsinki's lights glittering on the dark waters. The sky was clear and violet, with a moon and almost a sun, too. She had to take the plunge and hope that she could swim or at least tread water in these cold Finnish waters.

"I still don't think I can do it, Erkki. Marry you and stay here and raise Impi. Even though I've met Impi and your parents and have come to love Finland, I can't leave my work or my country permanently and play the traditional role of wife and mother. That's not why I left South Dakota or why I worked so hard to lose eighty pounds."

Erkki took her in his arms and she felt the warmth of his body against hers. He kissed her gently and deeply. "Also I do not know. My love is great for you but to press you, to force you I cannot do. You will think. I will think. After the race, we will talk. Until then I will not see you alone. But my heart you take with you."

"And mine with you," she replied and lifted her face for another kiss.

At the car she held his hand through the open window while he turned the ignition key, releasing it only when he was about to drive off. She squeezed the large bony hand one last time and stuck her head through the window to kiss the high forehead. Then she turned and entered the hotel, walking through the lobby without seeing or hearing anything but her own thoughts. She arrived at the bank of elevators and was surprised to hear someone calling her name.

"Lydia!" she exclaimed. "Why aren't you in bed?"

"Well, *you* aren't," was the indignant reply.

"*I* am not running one hundred miles tomorrow!"

"Look, who's going to be able to sleep tonight? We're all so jittery that it'll take a keg of beer to put us under. I thought of something better."

"I can imagine. Who was he?"

"*Was* he? He's still around, let's hope. After all!" But she obviously was pleased at the remark.

"Lydia, get your tail back into bed. You're ten jet lag hours from Palo Alto. This isn't Mammoth. You've had barely enough time to get your internal clock geared to Finnish time—"

"Okay, okay, Mommy," she said, grinning, looking tan, lean and healthy in pirate jeans and white shirt. "But I'd think you'd be shacked up with your intriguing Finn. Or would that be 'sauna-ed up'?"

Jeanne's face stopped her. If Lydia only knew the implications of what she had called Jeanne.

"Oh, so it's that serious? Well, good luck. I've got nothing against international relations. Hey, how many times do I have to give your lover the blood sucker my blood and other precious bodily fluids?"

"As often as you need a rest or a drink," Jeanne said. "You know that. He isn't going to yank anyone off the track. You give when you feel like it."

"Some of these world-class U.S. jocks he lured over here are not going to stop. You know that. A few of them can run the whole damned hundred without even *walking*."

"Then they won't be able to walk for half a year afterward, Erkki says."

"Erkki does, huh?" she grinned engagingly. "You two discuss athletics much?"

"Get to bed before I pull the fire alarm bell, Lydia."

The irrepressible runner darted away, light on her feet in string sandals, and took out her room key.

"Well, Jeanne, see you at the arena, where we poor gladiators will perform for old Caesar Erkkustus—tomorrow!"

Chapter Thirty-one

TODAY SIGHTSEEING WAS over. Maybe a dash to a shop for a carved silver pendant or a rya rug, but mostly today was for stretching, napping and psyching up for a tremendous physical and emotional effort. Not for speed, for no one could push hard for fifteen or twenty hours. For endurance, walk, run. Best to start early a pattern of walking part of each hour, before weariness begins to set in.

The runners would give their last prerace lab samples, dress in lucky shoes or socks or other paraphernalia—every runner had his or her own special talisman—supply their handlers with Vaseline, tape, sweatbands, changes of shirts and socks and anything else they'd need along the way.

The day was windy, which was good, unless the wind blew in a Baltic storm. The sun seemed farther away, milky through morning haze. This was nothing like a standard marathon for which you beg the weather gods for three to five hours of windless fifties, with a brief sprinkle welcome. For a ten-kilometer race, you need no more than a couple of hours of cool and quiet. But for this! Twenty hours of cool, perfect weather, please. Rain might be refreshing for the ultramarathoners, but it would be catastrophic for handlers and scientists. So keep it dry, at least until the end. *Anything* could happen in twenty hours.

Her worry lessened when Jeanne rode out to the course and saw the two tents—one for the sheltering of workers and equipment, and a bigger tent for the doctors and technicians.

Inside stood many racks of test tubes and flasks on tables, but only guards were present in the early afternoon. Stall toilets were available, stacked with paper cups and pencils to inscribe one's number when one gave a sample. Wonderful efficiency.

"How'll they know how far we've run when they take our specimens?" one of the women had asked.

"You'll record the time when you give the urine, and they'll record when they stick you or collect exhaled air. You will all begin running together, and the handlers will have lap times, so they can figure it accurately from there."

"Great," she'd replied. "I'll concentrate on running for science. Racing makes me very nervous."

Erkki was already there when she arrived. She glimpsed him darting in and out of the medical tent, giving orders to fleets of people from policemen to nurses. Handlers were stacking cots at various points for nappers or injured runners. Trucks brought in huge vats of liquid for the three hundred-plus runners, and she wondered how much of the fluids would be consumed. There would be food, too, although she herself was hard pressed to run five miles on a banana and a couple of cookies eaten beforehand or during. She got stomach cramps and bloodless legs, the blood ascending dutifully to her viscera to digest the food.

Sightseers had already begun to gather but stood back—mannerly, reserved Finns. She was taping last-day testimonials from the women and any race officials she cold catch in a rare unoccupied moment. The press was here, camping out to see the start.

The runners began to arrive in midafternoon. At four p.m. huge pans of spaghetti were set out, and runners lined up to eat. Pancakes and spaghetti were traditional marathon repasts. On stadium bleachers set up near the tents, runners and handlers sat eating and conversing. They would have six hours to digest their meal before the starting gun sounded.

Jeanne joined her American friends for a bowl of pasta. Spirits were high as the women downed their last meal before beginning the grueling race. Lydia spent less time eating than ogling and exclaiming over the male competitors. Carla chattered about the good luck phone call she had received from her husband and children. The kids had composed their own fight song for their mom, which they had sung to her at the end of the call. Mandy was, as usual, taking notes.

"Hey, I thought I was the journalist around here," Jeanne kidded her.

"You may be the journalist, but I'm the cultural anthropologist and you can never tell when a thought might come in handy," Mandy replied. She had been ribbed about the ubiquitous pencil and notebook, but took the joking with good humor.

Pat Prince was spending her last few hours before the race with her fiancé who had flown in that morning to be with her. They were to be married at the American Embassy two days after the race, after Pat had time to rest, and they would honeymoon in Finland

and then go on to tour Sweden, Norway and Denmark before returning to Oregon.

The group was rounded out by Peggy Epping, one of the New York women, who had made friends with Carla on the plane and had been included in their circle during the sightseeing tours. The usually lively New Yorker was quiet and subdued this afternoon. Jeanne asked if she were okay. Peggy said she was, just a bit jittery and jumpy.

After the meal Jeanne went to the medical tent to see if everything was under control. During the race she would record all samples taken from the American women, compiling a master list that would provide a double-check against the individual lists, which would be kept by the handlers. Jeanne would work two hours on, two hours off, sharing her task with one of Erkki's colleagues from race headquarters. During her off hours she could rest, eat or interview and take notes. The recording would be done at the medical checkpoint on the course, so she could watch the race at the same time.

By six p.m. the green grass was strewn with stretching or napping runners. Wearing two color-coded tags identifying her as a member of the press and a member of the medical team, Jeanne covered the grounds, tape recorder in hand. At the hotel and on the sightseeing tours her group had met some of the Swedes, British, West Germans and other runners, but she had not had an opportunity to interview any of the Russians. They seemed to be more restricted in their movements than the Western athletes.

Jeanne approached the brown-clad Soviet runners and looked for someone wearing a blue translator identification tag. She spotted a woman and asked if any of the women runners would like to express their feelings about the race for an American magazine. The woman frowned, spoke to the coach and then turned back to Jeanne. She could speak to the women but was requested not to tape the interviews. Jeanne agreed and took out her pad and notebook.

She asked how many of the women had raced one hundred miles before. Half had. Most had competed at fifty miles, though. What did they think of Lyudmila Bragina and Tatyama Kazankuna, two of Russia's great women runners? Jeanne's pronunciation of the name brought smiles and a few giggles. Comrades Bragina and Kazankuna were much admired. Next Jeanne asked how they liked Finland. There were shrugs and blank faces, and the interpreter raised her hand like a traffic cop. Jeanne had overstepped the boundary. There were to be no more questions. She thanked the Russian women and moved on, angry at herself that she hadn't thought about the implications of her question before asking it. She would have liked to continue speaking to the Russians.

She moved on to a group of quick, intelligent Swedes. They ranged in age from thirty to forty, like most of the women here, from whatever country. One didn't excel at these distances without some age. This wasn't swimming where you could be a has-been at eighteen.

The Swedes considered the race a lark. "One hundred miles on a track?" said one. "Can you imagine? Run four hundred times around? Never! But this is so pretty, with all the trees and bridges. And so large! Just twenty circuits. It will be fun. We shall see it as a relaxed time, an occasion to talk and run together."

Jeanne kept her eyes and ears peeled for the unusual—a very old or young runner; one recently a mother; someone who was pregnant, although she doubted that Erkki or any other doctor would let a woman carrying a child enter a race of this distance. Many women ran during pregnancy, but the long-term effects of ultradistance were still unknown. While thinking about running and pregnancy, Jeanne realized that her trust in Erkki had been restored after the jostling Mrs. Svenson had given it. They had both come through this test with flying colors, she thought.

Among the British women Jeanne found the oldest female participant. She was a sprightly grandmother of sixty-one who introduced herself as Victoria Sheffield from London. "A few years ago, dearie, I couldn't run around the block. Now I do ten miles a day, more when I train for these long ones, on Hampton Heath, which is more hills than anything else. I've got teenaged grandsons who can't keep up with me," she chuckled. "At least with this gray hair I'm visible on the course," she added happily. It was clear that Mrs. Sheffield was a favorite among her teammates, who affectionately called her Gram.

Jeanne made her way back to the American contingent for some last-minute interviews and to see if anyone needed anything. Everything seemed to be under control. Mandy had gone off to be alone the last few minutes before the race. Lydia was taking an opportunity to flirt with her Dane. Pat sat quietly with her fiancé. Carla was doing deep relaxation in the yoga corpse position, Shavasana. Only Peggy seemed fidgety, pacing back and forth aimlessly.

It was nearly ten now. A sizable crowd had gathered on the fringes of the track, giving the grounds a picnic air, for the spectators had brought lunches and blankets to sit on. Jeanne couldn't read the daily *Helsingen Sanomat,* so she had no idea how much publicity the race had garnered. However, today was Sunday. Tomorrow, when the race would end, was a Finnish holiday, so many people were free from work and could make the race a festive occasion.

The crowd was called to attention over the PA system. Throughout the race announcements would be made in Finnish, English, Swedish and Russian. One after another the announcers reviewed the rules of the race and filled the crowd in on suggested procedures for the runners. Runners should keep to the right to allow for other runners passing and lapping; liquids should be taken before feeling thirst. Locations of cots, food, toilets and medical aid were given. Race officials would cruise the course on marked bicycles. No other vehicular or pedestrian traffic would be allowed on the course.

The race would be starting in just a few moments now. For months it had been the focus of Jeanne's life as she traveled the United States recruiting female participants. It had been Erkki's work for more than a year, had taken him from Finland to the United States. The race had brought them together. In just a few hours, less than one day, it would be over. Jeanne had no plans for after the race. She had not thought that far ahead. She would go back to Washington and write her articles. But after that? Stay on at *Fancy Free*? Freelance? Or stay on in Finland with Erkki?

Jeanne stared at the translucent violet sky as if the answers to her questions might be written there. The wind dropped, holding its breath along with her.

The English-speaking announcer was asking the runners to begin assembling at the starting line. Jeanne walked with the American women to the start, pressing hands, giving last-minute advice as they jog-walked to the course. "Hold *on!*" she told them. "Don't worry about a slow start. You've got about seventeen *hours* to make up for three minutes' delay. I am so *proud* of all of you. You're all terrific."

Before going onto the course, the twenty-one women runners and Jeanne formed a circle, arms over one another's shoulders, for a moment of camaraderie, a gathering of strength and support, a final pause before entering the arena. Jeanne broke the silence. "This is it. My feet may not be running tonight, but my heart is with you. Go for it. You're lookin' good." With a cheer the women broke the huddle. Clapping hands, bouncing up and down, they took their places in the pack of runners.

Jeanne bounded over to the medical checkpoint to take her assigned station, nearly colliding with Erkki as she ducked under the checkpoint canopy. The shock of the encounter left them both breathless and a little embarrassed. Jeanne found her voice first.

"Well, this is it," she stammered. "I hope everything goes well for you tonight. You've worked so hard to make this all happen."

"As you have," he answered.

It was all Jeanne could do to keep herself from reaching out and embracing him, holding him close to her for a moment. Instead she sent him away. "You'd better get to the starting line. You'll be late."

"Yes," he murmured gazing down at her. "After the race we will find one another." Then he jogged off for the start of the race.

The atmosphere was electric. Spotlights had been moved in to illuminate the medical and supply areas. At these key spots, it was as bright as noon.

The starter mounted a platform, pistol in hand, white hair lifting in the night breeze. He raised his arm and on the signal from the official timer the gun went off.

With its forceful pop the hush became a roar, and the mass of colorful T-shirts and singlets oozed forward. Runners and spectators alike cried out in exuberance. Their feet made almost no sound on the soft duff. The first men were disappearing into the birch trees before the first women were jogging, then running lightly along. From her post Jeanne spotted a clump of green-clad women and jumped up and down waving her arms. "Go get 'em!" she yelled.

Then she stood alone, her shoulders slumping. This really was it. In less than twenty-four hours her life would have to change one way or another.

Jeanne had known her first shift would be easy. Few runners would stop until after the second five-mile loop. For the American women that meant about ninety minutes into the race. At thirty-five minutes of elapsed time the leaders began to pass her post. As the first runner to complete a single revolution breezed by, arms carried loosely, face intent, a cry went up from the spectators. His stride was so long he might have been doing a 440- or 880-meter sprint. He wore the brown singlet of the Soviet team. The Russian waved off the paper cup of water offered by his handler. It was cool this evening, but he ought to think about his body's depletion over the long, long haul, Jeanne thought.

A beige-shirted Dane came next. He did reach out for the liquid offered by his handler, waved to the crowd and took off after the Russian. Then a whole herd came by, heavy with green Americans, so the poor handlers, shoulder to shoulder, pouring and handing, jostled each other. But the system did work. She heard the click click of the hand-held lap counters of the recorders as they spotted their runners and looked at their stopwatches.

The first pulled muscles showed up around two a.m., after the fastest runners had covered more than a marathon distance. Limping racers asked for ice and sat down long enough to be ministered to. Then off they went. The sun rolled around the horizon just out of sight, but it would be back in just a few hours.

On her second off shift, four a.m. to six a.m., Jeanne felt very sleepy and picked out a cot so she could nap for an hour or so. She left instructions to be awakened at five thirty. Before returning to the medical checkpoint, she took the half hour to check on the American women's progress. As she picked them out of the crowd of runners she saw they were doing well. A few ran in pairs, talking to each other, hair flying, feet twinkling along, not sweating much. Round and round. She felt weary but had only to look at her friends for inspiration. Walking now and then, sitting down, stretching overworked and therefore shortened muscles, taking frequent refreshment, they didn't seem nearly as tired as she.

"It's good? How d'ya feel?" she asked whenever she spotted one of the Americans. She got smiles, nods, raised thumbs and even a few jokes in answer.

Jeanne had lost track of the leader. With runners lapping one another it was hard to tell who was in the lead. She would have to wait for the next announcement over the PA system. At the next announcement Jeanne learned that the Dane had overtaken the Russian for the men's lead. A Swedish woman led the female runners.

Her job at the checkpoint was grueling. She needed to make sure no handler passed her with a sample that was not recorded. It was not easy for the handlers to keep track of twenty-one people, especially when some of the handlers did not speak English. Her record-keeping partner was a Finnish woman named Raili, pronounced "Reilly," whose English, fortunately, was excellent.

Ten o'clock passed without a winner. No one had broken a world record here. Just after eleven a handler announced that his runner would be completing the full twenty laps in a few short moments. The crowd rose, rumbled, quieted and waited. So did Jeanne. She hadn't thought her heart could possibly accelerate, so tired was she, but it did. The figure sprinting exultantly toward the hastily strung tape wore light blue! A Finn!

Raili, who had remained at the checkpoint even though it was her off shift, began to jump up and down. She pulled Jeanne out of her chair and hugged her. Jeanne was astounded by this open display of excitement from the Finnish woman. She heard the loudspeaker announce the winner's name. He was Timo Ojala. The time was thirteen hours, eleven minutes, twenty-nine seconds.

A hometeam victory! The fans surrounded their hero, catching the man as he made it through the tape to pour water over him and hoist him onto shoulders. He was carried to the medical area, covered with a silver thermal blanket and lowered onto a cot. Medical personnel asked the crowd to stand back and give Ojala some air and space. The orderly but excited crowd began to disperse.

Jeanne looked around and saw many bottles of vodka emerge from picnic baskets as toasts were drunk to the winner. She looked around for Erkki, wondering where he was and what he was doing at this moment of exultation, but could not find him anywhere. She could not leave her post, for samples from the American women were coming steadily. It was still midrace for her friends. They would be on the course four more hours for the fastest, seven or eight hours for the slowest. The race was not over yet. Not by a long shot.

Ten minutes later, when excitement over the winner had barely diminished, the second-place runner crossed the finish line. He was wearing a green shirt. Now it was Jeanne's turn to jump up and down and hug Raili. *"All right! Lookin' good!"* Jeanne whooped.

Martin St. James of Santa Barbara, California, was given a hero's welcome by the still-excited Finns, and the American was hoisted on shoulders and carried to the medical area. St. James had missed beating the U.S. record by a mere quarter hour.

Finishers came in steadily after that, but it was nearly four o'clock before it was announced that three women runners were neck and neck on the last meters of the final lap. Jeanne craned her neck. As they came around the bend, she saw one yellow shirt and two green ones. Two green ones!

A sprint for the finish! Jeanne had tears in her eyes at the stamina in that final sprint after one hundred miles of running! *"Ruotsi,"* people were shouting. The runner in yellow broke the tape. Jeanne checked the clock. Seventeen hours, fifty-seven minutes, one and three quarters hours off the U.S. and world record.

Jeanne leaped out of her chair and called for Raili to spell her. Her shift was nearly over and she had to, just had to, get to the finish line. She sprinted from the medical checkpoint to the finish, never taking her eyes off the two green-clad runners. She finally made out their faces. It was Carla and Lydia! Carla edged out her friend by inches, and they fell into each other's arms, laughing and sobbing.

"I gotcha, Lydia! I took ya, after all!"

Laughing and sobbing herself, Jeanne embraced her friends. "Incredible!" she said over and over. "I can't believe this." Then Carla and Lydia were swept up by the crowd to be given the heroine's shoulder-carry to the medical area. Jeanne stayed by the finish line, looking for her other friends.

Mandy passed, wearing an ace bandage that hadn't been there when she began. She was moving slowly but steadily, still looking fresh with only one lap to go. Jeanne waved and gave the thumbs-up signal. Mandy returned it with a broad smile.

Then Peggy Epping passed, looking pale, feet dragging. Jeanne hesitated a moment, then, despite the rules, jumped onto the course and ran alongside Peggy. Her friend was more important.

"You gonna make it?" Jeanne asked.

"Or die trying," said Peggy, not looking around.

"How about if I run with you for a bit, for the company?"

"That would be nice. Thanks, Jeanne."

As they ran together Jeanne kept up a stream of chatter, trying to help Peggy take her mind off her pain. She told her about the male finishers, the sprint between Carla, Lydia and the Swede, goings-on at the medical checkpoint. Peggy was barely running, and Jeanne figured she was doing about a twelve-minute mile. This was Peggy's first one hundred miler. She had done two fifty-mile races but hadn't realized how much stamina this one would require.

Her face was set grimly. Only determination was keeping her upright and moving forward. Jeanne knew she was feeling pain with every step.

"Maybe you should call it quits, Peg," Jeanne suggested.

"No way. I've got a lap and a half now and I'm going to do it. Just run with me until the end of the lap, then I can finish on my own. But no more talking. Just be with me."

"Okay. That's the stuff."

Jeanne completed the circuit with Peggy and returned to the checkpoint. It was time to spell Raili. But the Finnish woman wouldn't hear of it. "The American women need you more now. The race is nearly finished. Not many are still on the course. You go to your friend. I see she is in much pain."

Jeanne hugged her new friend. You get close to people very quickly under circumstances as intense as these. They had shared a very special event.

Peggy was the last of the American women to finish, and her compatriots gathered to cheer her across the finish. She was running on pure guts and pride. When she came in sight of the finish line, the American women began to cheer. Come on, Peggy, come on, they screamed, clapping hard. Peggy came on. Suddenly she looked almost chipper. Her knees stopped caving together. She lifted her elbows, closed her fists and ran down the tunnel of clappers and cheerers to cross the line, just a moment after the clock clicked out the twentieth hour.

Peggy crumpled after her effort. Jeanne and Carla rushed to pick her up and carry her to the medical area, where a team of doctors hurried to her side.

Jeanne's official duties were over. But she stayed another hour until every runner had come in. Then she helped with the closing of the medical checkpoint. The runners had long since returned to their hotels. The spectators had dispersed. Only a few officials and members of the medical team remained.

Bone tired, Jeanne sank into a chair. She was asleep almost instantly. Then she felt a cool dry hand on her shoulder, shaking her gently. It was Erkki.

"It is over," he said. "Finished."

Chapter Thirty-two

THE SOUND OF trees sighing in the wind roused her from sleep. She felt Erkki lift her from the car and carry her into a building. She opened her eyes to find herself in a small primitive cottage smelling deliciously of woodsmoke and lumber. Suddenly there was a mattress beneath her, a sheet and blanket over her naked body. In the dusky night she slept deeply, curled like a cat.

When she woke her first sight was Erkki, lying next to her, staring at her. Not smiling, not frowning, just peering silently, as if to memorize her features. Her lids fluttered, closed and opened again. He didn't move.

She slid one hand out from the covers and found his chin, his cheek. Pressing her eyes shut, she familiarized herself once again with his facial planes, the hair in front of his slightly pointed ear, the velvety ear itself, the hollow temple, the sun creases beside his eye.

He seized her hand and pressed it over his lips hard.

"Oh, Erkki!"

"My Giini. Come home."

He said no more. Time had stopped in the almost eerie stillness of the cottage. Deeply they looked into each other's souls.

Jeanne closed her eyes, turned her head aside on the pillow and gave way to happiness. Slowly, slowly and tenderly, he kissed her face, then her neck, then the rest of her body. It was her turn now, with her fingertips, to rediscover the taut, strong wonder of him.

Their dance of passion was slow and deliberate. No others existed. They had endless eons to give and receive endless pleasure. Truly they became one body, one spirit, one mind, making no sound as they wove in, out and around one another. Even in their moment of ecstasy, reached together and sustained for infinite time, they did not break the cocoon of stillness. Together they slept, dreaming one dream.

Many hours later Jeanne stirred. She opened her eyes to find herself in a strange room. It took some time to clear her mind and remember where she was and what had happened. Then the scene rushed before her eyes, and she was flooded with warmth, aroused with passion. She woke Erkki with kisses, now loud and joyous, and they came together again, singing their love aloud.

Panting afterward, a loud rumble was heard from Jeanne's stomach. "Hey, I'm starved. Is there anything to eat here? And where are we anyway?"

She bounded out of bed and looked out the window onto a grove of birch trees and a lake beyond. Erkki explained they were at his cottage retreat, one hour's drive from Helsinki. If she opened the small refrigerator at the other end of the room, she would find some cheese and fruit and bread. Beer to drink. Erkki admitted his need for food, too.

They broke bread together and toasted their love. They spoke at the same time.

"We will stay here in Finland," Jeanne was saying.

"We will return to the United States," Erkki was saying.

Six months in each place, it was decided. Until Impi started school. Then one country for nine months. Summer vacations in the other. Erkki would continue his research. Jeanne would leave *Fancy Free* but continue as a free lance journalist.

The next question was when. With the race over, there was much work to be done. For both of them. In one month they would finish. They would stay here and be married. Jeanne's family would come from the United States. Next year the Haukkamaa's could visit in her country.

"We have come a long distance," she said to him. "When we met, we were both confused and ill prepared for one another. But our love has survived. It will carry us through the years."

"And it will grow, my Giini. And with it we will both grow, as we have already."

Jeanne held him close, listening to the strong, steady beat of his heart. "I love you."

"I love you, Giini."

Tuesday gone in a haze of love and joy, Jeanne and Erkki returned to Helsinki. They picked up Impi at the nursery to tell her the good news. She gurgled and cooed although she did not really understand what was going on. She only knew that *isä* was very happy and that she was going to have a new *isä*. "Mama," Jeanne told her, making her lips open broadly so Impi could imitate.

Next stop was the Haukkamaa's flat where the joyous tidings were celebrated with a hearty lunch of *karjalanpaiti,* a Karelian superstew of beef, pork and mutton layered with onions and seasoned with lots of allspice. The gravy that they poured over small, tart potatoes was thick and savory. There was pickled pumpkin—*kurpitsasalaatti*—and homemade thick bread. For dessert, berries with cream. Jeanne asked Erkki to tell his mother that she wished to begin her Finnish cooking lessons as soon as possible. There was so much new and exciting to learn.

While at the Haukkamaa's they put in a transatlantic call to Elmton, South Dakota. Jeanne informed her flabbergasted parents that they were soon to have a son-in-law and a grandchild. Plans were set in motion for the Lathrops to get to Finland for the wedding.

Another call went to *Fancy Free.* Ron, Kerry and Nancy whooped with delight over the news, although they were sad to be losing Jeanne. Ron promised to keep her busy with freelance work, though, and was anxious to hear about the race and to see her articles. She told him a little bit about the ultramarathon before ringing off.

Leaving Impi with her grandparents, they returned to the hotel to collect Jeanne's things. Mandy was just finishing her packing when Jeanne walked in. They hugged hello and Jeanne blurted out her engagement plans. An overjoyed Mandy pranced around the room, crowing with delight. Then she got on the phone and called the others who were in their rooms doing last-minute packing. They were to leave in thirty minutes for the airport, just enough time for a quick toast to the happy couple.

Lydia was resplendent in a geometric-patterned blue and white cotton Marimekko dress. "I knew it all along, darlings," she drawled, taking the opportunity to kiss the groom, in a more friendly manner than Jeanne preferred. But that was Lydia.

Pat and her fiancé pretended to be a little miffed that someone had stolen their spotlight. Since Hal's arrival they had been petted and poked as the team's official lovebirds.

Peggy was still tired from the ordeal, but Jeanne could see the happiness in her face. "Don't go out of my life, Jeanne," Peggy said. "Just because you're far away doesn't mean you can't write and visit me in New York when you're in the States." Jeanne promised to stay in touch with all her newfound friends. It was the first time in her life she had really close women friends. She was not about to go backward. Only forward from now on.

Carla told her that she and Erkki and Impi were welcome any time in Palo Alto. She had a houseful, but there was always room for a few more in the Silver home.

Champagne was ordered and a toast drunk to the new couple. For the second round, Jeanne and Erkki offered a toast to the runners and their superhuman effort.

The bus was waiting outside, the departure could be delayed no longer. As the group walked slowly through the lobby, Lydia came up behind Jeanne and put her arm around her. "Take care of your new little girl, South Dakota. I really envy you. I lost my kids, the court wouldn't give me custody in the divorce—the drinking, you know—and not a day goes by that I don't miss them."

Jeanne was deeply moved by this declaration by

Lydia. There was Lydia, with more houses, furs, jewels and money than she would ever have, but not surrounded by people who loved her. "Things can change, you know, Lydia. Take a look at the July *Playgirl* when you get home. There's an article by Alice McCoy, you know, the real McCoy. I think you'll find it very interesting." Jeanne hadn't thought of her transformation article in days. So much had happened since she had written it.

They had reached the bus, and Jeanne and Erkki were hugged by one and all. All but Pat and Hal boarded the bus. The four lovers stood at the curb and waved until the bus was long out of sight. Jeanne and Erkki were invited to attend Pat and Hal's wedding at the American Embassy the following day, and they accepted the invitation happily.

The Haukkamaa's would be taking Impi that evening, so Jeanne and Erkki returned to the little cottage.

"Always this will be our place, my Giini. Each year once alone we will return here to renew our vows to one another, yes?"

"Yes, my love. Yes."

Epilogue
April 1982

THE CROWD CHEERED and clapped. "One mile to go,"
Jeanne heard someone yell. With every ounce of determination she willed her legs to move, one in front
of the other. One step, then another, then another,
covering ground.

It was her first marathon, and she had one mile to
go. She had hit the wall about five miles back. With
the end in sight she felt her strength returning. Adrenalin flowing now, she pushed. Rounding a corner, she
saw the bright plastic banners that marked the chute.
A band was playing somewhere. Hands were clapping.
Cries of "Lookin' good" and "You've got it" reached
her ears.

She was close enough now to read the clock. 3:57:22.
If she sprinted, she could make it in under four hours.
Closer and closer she came. But her energy was flag-
ging. She couldn't keep it up. She must. She must.
And then she saw them. Erkki and Impi. Impi sat on
her father's shoulders. In her chubby fists she held two

little flags. The Stars and Stripes in one hand, the blue and white Finnish cross in the other. Erkki called her name. Her feet flew.

The last time she looked at the clock it read 3:59:50. She had done it. Wet and dizzy, she staggered through the chute. Erkki stood at the other end, and she fell sobbing into his arms. Jeanne felt a tugging at her leg.

"Don't cry, mama," Impi said in her childish lisp. "You won."

REACH OUT FOR ROMANCE
...PURSUE THE PASSION

Purchase any book for $2.95
plus $1.50 shipping & handling for each book.

___ **ROYAL SUITE** by Marsha Alexander
___ **MOMENTS TO SHARE** by Diana Morgan
___ **ROMAN CANDLES** by Sofi O'Bryan
___ **TRADE SECRETS** by Diana Morgan
___ **AFTERGLOW** by Jordana Daniels
___ **A TASTE OF WINE** by Vanessa Pryor
___ **ON WINGS OF SONG** by Martha Brewster
___ **A PROMISE IN THE WIND** by Perdita Shepherd
___ **WHISPERS OF DESTINY** by Jenifer Dalton
___ **SUNRISE TEMPTATION** by Lynn Le Mon
___ **WATERS OF EDEN** by Katherine Kent
___ **ARABESQUE** by Rae Butler
___ **NOTHING BUT ROSES** by Paula Moore
___ **MIDNIGHT TANGO** by Katherine Kent
___ **WITH EYES OF LOVE** by Victoria Fleming
___ **FOR LOVE ALONE** by Candice Adams
___ **MORNINGS IN HEAVEN** by Perdita Shepherd
___ **THAT CERTAIN SMILE** by Kate Belmont
___ **THE RAINBOW CHASE** by Kris Karron
___ **A WORLD OF HER OWN** by Anna James
___ **BY INVITATION ONLY** by Monica Barrie
___ **AGAIN THE MAGIC** by Lee Damon
___ **DREAMTIDE** by Katherine Kent
___ **SOMETIMES A STRANGER** by Angela Alexie

Send check or money order (no cash or CODs) to:
PARADISE PRESS
8551 SUNRISE BLVD. #302   PLANTATION, FL 33322
Name _____
Address _____
City_____ State_____ ZIP_____